PURE PLEASURE

We glared at each other for at least thirty seconds. Then I began to laugh.

"Kiss or kill?"

"What?"

"Didn't you ever take Directing 101? 'Kiss or kill.' When two characters are in a tense scene and they get closer than two feet to each other, one of two things has to happen."

His expression softened for the first time since he'd surprised me under the sofa.

"I get it."

He did, too. He grabbed me, put his lips to mine, and began the more pleasurable of the two choices. Lips were exploring lips, tongues getting entangled, arms were clenched around bodies, and hands were starting to roam. I was giving back as good as I was getting and enjoying the whole process far too much. Lida Rose would be proud.

BOOK YOUR PLACE ON OUR WEBSITE AND MAKE THE READING CONNECTION!

We've created a customized website just for our very special readers, where you can get the inside scoop on everything that's going on with Zebra, Pinnacle and Kensington books.

When you come online, you'll have the exciting opportunity to:

- View covers of upcoming books

- Read sample chapters

- Learn about our future publishing schedule (listed by publication month *and author*)

- Find out when your favorite authors will be visiting a city near you

- Search for and order backlist books from our online catalog

- Check out author bios and background information

- Send e-mail to your favorite authors

- Meet the Kensington staff online

- Join us in weekly chats with authors, readers and other guests

- Get writing guidelines

- AND MUCH MORE!

**Visit our website at
http://www.kensingtonbooks.com**

Ghost of a Chance

Flo Fitzpatrick

ZEBRA BOOKS
KENSINGTON PUBLISHING CORP.
http://www.zebrabooks.com

ZEBRA BOOKS are published by

Kensington Publishing Corp.
850 Third Avenue
New York, NY 10022

All Kensington titles, imprints and distributed lines are available at special quantity discounts for bulk purchases for sales promotion, premiums, fund-raising, educational or institutional use.

Special book excerpts or customized printings can also be created to fit specific needs. For details, write or phone the office of the Kensington Special Sales Manager: Kensington Publishing Corp., 850 Third Avenue, New York, NY 10022. Attn. Special Sales Department. Phone: 1-800-221-2647.

Zebra and the Z logo Reg. U.S. Pat. & TM Off.

First Printing: August 2004
10 9 8 7 6 5 4 3 2 1

Printed in the United States of America

To Ed, my Non-Sequitur Man, with love.

In memory of Bob Schmidt, the best villain I ever knew.

Chapter 1

"Kiely! You're needed. Airport. Now. Bring that lace dress. The spiky boots. And your character shoes."

"Nice to hear from you, too, Lida Rose. Hello? How are you? How's the weather in Texas? How's your veggie garden?"

A distinct snort could be heard long distance.

"Terrific, hot as hell, wilting. Ticket waiting at La-Guardia. Terminal B. Noon. Be there."

I was getting worried. I'm accustomed to Lida Rose's abrupt style, but this was beyond crisp.

"Wait. What's the problem? Why am I needed? Are you about to be a grandmother or something?"

She sighed and switched her tempo to one a bit less frenetic.

"No. The twins are in Europe on junior year abroad stuff. As far as I know, neither of them is planning any little surprises for me. Why would I bring you down here for that, anyway? You'd just buy tons of ridiculous baby clothes and make up inappropriately absurd names. Kiely. You're getting me off the subject. Just be quiet and listen. We're doing a revival of a very old melodrama here. I need you to choreograph about six numbers and play a slutty dance hall girl. I originally just needed you to choreograph, but

I lost a dancer, and you do sluts better than anyone I know."

"Thank you. I appreciate your high opinion of me."

I try and help out Lida Rose in emergency situations when possible, but I did have a question for her.

"How'd your dancer break her leg?"

"Oh—rollerblading while a teensy bit inebriated."

"You can really pick 'em, can't you? You are the worst casting director to be the best actual director I know."

She ignored this last comment.

"You have four hours and seventeen minutes left to make it to LaGuardia."

"Lida Rose, I have just gotten off a nine-month tour of *42nd Street*. I'm negotiating to go to Florida to play the tango dancer in *Grand Hotel* at some chichi dinner theater. I can't remember the name. My agent has the info. Why come to Texas?"

"Oh, sweetie. You've played the tango dancer at least a thousand times. This will be fun. Totally different. A real live melodrama. I have money. Good money. Far better than dinner theater pays. And remember Ted and Margaret?"

Ted and Margaret Wyler are financial wizards and great patrons of theater and other arts. Lida Rose and I have known them for eight years. She's sucked them dry for at least seven.

"Sure. What have they got to do with this?"

"They're going to Cancun for three months and need a house and dog sitter. They just rescued a puppy and don't want it given away to some awful person somewhere. You love dogs. You can never have a dog, since you're touring all the time. We haven't done a show together in three years. I miss you. And you'll love this theater. Lights, sound, and house are totally renovated. Well, almost. But there's a brand-new stage."

She paused for breath.

"And, Kiely? This is perfect! There are six, count them, six gorgeous men in this show. All single. And straight. I think. I'm not that great at telling."

Warning bells screamed louder than the car alarm wailing on the street below.

"You almost had me, you witch! A fun show, a dog, a house to live in. Then you had to poke your prying, pimping, surgically altered little nose into my life. Leave me alone!"

"Now, don't go getting your drawers in an uproar. I won't set you up with anybody if you don't want. Honest. And I do need you to choreograph. I'm being absolutely sincere. Now be quiet and listen for a change. The East Ellum Theatre has been in existence for over a hundred years. They did melodramas for the first seventy or so. We're bringing back the good old days. *Bad Business on the Brazos* will be the hundredth anniversary gala event. And the theater's haunted. So it's going to be an even bigger deal here and be written up in all the papers in North Texas, and I want it to be a great show. Please come?"

I missed this entire explanation. My ears and brain were impervious to everything after "Kiely! This is perfect!" Four little words that portend nothing but trouble when spoken by Lida Rose Worthington, my best friend and worst plague since we met performing *The Best Little Whorehouse in Texas* twelve years ago.

I was backstage doing warm-up stretches before rehearsal for the "Hard Candy Christmas" number when a soprano voice pierced the dark quiet.

"Holy mama! Splits against the wall. Effing amazing! Painful, but amazing."

A witch's cackle rang out. I lowered my leg, turned, and got an eyeful of what appeared to be an overripe gypsy. Costumed in a fuchsia T-shirt and multitiered, multicolored ankle-length skirt with a gold sash dissecting top from bottom, the woman stood five-foot ten inches tall in flat pink sandals, and displayed a bust a ship's prow might envy. Bottle-dyed, black, big Texas hair framed a porcelain complexion. Her expression was that of a child swiping the last cookie from the jar.

No gypsies in Best Little Whorehouse, *I mused. Carnival escapee? A reader from the Ukrainian tea room in Deep Ellum?*

Chubby fingers boasting a ring on each digit grabbed my hand and squeezed.

"Lida Rose Worthington. Playing Miss Mona."

"You've got to be kidding."

"Wait. Let me explain. I have a whole routine you need to hear."

She took a breath, then launched into a monologue about her birth.

"Eugenia Grace Worthington's contractions began in the middle of Act Two, Scene Two of *The Music Man*, May 9, 1957. Eugenia Grace anticipated this possibility. Being a polite, as well as avid, theatergoer, she had requested, and been given, an aisle seat. Eugenia Grace and her husband, William James Worthington the Fourth, calmly and quietly walked up the aisle and out of the theater. It surprised neither that a taxi waited curbside.

"Less than thirty minutes later, Eugenia Grace brought forth a baby girl in the delivery room of St.

Luke's Hospital on West 59th Street. Still feeling somewhat loopy from the nitrous oxide, Eugenia Grace insisted the child be named Lida Rose. William James was in the waiting room reading the *Wall Street Journal*, fuming, then phoning his broker. He learned about the name too late to object. 'Lida Rose Worthington' had been entered on the birth certificate by an overly enthusiastic young nurse.

"Thus, as Robert Preston was belting out the last notes of *Seventy-Six Trombones*, I was belting out my first notes of life in the very same key."

About a year after hearing this monologue, I expressed my opinion to Eugenia Grace that if she had to pick a song title from *The Music Man* for her darling daughter, it should have been *Trouble*. I say this because Lida Rose causes a maximum of trouble—usually for someone else. The someone else on the receiving end is most often *me*. I admit that gullible is my middle name. But Lida Rose doesn't have to keep that item stored in the scrapbook of her brain and take advantage of it on a yearly basis.

But I digress. Backstage that day, I didn't know the full extent of Lida Rose's ability to create mischief. I was so impressed with the tale of her birth, I forgot my manners and stood silently gawking until Lida Rose nudged me.

"So? Who are you? Other than some leggy contortionist."

"Oh, sorry. Kiely Davlin. Playing one of your girls." Her face brightened.

"Keeley? What kind of name is that?"

"One *i*, one *e*. You had it pronounced right. Like 'key.' From my grandmother's side. County Cork, Ireland."

I bowed.

"Aye, lassie, ah'm one o' those. Irish on both sides of the lucky penny."

She nodded so vigorously I feared her pendulous earrings would tear her lobes out; then she immediately changed the subject.

"I must admit, Ms. Davlin, your split against the wall *was* intimidating. I, however, have a pure four-octave range, which is how I can play this ridiculously low role when in reality I'm a coloratura soprano."

"But can you cook?"

She grinned, flashing white, pointed teeth.

"Best blintzes outside of Brooklyn."

"Brownies," I stated stoically. "With chocolate chips, walnuts, and Kahlua."

We sighed, contentedly in sync, and became best friends on the spot.

Since Lida Rose was playing the proprietress of the infamous Texas Chicken Ranch, I naturally began calling her "the Madam." I still do. She has always had the grace not to call me "one of the best little whores." I appreciate this.

Lida Rose. Trouble. The words go together like tequila and sunrise. Like narrow and escape. Like sun and burn. The inferences are too numerous to list.

Every summer since we first met, she's done her best to ruin my life. Admittedly, there are signs that such ruination is imminent. *The words "Kiely, this is perfect!" is a good clue.* Upon hearing them, I try to run toward the imperfect, the past perfect, or the pluperfect. Anywhere Lida Rose is not.

Other than that first summer, when she dyed my hair platinum blond, the trouble has been primarily male-related. (I'm a curly redhead with the freckles and blue eyes that often accompany the same. The result of the yellow dye job was me resembling one of those best little you-know-whats with bad fashion sense.)

Lida Rose's efforts then veered almost exclusively toward matchmaking. The role of Miss Mona obviously went to her head. She believes she truly *is* a madam. I've repeatedly told her I don't need a seventh-generation-Manhattan-Episcopalian-turned-Southern Baptist yenta in my life. But the woman possesses a low learning curve when it involves the concept of single and happy. This is the fault of George Rizokowsky, with whom she's shared wedded bliss for over twenty years. George is five-foot seven, with a slight build, balding head, gray eyes, a brilliant mind, and a gentle disposition. He's also a tiger in the bedroom and the best chef this side of Paris. (The last two tidbits are courtesy of Lida Rose's confidences.) George teaches European history in a Dallas high school where, I'm told, the students worship him.

George and Lida Rose met at Dayton preschool in New York when they were three, fell madly in love, and stayed that way. I don't think either ever dated anyone else. Lida Rose just keeps the Worthington name professionally. It looks better on a marquee and she hates trying to spell "Rizokowsky" for the media.

Because she was lucky enough to find this paragon as her mate, Lida Rose assumes I, too, am searching for that perfect significant male other. I've tried to explain that I'm happy dancing my way across America and that her taste in men (aside from George) is unbelievably atrocious. Nonetheless, she persists.

Case in point: Three summers ago she was directing *Pippin* in Dallas. I stupidly accepted her invitation to come choreograph. (I say stupidly because in my haste to do this show, I neglected to listen to those words, "Kiely, this is perfect!" as Lida Rose was uttering them.) She already had three men lined up for me.

Bachelor number one was a cattle baron from Fort Worth who stood all of five feet tall, had crooked teeth, and smelled like a stockyard. Mind you, I'm not totally adverse to dating men shorter than my five feet eight inches. I've even been engaged to two. But I have a good nose for bad breath and Brahma bulls. I also failed to understand why anyone this wealthy couldn't shell out a buck or two to get his teeth fixed. Exit the beef.

Bachelor number two was a drag queen who spent his weekends impersonating Bette Davis in gay bars. I enjoyed watching Andy perform his routine and we became great friends, but I kept envisioning annulment papers citing "lack of conjugal consummation" tacked to my door.

Bachelor number three. I shudder. Not that he wasn't cute. *Au contraire.* He looked like Mel Gibson in *Lethal Weapon.* And he was undeniably charming and intelligent and (unlike Mel) over six feet tall. But, as I later told Lida Rose, I just wasn't comfortable being involved in a car chase down Central Expressway that lasted twenty minutes. Watching as my date was hauled off in handcuffs for stealing the new Corvette we'd been in made me nervous. Luckily, one of the cops handling the arrest was a high school buddy of mine who loves theater. He knows Lida Rose. In fact, if he hadn't been happily married with three kids, she would have tried to match *us* up. No explanations were necessary once I mentioned Lida Rose's involvement. He understood the situation and kindly gave me a lift home.

***

I tried to pull my focus back to whatever information I'd just missed from the troublemaker on the other end of the line.

"What's the name of this extravaganza again?"

"*Bad Business on the Brazos.* Last performed fifty years ago. Same theater. Very historical."

Visions of puppy dogs danced in my head. I also liked the idea of working at a famous old theater.

"Kiely? You now have four hours and thirteen minutes before your plane takes off. Enough time to grab a couple of drinks at the airport so you forget you're flying."

I was silent for a moment or two. It did sound more fun than dancing a role I could now do in my sleep. But I've learned not to give in too soon with Lida Rose. It only encourages her to think up more ways to ruin my life.

"Tempt me some more. What's the plot of this thing?"

She knew I was leaning. Caving in was closer to the truth.

"Pretty basic melodrama. Rancher gambles away his ranch in a card game to a villain who cheats. His daughter wants it back. She tries to enter the game on a riverboat going up the Brazos. The hero gallantly offers to take her place since he also has a score to settle with the villain. Lots of great characters, fun songs. And Kiely. Remember Joe Hernandez? He just opened a place two doors down from the theater. He's calling it *El Diablo's.*"

Ouch. That got me like nothing else could. My last authentic Tex-Mex meal had been nearly a year ago.

Manhattan is many wonderful things and offers many wonderful restaurants. Authentic Tex-Mex isn't one of them.

Tex-Mex two doors down from the theater. Tex-Mex owned and operated by my favorite cook in Dallas. I added visions of tacos to the chorus line of puppies in my head.

"All right, you evil woman. I'll do it. For whatever pay you can offer. Doesn't matter. Just meet me at the airport and drive me straight to El Diablo's. The devil. Perfect. What'd Joe do, anyway? Name it after you?"

She wisely ignored this last rhetorical question. We went on to discuss my salary, the flight arrangements, and the schedule for the show. Then she casually tossed in one last possibly relevant piece of information.

"By the way. Did I mention the theater is haunted? I'm sure I did. You were in another time zone or you would have snapped that one up."

I was silent for so long Lida Rose started tapping the phone, checking to see if we were still connected.

"Kiely? Are you there? Kiely! Answer me!"

"I'm here. And after that last remark, it's where I'm likely to stay. Have you lost what's left of your mind? Or have you dyed your hair so many times your brain has absorbed all those toxins and just shut down?"

She sounded slightly miffed.

"I am *not* crazy. The theater is haunted by the ghost of the actor who played the villain when they did *Bad Business* fifty years ago."

"Lida Rose, I will come down and do this show primarily because I want Tex-Mex three times a day and I miss not having a dog. But do not go out there and play your version of Dolly Levi and try and get me married off. And don't scare me every five minutes with stories of headless actors wandering the theater howling at the moon. You hear me?"

"Of course I hear you. All of Manhattan probably hears you. Really, Kiely, there's no need to shout. I'll meet you at the airport late tonight. Bring cool clothes hon—it's already a hundred degrees here."

"Okay. I'll see you later."

The receiver was in my hand. In the act of replacing it, I realized the Madam had completely ignored my comments about matchmaking and ghost stories. I desperately wanted to know why she thought the theater had a ghost, but again, one does not provide the ammunition for Lida Rose to fire up her schemes. Her voice came back over the wire.

"Oh, Kiely?"

"Yes?"

"Did I tell you why the villain haunts the theater?"

"Oh, Lida Rose?"

"Yes?"

"Did I tell you I don't want to know?"

Chapter 2

"I have bad news."

"Oh, crap. I've been on solid ground for . . . what? Five minutes? What's the problem?"

"El Diablo's is closed. We have to go somewhere else for Mexican food."

I stared at Lida Rose.

"I thought it just opened."

One small tear trickled down her plump cheek.

"Joe had an accident. He's in the hospital. I don't know when Christa is reopening."

Two hours ago Lida Rose had promised me a fun melodrama, gorgeous men, and the real clincher, Joe Hernandez's cooking at his new restaurant. Beyond the jolt to my Tex-Mex cravings was the punch in the stomach I was feeling at hearing bad news about a terrific guy. I adored Joe.

"What the heck happened?"

She shrugged as she wiped away that tear.

"Honestly? I don't know. I called El Diablo's to tell Christa you were coming in and some kid rattled off Spanish so fast I couldn't keep up. Sounded like *tragico manodata encallar a noche media.* Which would make a great title for a bad Spanish pulp novel. We'll get over to El Diablo's as soon as Christa reopens, and get the full scoop from her."

"From your chopped Spanish I gather Joe was running around in the middle of the night slapping journalists. Which doesn't add up to an accident."

"Sorry. As I said, the kid was on high speed and my Spanish language skills are limited at best."

I nodded and figured I'd simply have to wait for the truth to surface from Christa Hernandez, Joe's wife. I stayed silent for a moment, sending up a prayer that Joe would recover fast and making a mental note to visit him first chance I got.

We managed to get my bags, find Lida Rose's car, then leave the airport in less than thirty minutes. Lida Rose headed down Northwest Highway toward another Mexican restaurant. I struggled not to fall asleep from the airsick pill I'd popped at LaGuardia.

"He was murdered."

"I beg your pardon? I thought you said Joe was in the hospital?"

Lida Rose shook her head, made a ridiculously sharp left turn, then squealed to a stop at Chimichanga's. I was suddenly completely awake.

"No! No. Not Joe. Don Mueller. Our resident ghost. Right at the end of Act Three. Shot down by the hero in full view of the seven hundred and fifity patrons enjoying the show. At least up to that point. I think they pretty much got the hell out of Dodge after he fell. Mr. Mueller, however, hung around. For the last fifty years. It's wonderful."

I waited until we'd been seated in a nice booth overlooking the parking lot. Lida Rose requested that spot so she could keep an eye on her car, which currently has no working locks on the driver's side. I waited until

our order was filled. Then I scooped an enormous
amount of salsa onto my soft tortilla, and dipped it in
the refried beans. I took an equally enormous bite of
the mixture. I chewed. Thoroughly.

Lida Rose waited. I signaled to our waiter.

"Another margarita, please."

Lida Rose shook her head.

"Kiely. How many does that make?"

I glared at her.

"Just three. Plus the two in the airport in New York.
I don't deal well with flying. You know that. Tequila
helps with the claustrophobia. I've tried bourbon but
it doesn't have the same effect."

She sighed.

"You need to get over this, you know."

"I've tried. I even consulted a shrink in Manhattan—
doesn't everyone? He said the claustrophobia is really
my fear of commitment. L. R., I swear my bullshit meter
flew higher than an eagle on acid. At least the man got
me a prescription for Paxil. It sort of helped. I can now
travel by subway. I still can't take elevators. I am absolutely unable to ride in tunnels. Which is nice
crossing into Jersey. Bridges only. And I have to get
schnockered before boarding a plane. So don't hassle
me. Just go on with this outrageous story. Theater
ghost, wasn't it? Yawn. Doesn't every theater own one?"

Lida Rose rolled her eyes heavenward.

"Don't be so cynical. East Ellum really is where Don
Mueller resides. And besides his murder, the whole
melodrama is cursed."

I moaned.

"I may get back on that plane. I don't remember
you mentioning that fact. Why is it cursed? And do I
really want to hear this?"

"Of course you do. I'm not real sure about the curse. I'm working on it."

I eyed her suspiciously.

"Working on it? Do you mean you're fabricating a story to give to an unsuspecting press merely for the purpose of drumming up publicity?"

Lida Rose beamed at me as though I'd just won the state spelling bee.

"You're so bright! What a great idea! Thanks."

I screamed. Softly. I was in a public place. She relented.

"All I know is that something not so great happened to three of the actors who were in the original version that was produced about a hundred years ago. Disappeared or went mad or got shot. That may not be enough to really peak the interest of the rabid press."

She moped for a few seconds as a song began playing in my head. Even after five drinks I recognized slightly altered lyrics from the original *The Music Man*:

> *Oh, we got trouble! We got terrible, terrible trouble.*
> *With a Capitol 'T.' And that rhymes with 'G.'*
> *And that stands for 'Ghoul.'*

Lida Rose. Trouble. The words go together like root and canal. Like fire and cracker. Like grave and yard. Like—

"Kiely. You're not listening. Stop singing."

"Sorry. You were saying?"

"I've been *trying* to tell you for the last five minutes who all's in the show. Where was I? Ah. Hank and Ham Humble. Twins. Big strapping boys with brains and brawn and money. Playing twin ranchers Billy Joe Bob and Bobby Joe Bob Travis."

I put a hand up to stop her. "Hold on. Billy Joe Bob and *Bobby* Joe Bob?"

She shrugged. "I didn't write the script, honey, I just cast the show. And that's how it is in the script. Oh, the only drawback to the Humble boys is they can't dance. But I'm sure you've taught and dated worse. Jason Sharkey. He's playing Lance Lamar, the hero."

She gave a low growl. "Holy mama! Hunk, hunk, and more hunk. Blond, blue-eyed, tall. Good actor. I did a great job of getting men over the height of six feet for this show, by the way. I should pat myself on the back."

She suited the gesture to the words, then returned to her description. I continued to eat my way through combination numero tres. At least she'd quit the ghost tales for a while.

"Where was I? Oh, yes. Jason. Done him. Come to think of it, so has every female in Dallas! Anyway, next we have Theo Stafford who is playing Ace Royale and is just cute as they come. He's funny. He's playing a card shark and I swear he's never played a game of poker in his life. Rafe Montez. In a word. Wow. The man put the 'some' in handsome. He's playing Nick Nefarious the villain. I believe you share a nice kiss with him in Act Two. I'm extremely envious. Um, Charlie Baines. He's our tech director. Sexy in that dark, long-haired, wiry-bodied techie way. Even the box office personnel is cute—Neil Kincaid is cherubic looking. Like an impish choir boy."

She stopped long enough to gulp down a few swallows of iced tea, then eyed me intently.

"Well? Doesn't that sound great?"

I smiled. "So, we're doing a drag show?"

"What?"

"A drag show. You know. Guys dressing up as women. I've read this script, L. R. There are parts for at least six girls. And since you've not mentioned a single female in the last ten minutes, I must assume there aren't any."

She rolled her eyes and wrinkled her nose.

"You have a demented sense of humor. Did I ever tell you that?"

"Constantly. For twelve years."

"For your information, I have cast numerous wonderful ladies. Remember, you're one of them? Delilah Delight. I just thought you'd be more interested in hearing about your intended mate. And geez, Kiely, it's not like I'm not giving you a nice variety. I think all these guys even live in Dallas and you could marry any of them and stay down here and do shows with me all the time."

"You're worse than my mother, you know that? At least *she* doesn't care if I'm married or not. She just wants me back in Texas."

"Well, listen to her every now and then, you ungrateful child. Your mother is a brilliant wonderful woman and she's usually right. Especially when she agrees with me."

There was no good response to that statement. I poured more salsa on my rice and quickly began to tell Lida Rose about all the changes to my apartment building since she'd last visited. She knew I was avoiding more discussion concerning marriage and moving, but she let me drone on about the renovated lobby anyway. That's why she's my best friend.

We left a huge tip for our doubtless illegal waiter, then Lida Rose drove me to my new home. She'd been uncharacteristically reticent the entire ten minutes it had taken to get there. She'd avoided all mention of men, ghost hunting, and curses. Instead, she'd given me a quick rundown of the women in the cast of *Bad Business on the Brazos*. I was gratified to hear that at least two out of the six had had formal dance training.

"This is it, Kiely. Your new abode. Isn't it terrific?"

It was.

My hosts, Ted and Margaret Wyler, had bought an old Victorian-style house on Bennett Avenue. It's a funky neighborhood. Every ethnicity and economic status except very rich is represented. (How the Wylers got through this intangible opposite wealth barrier, I have no idea.) The location boasts good grocery stores within walking distance. The nights on Bennett are filled with the sounds of reggae drums, Celtic fiddles, and mariachi guitars. Scents of zeppolis, dim sum, and fried chicken mix with jambalaya and curry. It reminds me a lot of Manhattan neighborhoods, just less crowded with bigger apartments and wider streets.

Upon my arrival I was greeted by the next-door neighbor bearing keys and a sixty-five-pound black-and-white dog of uncertain ancestry. The Wylers had entrusted the keys and the canine to this woman, then flown off to Cancun. The dog immediately jumped up, put both paws on my chest, and proceeded to lick my face, removing any makeup hardy enough to remain after the three-and-a-half-hour flight. I forcibly shoved his bottom to the floor.

"Sit. Good dog. No, don't get up again. Sit. Good dog."

I needed at least one hand free to accept keys and his leash. Once the transfer was successful, I squatted down to get a better look at my new roommate. His tail flapped happily on the ground behind him.

Pedigree-challenged aptly described the puppy. He was a black Labrador wannabe whose mom had been involved in a run-in with a Siberian husky. The personality was all black Lab. And his looks were close to what I normally associated with the breed. Except that his tail was all Siberian husky. Curly and sort of a brownish-white color. His ears were undeniably lopsided, and when he quietly stared into my eyes, I realized he had one brown eye and one blue. Perhaps that accounted for the fact that he was cross-eyed as well. The tag on his collar read "Jedidiah." Jed. I hugged him. For once Lida Rose had matched me with a male I could honestly love.

The house was as much fun as the dog. The bedroom had been converted from a sundeck, so it was light and airy and overlooked the street. The kitchen had an island in the middle, more cabinet space than I'd need for a year, and countertops boasting the latest in programmable coffee machines, juicers, and vegetable-chopping devices that were technologically frightening. I would be able to dance in the living room without knocking into furniture, especially when I moved the quilted floral sofa against the wall. There was even a library with a selection as varied as a used bookstore after Christmas.

Jed and I spent a nice afternoon bonding. He took DNA samples of my belongings by chewing on my blusher brushes and the bottom of the jeans I'd removed after the plane trip. A few "No! No! Jed!'s" convinced me that negatives were *not* part of his limited vocabulary. Luckily, I discovered chew toys bigger than my makeup case in a pantry, along with a fifty-pound bag of puppy food. I quickly became the recipient of Jedidiah's undying gratitude, loyalty, and love upon offering a fresh toy, then filling the food dish marked "The Dog" to overflowing.

Once fed, Jed settled down but continued the bonding process by plopping on my bed, although he graciously allowed me a spot on the edge. Every dog I'd had as a kid had done the same thing. I didn't try and kick him off. There is something ultimately soothing about feeling the warmth of a canine companion snoozing and twitching while experiencing their puppy dreams.

Following a long sleep, I'd been ready to meet new people and start rehearsals. Lida Rose, bless her, had suggested I bring Jed to the theater so as not to worry about leaving my new buddy to do what seven-month-old puppies do when home alone.

Chapter 3

"Gennel'men. Ah b'lieve the last hand is mine. Excuse me whilst I take m'winnins."

"Ah don't rightly think so, Mr. Travis. Seems to me that four aces beats three of a kind every day, includin' Sunday. Now, ah'll jest take that pot."

"Not so fast, Mr. Lamar. I'd say my royal flush make those aces look pretty puny. Nothing personal, you understand. But *this* round goes to me."

"Jest hold those hands off'n the table, Nick Nefarious. If I 'member m'poker rules, a royal flush starts ace high, don' it? And since I've got four of 'em, you, sir, are cheating."

The sound of five chairs crashing to the ground and five guns cocking back filled the air.

"Daisy? Daisy! Where the hell are you? Your cue is 'this round goes to me.' Damn it, this is a run-through of the entire scene, not just a blocking rehearsal. Daisy!"

Our flushed accompanist hurried down the aisle toward the piano to strike the opening chords of "Gamblers We," the song that interrupts the gunfight before it escalates further than bravado.

"I'm *so* awfully sorry. I was backstage drinking a coke, and lost track of where I was."

Lida Rose lifted violet eyes heavenward and sighed audibly.

"That's okay, Daisy. Just please stay at the piano during the run-throughs, all right?"

Lida Rose surveyed the stage.

"Take five, everybody. Coffee break time."

"Damn straight! My butt's killing me sitting this long."

Jason Sharkey winked at me.

"Hey, Kiely. Want to go get coffee with me? Maybe share a cup? Maybe share some time? Kismet's available and quiet."

I smiled sweetly. "Not on your life, Jason. A coffee break with you is more like the chase scene in this play. I'll save my energy for dancing, thanks."

Jason laughed and extended the same offer to Macy Mihalik, the dance hall girl with the face and body of a Dallas Cowboys cheerleader. She trotted off behind Mr. Sharkey. Macy's very young. She wouldn't know a rounder from a roundoff. I debated the merits of giving her a short facts-of-life lecture concerning certain leading men, but nixed the idea. With those stars in her eyes, she'd ignore me, then resent me for interfering.

I jumped off the stage and headed toward the lobby where Lida Rose keeps pots of coffee going during marathon rehearsals. I was in luck. There was one freshly brewed, hot, and there were cups available. Only one other person was in line—Rafe Montez, who played Nick Nefarious, the villain.

I nodded. He nodded. He walked away; coffee cup in one hand, the other clutching a bag of freshly popped popcorn. He hadn't said more than two words to me since I started rehearsals six days before. It irked me. I admit it. The man was gorgeous. Thick, wavy black hair and deep-set eyes the color of a midnight sky. The longest, darkest lashes this side of Maybelline. Bronze skin, chiseled jaw, full lips. A body designed by a Greek sculptor on a very good day. Strong chin. Roman nose. Four hundred years ago, he would have been wearing armor, conquering Peru. I would have been first in line volunteering to be conquered.

I had to keep that thought away from my mind before Lida Rose picked up on it. She'd be on me to mate with Mr. Montez like a june bug on a tick. So far, rehearsals had been blissfully free of The Madam's matchmaking. I hoped to keep it that way.

My first few days at the theater had gone by almost too smoothly. I'd been busy learning names, choreographing dances, and memorizing lines and songs. Lida Rose had been busy directing and having production meetings, and hadn't started bugging me about the men in the show.

I knew her noninterference policy couldn't last. I was right. As I sipped coffee, watching Rafe Montez striding away from me, and Lida Rose marching toward me, I could feel my peaceful existence rapidly slip away.

"Kiely. Are you finished with your coffee?"

"No, Lida Rose, I am *not* finished. I've barely begun. What do you want?"

"I need you to come backstage and look through these costumes the historical society sent over. I think there's at least four we can use, but I'd like your input."

"Why ask me? Why not Thelma Lou? Or her assistant? What's his name—Larry?"

"Thelma Lou is looking at fabric. Larry has gone over to the Undermain Theatre. They're donating."

I followed Lida Rose to the back of the theater,

passing by our ninety-something-year-old costumer, Thelma Lou Treeberry, who was perched on a comfy chair in the wings. The brocades and laces on her lap failed to obscure the Dallas Mavericks T-shirt and faded cut-off jeans. A Yankees cap faced backward over sparse platinum-blond hair. I nodded. She nodded. She returned to the mass of fabric now spilling onto the floor. I picked up a stray piece or two, gave it to Thelma Lou, then hurried off after Lida Rose.

We spent the next fifteen minutes wading through leather chaps, satin gowns, feathers, petticoats, and early Levi's. I wasn't much help. Lida Rose knew exactly what she wanted. That should have warned me. This was no business meeting between director and choreographer. She didn't care what I thought about the leathers and laces. This was girl chat time.

"So, Kiely? Whatcha think of the guys?"

"Don't start with me, Madam."

"Now, now. Let's not be hostile. You must admit, I've collected a nice batch of unattached attractive males."

"Yes, you have. And I suppose you're just aching for me to rate them. After all, it's been, what, a week since I got here? By your standards I should have a giant engagement ring flashing by now."

She nodded. I stopped her before she began giving her opinion of nice china patterns.

"Don't look so happy, L. R. I haven't started my critique yet. Would you care to hear general objections? Or would you prefer *specific* objections?"

This question elicited the classic Bronx cheer from my genteel friend.

"Go ahead, Ms. Davlin. Pick them apart. At this rate you will *never* find a husband."

"I wasn't aware I was looking."

"Oh, sweetie, every girl over the age of twelve is looking."

I took a deep breath, intending to dispute that statement. But arguing with Lida Rose is useless. I know this well. So I launched into a review of the gentlemen of East Ellum Theatre currently onstage for *Bad Business on the Brazos*.

"Okey-dokey. Jason Sharkey is an egocentric, lady-killing smarmy, heavy drinking SOB. Oh, by the way. What is this bit about 'Kismet' being quiet and available? Is that a code for his van or something?"

A sliver of a grin appeared on my friend's face.

"'Kismet' is what everyone calls the old prop room. Holds every last item from when the theater actually did *Kismet* about a thousand years ago: beads, bangles, baubles, scimitars, magic carpets, you name it. There's a highly comfortable sofa-type bed up there that's been used for, shall we say, recreational activities throughout the years."

Her grin grew broader.

"At least, so I've been told. I prefer to do my aerobic amours with George at home in the four poster. Anyway, forget it. I can't see you rolling around a floral loveseat for illicit purposes anytime soon. Go on. Jason's out. I agree with you on that one. What do you think of Theo?"

"Theo Stafford is a doll. He seems more interested in Lindsay than me, which is fine. She's a doll, too. I wish them years of happiness. Um. Ham and Hank Humble are a great twin act. I can't tell one from the other. Yet. I don't know if I want to try, although they're very cute and seem to have some smarts even if they have four left feet between them. Let's see.

Larry Creighton is a wonderful costumer. I question his proclivities as to which gender he prefers, but that's his business and not mine. Charlie Baines, the techie, is married. Don't you look at rings? And then there's Neil. The box office cherub. I haven't seen him yet, but apparently he's a child. I mean, what is he, fifteen or something? I'm so sorry to disappoint you, but I draw the line at jailbait."

Lida Rose frowned at me.

"Aside from Larry being gay, Charlie being married, and Neil being young—ha! That's a good one. Neil. Young. Get it?"

I stifled a giggle. It's best not to encourage the woman when she's being funny. She went on.

"Actually Neil's eighteen, and I don't see a problem with the others. Well, except Jason. And excuse me, but why haven't you mentioned Rafe Montez?"

I stopped. Why *hadn't* I mentioned Rafe Montez?

Fortunately, we were interrupted by the appearance of Daisy, the rehearsal pianist, wandering into the costume shop and spilling coffee all over the floor, barely missing a beaded ball gown, circa 1889. Daisy Haltom seems to possess the grace of a bull and the brains of a cow. Her mother doubtless bore the name of Elsie and decided to hand the bovine-name theme down to the next generation. I *should* feel sorry for Daisy. Instead, I keep wanting to slap her. Lida Rose feels the same way, but Daisy is such an excellent musician, she can't afford to dump the girl. Ms. Haltom plays organ at the Baptist church in Balch Springs and dresses like a stereotypical spinster from a 1950s movie starring Joanne Woodward: brown shirtwaist dresses, low-heeled pumps, and not a smidgen of makeup.

"Daisy? What is it?"

"I'm sorry, Lida Rose, but I have to leave rehearsal. I'm playing a funeral today in Balch Springs. I forgot."

The sound of grinding teeth emanated from Lida Rose. I winked at her. She took a breath.

"Fine. Go. Any other conflicts you've forgotten?"

"Oh no. Least, I don't think so. This was kind of an emergency situation. Mr. Brewer died yesterday evening and his wife said she wanted him planted in a hurry on account of she's leaving for the Bahamas tomorrow."

I dove facedown into a pile of lacy undergarments in an attempt to stifle my mirth. Lida Rose choked, but shooed Daisy out the door, then collapsed on the petticoats with me.

"Kiely, please tell me this show is going to go off without a hitch. Please?"

I assumed my "good dog, Jedidiah" voice. "It'll be fine. What could go wrong? No, wait. Don't answer that."

A gleam appeared in Lida Rose's eye.

"Maybe our ghost will decide to make an appearance. Pull some poltergeist stuff and knock down the set. While we're onstage. Or, let's see—take possession of one of the guys. Although I guess it could be one of the girls. Are ghosts gender conscious when occupying bodies?"

Lida Rose was watching me like a child waiting to be led to her birthday cake. I can't resist that face.

"I'm not an authority, Lida Rose. Why don't you call 1-800-Haunts-R-Us and ask?"

That gleam grew brighter.

"I must admit I've been waiting for Don Mueller

to do something to take revenge on the theater responsible for his murder."

She settled up against the wall and happily began to play with the laces on a black corset.

"After all, he was shot right on stage during the last act of *Bad Business*. This very show. He died mere seconds after a bullet fired from the gun of the actor playing Lance Lamar entered his chest. He's remained here ever since. It's so neat!"

I glared at her.

"You have kinky ideas of neat. I think it's very sad. Why is he supposed to haunt the theater?"

"Hell, I don't know. Legend has it his lady love also died here under mysterious circumstances and he's looking for her."

"Does that mean she's here, too?"

Lida Rose beamed, then grew morose.

"No. I haven't heard about any ghost sightings of females. Although there is a rumor about the very first Delilah Delight. From a hundred years ago."

Her voice trailed off. A gleam appeared in her violet eyes.

"Never mind. Only a trace of a story. So far. Anyway, the only ghost I know of for certain is Don. He roams around still dressed in his villain costume. Stovepipe-crumpled black hat, black tuxedo jacket with tails, black trousers, black cape. And white sneakers. Just like that picture of him in the lobby."

I'd seen the photograph to which she referred. It portrayed a man in a villain suit straight out of a Snidely Whiplash cartoon. The actor himself possessed a wonderfully expressive face and kind eyes. I'd felt an immediate rapport with him, not knowing he floated around the theater without a flesh-and-blood body.

Lida Rose said wickedly, "I'm going to dress Rafe in that same style costume since he's playing Nick Nefarious. I hope he's not superstitious."

I shivered again. I needed to get out into the sunshine. I hoisted Lida Rose off the petticoats.

"So, Director Lady, since Daisy crapped out on us, are we done for the day?"

"Oh, shoot. Where's my mind? Yeah, we're through. Let me tell the others. They should be back from coffee break by now. This'll give everyone a chance to study the script. I've never heard so much ad-libbing from professionals who should have had lines off last Thursday."

She hurried off. I picked up a few of the petticoats and started putting them back on the hangers. A shadow fell across the wall. I squinted. Maybe I needed a new prescription for my contacts. I could have sworn the shadow was cast in the shape of a man wearing a tux. A stovepipe hat sloped rakishly on top of his head.

Chapter 4

I *had* planned on getting to the theater early the next day to choreograph. The biggest number for the dance hall girls was still swirling around in my brain, but wasn't yet on paper. I foolishly believed that if I had a bare stage and no one around, I'd actually have a chance to finish it. Lida Rose had given me the theater keys the day I got to Dallas. The idea was that I wouldn't have to bother anyone else (i.e., her) at eight in the morning.

Jed and I jogged from the house on Bennett with only a few stops along the way for sniffing and watering bushes (Jed, not me). I allowed the dog one more elated swipe at the mulberry tree ten feet from the theater entrance while I rooted the keys out of the top of my dance bag. They weren't needed. The doors were unlocked. Actually, they were wide open. Some other fool was up. The aroma of hazelnut coffee coming from the kitchen tingled my senses.

"Hey, Thelma Lou. How's it going? What on earth are you doing here so early?"

"Lookin' over costumes Larry brought in after y'all left yesterday. My hands ain't in the best of shape, but I still got a good eye for what's needed. I figured I'd sort through 'em, see if anything matches what we used years ago."

I smiled and nodded thanks as she placed a steaming cup of coffee into my eager hands.

"That's right. You were costumer the last time the theater did *Bad Business on the Brazos,* weren't you?"

She nodded. My curious nature took over. Here was someone who might know a bit more about the ghost of Don Mueller. But how did one delicately ask about the death of a man an elderly lady had costumed fifty years ago? A man who'd been her friend. Thelma Lou quickly solved my dilemma. She opened her mouth and a monologue spewed forth that rivaled any Lida Rose had ever delivered.

"We put on a good show back then. Great cast. I 'member Fran Watkins played Bathsheba Bombshell, one of the dancers. She wasn't as pretty as you or these other girls, or even as good a dancer, but she was a heck of an actress. Played lots of ingenues in the regular season shows. Part owner of the theater now. Rich. Big friends with that idiot Kincaid woman. *She* played one of the dancehall girls. Can't remember which. She's t'other owner, didja know that? Her grandson works box office for us and he's as big an idiot as she is. Lessee. We didn't have *real* twins to play Billy Joe Bob and Bobby Joe Bob Travis, like those Humble boys, but we had two fellas who were terrific actors. Ain't those Humble boys cute? And a' course, there was Don."

I stopped midsip. "Yes?"

"Best damn villain this theater ever saw. He was one super actor all the way around. Every show he did, he gave a hunnert percent."

"Tell me about him, please?"

She looked up at me. "Why you interested, hon?"

"I don't know. I guess because I've seen his pictures and heard these stories about him haunting the theater. Maybe it's only curiosity. Whatever it is, I feel a link with him."

She nodded. "You seen him?"

"What?"

"His ghost? Seen him? He was here, ya know, watchin' your dance rehearsal two days ago. He likes you."

I sank onto the kitchen stool. Jed, who'd been sleeping under it, licked my ankle, then promptly faded out again.

"What do you mean?"

"He's been watchin' different rehearsals here for the last fifty years. If he don' like somethin' he just goes away. He likes you, though. Stayed for the whole rehearsal."

I was more than a little fascinated.

"Where was he?"

"Up in the balcony. Well, what used to be the balcony. It's the light booth now. You'da liked Don. Kindest, most honest, most generous man I ever knew. And funny. Lord a' mercy, he could make people laugh. Things would be reachin' that stretchin' point in a rehearsal where tempers start to go. And Don would make a joke and you could feel everybody relax. He could handle an audience, too. We always had the rule that popcorn was all you could throw during a show, but sometimes people would try and get a little rowdy and toss ice or coins and stuff. Why, Don'd just stay in his villain character and step right down to the front of the stage and talk to the boys pullin' that kinda nonsense. They'd quiet right down. 'Course, if they did throw popcorn, he'd want to eat it. That man loved popcorn like it was steak and potatoes."

I laughed. "Must be a villain thing. I have yet to see Rafe Montez without a bag in his hand when he's not onstage. Or when he *is* onstage, for that matter. I guess he's practicing his aim toward the audience."

Thelma Lou winked at me.

"Could be. Could be he just likes popcorn. Like Don. Who was also a wizard at tossin' ad-libs back at the audience. Better 'n the script most of the time."

I poured another cup of coffee. My choreography could wait. I didn't know why I was so interested in hearing about Don Mueller, but since Thelma Lou was on a talking jag, I wasn't about to shut her up.

"All the ladies loved him. Funny. He wasn't really a looker. Kind of a hooked nose. Think he broke it doin' a stunt in one of the shows. Big, sad, dark blue eyes. Brown hair. Tall, thin. Sort of a rubbery face. Great for an actor."

"Was he married?"

Thelma Lou got a funny look on her face. "No, honey. Was a bachelor for years. Then he got sweet on some little girl. Noemi was her name. She was supposed to play one of the dancehall girls in *Bad Business* with Fran and Shirley. Come to think of it, was your character, Delilah Delight. I remember some of the other girls weren't too nice cause she was Mexican. Stupid. Why do people do that? Anyway, she took off about a week before the show opened. Don't know what it is with Delilah Delights. First one ran off, too. A hundred years ago. Where was I? Oh, yeah, Noemi. Don got real sad. Then he got shot."

I nearly spilled my coffee. "Can you tell me what happened? Lida Rose doesn't really know details. I'm sorry. Only if you don't mind. Obviously you were a good friend of his. I don't want to bring up hurtful memories."

She patted my hand. "It's fine. I've had fifty years to get over it, and since I see him occasionally at the theater, it don't pain me so much now."

She headed toward the house of the theater, motioning for me to follow. We opened the doors leading in from the lobby, then hiked up the aisle to the stage. Once we were on the stage itself, she pointed to a spot close to the wings on the left side.

"It was the last night of *Bad Business*. We got to the part where Lance Lamar is supposed to shoot Nick Nefarious. Cyrus Boone was playin' Lance. Normally Don would get shot, then go through about a minute of dyin' all over stage. The audience would go wild, hootin' and yellin' silly stuff at him."

She lifted her chin and closed her eyes, remembering. Then she opened them and said, "I watched every night and just about wet my pants laughin'. Don could die like nobody you've ever seen. He'd stagger around, switchin' his right hand over his heart, then his left, like he didn't know where he'd really been shot. He'd be yellin' out jokes to the audience and finally fall on his back with his feet up in the air like some ol' cockroach just been sprayed."

I could see him fake his death scene in my mind as she described the antics. I smiled along with her. Then her tone and demeanor changed.

"But this night Cyrus shot the gun . . . and Don? Well, he just dropped. I was standin' in the wings like I always did and I could see Don's face close as I see you now. He looked—I don't know, surprised for a second—then he fell. Everybody knew. The actors, of course, but even the audience. Most of 'em were regulars who'd seen the show more'n a few times."

She paused and shook her head. "I'll never forget poor Cyrus. He looked like *he* was the one died. He kept shakin' that gun and crying. Left the actin' business for about ten years. And I've heard since that night he ain't never been the same, either. Too quiet. Cyrus adored Don. Don was older and Cyrus followed his every move like some puppy dog. Don was his hero. The hero worshipping the villain. We all used to laugh about that. And afterwards it seemed to make it worse."

I was almost crying myself. I could see the tragedy unfolding before my eyes on this stage as vividly as if I'd been there the night it happened.

"Did the police find out what had happened? Who switched live bullets for the blanks?"

She looked at me and shook her head again.

"Nope. Never did. Part of the problem was there just didn't seem to be a motive. Who would want Don Mueller dead? It wasn't like this was some big Broadway show or somethin' where the understudy would want to take over. He didn't have a family to inherit, and even if he'd had, the man didn't own more than a little house. And he wasn't playin' fast and loose with nobody's girl, and far as I recall, nobody else was hankering after Noemi. The whole damn thing just never made sense. Lots of the cast used to do target practice outside when they'd get bored during rehearsals. And a' course, all of 'em carried a gun onstage. The guns were real. Just the bullets were fake. Somebody might have left a gun they used for target practice backstage and it got mixed up and the wrong bullets got put in. We didn't have a props man; just everybody lookin' after their own things. It was pretty messy backstage. So the police called it accidental. A sad mistake, they said."

Derision dripped with that last statement. I looked down at this tiny woman with the wrinkled face. She was dressed today in pink bermuda shorts nearly covered by an oversized gray Dallas Cowboys sweatshirt. The platinum-blond hair was pulled back under a black Dallas Burn cap and she was sporting the reddest lipstick I'd seen outside of what I planned to wear as Delilah Delight. Her expression was grim.

"Thelma Lou. What do *you* think?"

"He was murdered."

She turned and walked away toward the costume area. The conversation was over.

I stayed out on the stage. Jed had followed us from the kitchen and was now drooling on my feet, chewing the laces of my jazz shoes. I knelt down and quietly took them out of his mouth, replacing them with one of the toys I kept in my dance bag. He contentedly began destroying the plastic Daily Growl chew toy. I stroked his soft head as I appraised the theater.

The *East Ellum Theatre* had been built over a hundred years ago. It started life as a small opera house, one of many that sprang up during the prosperous cattle-driving years in the Dallas-Fort Worth area. There was a proscenium stage with moderate wing space, and a real-live orchestra pit below. The house itself only held about 750 seats. The balcony had been replaced ten years ago with an ultramodern light and sound booth, and extra seats had been added downstairs on the sides so the seating area for the audience was now shaped more like a horseshoe. The stage had been enlarged at the same time. Costume, prop, and scene shops were still in the process of being added to the left side of the theater. They would connect to the wings on that side. A catwalk above the stage and theater house had remained, after being reinforced with steel. The orchestra pit was still down front below the stage, but a hydraulic lift system had been added, and if one needed the extra space for shows not requiring music, the pit could be converted and extended downstage toward the audience.

The renovations to the theater had added space, modern lighting, and sound, but thankfully not removed the charm of the old place. Obviously Don Mueller was still comfortable here. I didn't know if he was the kind of ghost who'd get pissed and start throwing things if a production didn't live up to his expectations, but even if he remained benign I wanted to believe I had his approval for my dances.

Thinking about my dance rehearsals reminded me of why I'd staggered out of the house so early. I had real work to do. Ninety minutes remained before the rest of the cast would show up. I needed to put that time to good use. I couldn't spend it mooning over the tragic story of an actor who'd died fifty years before I'd had a chance to meet him.

Chapter 5

I dragged my small tape player out from the bottom of my dance bag and proceeded to pop in the cassette Daisy had hastily put together two days ago. The tinny sounds of a piano filled the theater as I tried out various steps, pausing to write down good ideas when they hit. I could hear nothing but the music. Thelma Lou was hip deep in fabric in the costume shop. The dog and I were the only beings in the theater proper, so I was startled when Jed's ears perked up and his tail started maniacally thumping against the stage floor.

I looked out into the audience to see if Lida Rose had arrived. And saw a man dressed in the villain's costume staring at me. My breath caught. He looked awfully real from where I was standing.

"The dance looks good."

I nearly fainted. The ghost was talking! Then I looked again and realized the ghost was also walking.

Jed's tail started beating a rhythm that mimicked the pounding of my heart.

"Jedidiah! Shouldn't you be howling or something? Aren't dogs supposed to be scared of ghosts?"

"What ghosts?"

The villain began marching down toward the orchestra pit. I screamed. I shut off the music and screamed again.

Rafe Montez stared at me from the edge of the stage. I pursed my lips together.

"Oh, hell and damnation fury! It's only you."

"Thanks. Such a nice way you have of greeting a fellow actor. Really gives one a warm and fuzzy feeling."

I blushed. "I'm so sorry. I really didn't mean it the way it sounded. I was petrified. Well, maybe a bit excited, too. I thought the ghost of Don Mueller had decided to join me for a little waltz onstage or something."

One of Rafe's black eyebrows lifted about an inch. I've always both admired and resented people who have perfected that wonderfully sarcastic gesture. I can never get just one brow to lift. I believe this to mean the *raisee* possesses gifts of phenomenal talent and intellect I can never comprehend. This particular talented intellectual was staring at me as though I'd just turned green and grown Vulcan-style ears.

"Did you say the ghost of Don Mueller?"

"I did. Hey, you ought to be worried. Here you are running around in his costume, taking over his part. He may decide he's envious and try and scare you out of the show."

I was kidding, but Rafe looked concerned.

"You're weird, you know that?"

I didn't appreciate the insult. And I was miffed that he thought I was a kook.

"Am not. What makes you say that?"

"Because it sounds like you actually believe this character is haunting the theater. No offense, Miss Davlin, but that's a large load of cow poop."

Okay. He was getting my Irish up. Davlins and Rileys. Both sets of ancestors.

"Well, excuse me, Mr. Zero Imagination. Not only am I convinced he's here, but I have reason to believe it. I've seen him. Really."

Oops. Hadn't meant to let that slip out. His other eyebrow lifted. Damn. Ambidextrous movable brows.

"Care to share your little ghost story? Or is it reserved for dark and stormy nights around a campfire?"

I shot him what might be termed a hostile look. The man hadn't bothered to talk to me for the six days I'd been here. Now that he was making an effort, it was only to ridicule me.

"Fine. Laugh at me. But I know yesterday I saw him in the costume shop just before I left. Dressed in the same full villain's gear you've got on now. And I swear on my dog's nose, it wasn't you, unless you can fade away like a Cheshire cat into a wall."

"I seem to remember you and Lida Rose going off in that direction yesterday. Did she happen to regale you with her little ghost stories before you saw this so-called apparition?"

"Well, yes, and she did mention that she thought he might be ready to put in an appearance soon. But I *didn't* imagine seeing him. I'm not that suggestible."

"Uh-huh."

This was no way to start a friendship. Or anything else.

"Believe what you like. Now, if you'll excuse me, I have to get back to work before anyone else shows up."

"So you do. I'm sorry I disturbed you. The only reason I'm here early is to try on this costume our director seems determined to have me wear. I'll leave you alone."

He whirled away before I could apologize. Perhaps

I *had* been a bit snippy. He suddenly turned around again.

"The dances are good, Kiely. My mother was a dancer with New York City Ballet. I recognize talent when I see it."

I did blush then, until my face matched the color of my hair.

"Thanks. I appreciate you saying that."

Rafe smiled and my heart started thumping rather on the order of Jed's tail.

"No problem."

He headed off toward the costume shop. I was amazed I hadn't heard him earlier. I could have sworn he'd only now entered from the theater house. The man rivaled my ghost in silence.

I turned my attention back to my choreography. No one else entered the theater for the next half hour. At least no one I was aware of.

"Kiely! Guess what?"

I looked up from the notebook where I'd been frantically writing out my own shorthand version of the steps I was creating. It was ten A.M. Lida Rose stood in front of me, flanked by Jason Sharkey, the Humble twins, Amber the ingenue, and my two female dancers, Lindsay Carmichael and Macy Mihalik.

"What?"

Lida Rose was literally jumping up and down in gleeful excitement. With her anatomy, I feared she'd knock herself in the chin and pass out. I grabbed her to stop the movement and asked, "What?"

"They've accepted. Every one of them."

"Who? Every one of what? Madam Worthington, you are the most exasperating source of information I've ever known. Tell a person what you're talking about just once so they'll have an inkling as to whatever is in your head."

She looked not the least embarrassed. I am always telling her she is generally three conversations ahead of the rest of the world. She knows this. It doesn't bother her. She simply expects the rest of humanity to read her thoughts and catch up.

"Kiely! Quit blathering and pay attention. I'm talking about the original surviving cast members of *Bad Business on the Brazos*. I had the publicity office send out invitations asking if they'd like to attend the grand reopening of the theater as our special guests. And they're coming. Those that are still alive, that is."

Rafe would be glad to know a collection of ghosts were not about to invade the theater.

"Who all's accepted?"

Jason stepped forward to answer, possibly because Lida Rose thrust the list into his hands. Her reading glasses were nowhere in sight, so he'd been elected as speaker. He cleared his throat and began to announce the names in tones similar to those of an anchorman reciting the local news.

"Fran Watkins, the original Bathsheba Bombshell, who also happens to be one-half owner of East Ellum Theatre. Shirley Kincaid, the original Sultry Salome, who just happens to be the other half. Let's see . . . Nathaniel Bollinger, the original Ace Royale. My counterpart, Lance Lamar, one Mr. Cyrus Boone. Jeez, what a name. Sounds like a regular old geezer, doesn't it? Probably doesn't have a tooth or a thought left. Actually, didn't he go nuts after that old actor died? The spook haunting the theater?"

Lida Rose glanced at me. I was too angry at Jason's insensitivity to notice.

Several more of our cast had gathered 'round. Theo Stafford, the current Ace Royale, shot Jason a less-than-cordial look. "I wouldn't be quite so quick to put down the man who received more rave reviews for his performance in the New York Public Theater's production of *King Lear* than you've been granted in your entire theatrical career. As for the tragedy years ago—can you imagine how awful it must have been for him? Killing someone, even as an accident? I'd've spent *my* next twenty years in a nice sanitarium."

Jason ignored him and continued to read.

"Okay, there's one other name—Noemi Trujillo. Who doesn't seem to have a reason to be on this list. I can't find a character name given and there's a question mark by her name."

My head shot up. I knew that name. Noemi. Pretty name. Thelma Lou said she was the woman who'd been in love with Don Mueller, then taken off and broken his heart.

"Let me see that."

He handed me the list. There it was. I looked at Lida Rose.

"Was she in the show? I thought Thelma Lou said she left a week or so before they opened *Bad Business.*"

Lida Rose smiled at me.

"They didn't list her in the old cast program. Thelma Lou's correct. The lady disappeared before opening night. The programs must have been printed after she'd gone."

"Noemi was supposed to play your character, Kiely. Delilah Delight. I hear they didn't replace her. They just did without one dancehall girl and gave her lines to Shirley Kincaid. Rumor has it she was engaged to Don Mueller. Noemi, that is. Not Shirley."

She stated, "I just stuck her name on this list because I wanted to ask the other old cast members if they knew anything about her."

Macy was hanging over Jason's shoulder. He didn't seem to mind.

"So who's *not* here?"

Jason handed the list to me.

"Kiely, you seem to know all about these people. Any idea who's missing?"

I took the paper from him.

"I don't know *all* about the cast. Thelma Lou told me mainly about Don Mueller. As for this list, I imagine since we're doing the same show, then whoever our counterparts were back then, and aren't listed here, are those missing. Definitely the rancher twins, Billy Joe Bob and Bobby Joe Bob Travis."

Lida Rose beamed at me. "Very succinct, Kiely. I understood that completely."

I quickly perused the names. "Okay. Aside from the Travis boys, we seem to be minus one ingenue, the villain sidekick Jackson Wild, and of course, the villain. Five of the original cast members are missing. Well, six if you count Noemi Trujillo. Are these others deceased?"

Lida Rose nodded.

"I think so. Of course, we know about Don Mueller. And all these people are at least in their seventies now, so I wouldn't be surprised if several of the others had passed on to the great melodrama in the sky at some point."

"I'm here."

We all turned. Daisy Haltom had arrived and was running down the left aisle of the theater unintentionally banging into chairs and railings. The woman was a walking disaster.

I glanced at Lida Rose. She was in the middle of proclaiming, "Who gives a rat's derriere?" at the accompanist, who was now fifteen minutes late for rehearsal. I poked her before she could finish muttering the question. For now, we needed Daisy. She might be a pain in that rodent's behind but she was an excellent musician.

Lida Rose clapped her hands together to command the attention of the cast. "Okay. Y'all had an unexpected break yesterday. I assume that being the good little actors you are you took full advantage and went home and memorized your lines? Of *course* you did. At any rate, we've got a long day ahead, so plop your bags down and come sit in the first few rows for a vocal warm-up. Kiely? I need to see you for just a minute."

The rest of the cast did as they were told and started singing the first notes of a scale. Lida Rose pulled me aside.

"Yes, oh director mine? Is this a fast and minimal production meeting?"

She immediately looked guilty. I've noticed in the week I've had him, that Jed gets that same expression on his face after he's eaten the Kleenex from the trash and the chicken bones from anybody's garbage.

"This is not a production meeting. You know what you're doing dance-wise. You always do. This is purely personal. I ran into Rafe just before I came into the theater. He told me you'd seen Don Mueller. I'm so excited. Did he say anything to you?"

Fortunately, she was whispering, but I glanced down into the rows where the cast was sitting just in case ears perked.

"Sshh! This is *just* terrific. Why the hell did he tell you that?"

"Because I asked him what you thought of his costume. He blurted out that you thought he was Don. Rafe wasn't telling tales, Kiely. Honest."

I felt a little better.

"There's nothing really exciting to relate. I saw your ghost in the costume shop. That is, I assume it was your ghost. Now that I think about it, it was probably a shadow."

My friend shook her head vigorously.

"It was Don. This is too much fun. You know he really likes your dances. Thelma Lou and I peeked in here after Rafe told me you thought he was Don. She said he was watching you while you worked. He was bobbing his head up and down and smiling."

I stared at her. My best friend was a lunatic. I'd suspected it for years. Now I was sure.

"You are out of your skull. Ya know that, Lida Rose Worthington Rizokowsky? Now, don't misunderstand. I might *just* believe that there are such things as ghosts. In fact, I think it's in the actor's handbook that performers must work in at least two haunted theaters on a yearly basis. I've also heard ghost theories that explain that maybe the spirits are an essence of someone's presence remaining, some sort of shadow of energy. But to have you stand there and tell me that Don Mueller is acting like some choreographic critic keeping an eye on my work is beyond nutso."

She smiled.

"Just wait, Kiely. You'll see. Okay, I've kept you long enough. Go sing."

I hurried off the stage to join my castmates. Rafe eyed me with his left eyebrow up this time. I gave him a huge smile, opened my mouth wide, and joined the others, hitting the top notes of an F minor scale. Jed added his own interpretation of the scale from the orchestra pit where I'd left him. He loves high notes. Our soprano, Amber, was already finding it difficult to sing her solo with Jed accompanying.

We finished warming up, then sang through the five songs we'd learned so far, including "Gamblers We," the number we'd been about to sing yesterday before Daisy's desertion. Lida Rose came down and listened, then waved at the accompanist to stop playing.

"Let's start there. Everybody? Onstage, Act Two, Scene Two. Um, let's take it from the beginning where the poker game is getting heated."

For the next three hours we ran the scene until it met Lida Rose's high standards. The woman may come across as a scatterbrain, but she's a killer director. Very picky, very knowledgeable about what she wants, and very adept at getting it. Exhaustion was setting in when she finally called "Break."

We had an hour off for lunch. Lida Rose had heard from Christa Hernandez that El Diablo's was open again, so we'd decided to lend monetary and moral support and go en masse for real Tex-Mex.

I grabbed Jed, who was now happily gnawing the chairs in the back row, and penned him in the kitchen where I figured he could do the least amount of damage. I gave him water and two more chew toys from my bag, then delivered a stern lecture about staying out of trouble. His eyes never left my face and his expression oozed pure adoration and angelic acceptance. I had no doubt the moment I left he would find a way to open one of the locked pantry doors and devour the unpopped popcorn from the sealed bags.

Heck, with his talent, he'd probably find a way to pop them in the microwave—with extra butter.

In that case I just hoped he'd share with Don Mueller.

Chapter 6

The cast, minus Jason, Macy, Daisy, and our ingenue, Amber something (I had yet to learn her last name and doubted I ever would), was already seated at a huge round table at El Diablo's. Chips and salsa and water glasses had been set down, and the waitress was standing near Theo, waiting for the order. I hurried in and took the empty chair next to one of the twins—Ham, I think. That put me directly opposite Rafe, who nodded politely at me.

"How's Jed?"

"He's fine. There might not be a kitchen when we get back, but he seemed happy. Actually, Thelma Lou came in as I was leaving and said she'd stay with him, so the theater may be safe for the moment. More important, how's Joe? Is Christa in today?"

Lindsay Carmichael, a tall, gorgeous dancer with mocha skin, an incredible figure, and a constant twinkle in her brown eyes, lifted up a chip dripping with sauce and waved it at me. Little red dots flew around the table.

"Christa hugged every one of us as soon as we burst through the door. Joe is apparently encased in a full body cast and will be enjoying the accommodations at the hospital for an undisclosed time. Probably until the insurance company says enough."

Rafe added, "We need to arrange a visit. Preferably get about ten members of *Bad Business* in at the same time. Joe loves crowds. It'll piss off the hospital staff, but be worth it for him."

I did like the way Rafe's mind worked. But I was curious.

"How do you know Joe?"

Rafe replied, "We're cousins. We're just about the same age and we pretty much grew up together. I was sampling the cuisine at the Hernandez household long before Joe ever decided to open a restaurant. You think he's good? You should be there at Thanksgiving when my uncle Jess is cooking. Deliciously sinful."

His tone changed. "Needless to say, though, I'm damned upset about his accident."

"What really happened? Anyone know?"

"Apparently Joe had just finished locking up here and was heading for his car, which was parked across the street. Some sonovabitch plowed into him. There were no witnesses, naturally. It's not exactly booming in this neighborhood after midnight."

I looked around El Diablo's. "I can't believe this happened so soon after he opened. It's really a fun place. I love those funky 'Early Juarez Tourist' velvet paintings on the walls. Joe does have a wonderful sense of humor."

Rafe laughed. "He told me he wondered how many people would think *he* believed those were serious pieces of art—"

Lindsay interrupted before Rafe had a chance to continue. "Art, schmart. We're half through with lunch and I want info on my fellow *Bad Business*ers. So, is everyone a Texas native, except for Kiely?"

I tried to emulate Rafe's one eyebrow technique but succeeded only in raising both.

"Lindsay, my friend, I'll have you know I *am* a Texas native. Well, sort of: born in Virginia, raised in Dallas from age nine on. Went to the Arts Magnet High School and everything. I only became a Yankee citizen ten years ago. Do you mean to tell me you can't hear that little twang in my voice? I'll have to call my vocal coach in Manhattan and tell him what an amazing job he did."

She smiled.

"I know. Lida Rose told me all about you when she said you were coming to choreograph. I just wanted to bug you a little, sauntering in from the big city to help out the home folks. Anybody else?"

"I'm not native, Lindsay," said Lida Rose. Here it came. Eugenia Grace and *The Music Man*. I winked at her and nodded. It was a great story. Never failed to delight an audience of theatrical trivia buffs.

"Anyone else want to fess up to being a carpetbagger?" Lindsay questioned as Lida Rose finished up with "I was belting out my first notes in the very same key."

Theo turned as pink as was possible for a man whose skin color was a deep brown. "I have to admit it. I was not born in Texas. Nowhere near."

Lindsay poked him in his side.

"Yes, yes. Give."

He smiled sheepishly. "Actually, my dad was in the service, so I wasn't even born in America. We were living in Germany at the time. But I did go to college at Sam Houston. Am I forgiven?"

The look Lindsay gave him made it clear he could

have robbed a bank and been forgiven. I had that one pegged right. I was glad. They were a great couple. Plus, since Theo had been nabbed, Lida Rose would have one less bachelor to bug me about. Theo looked at the twins.

"Where you guys from?"

Ham and Hank chuckled. In unison. With the last name of "Humble" and those first names, they had to be Sons of the Texas Republic. Their ancestors had probably elected the first governor, signed treaties with Mexico, and imported the original longhorn steers.

I was right. Ham stopped chewing on a taco long enough to announce the Humble brothers as natives of San Augustine, the oldest city in Texas. Lindsay squealed and stated she was from Lufkin, only forty miles away.

That started the "where were you the year San Augustine beat Lufkin?" routine. The beating referred to was, of course, football. Yep. I was back in Texas.

Rafe had stayed silent. Lindsay, the instigator of this roots interrogation, eyed him and stared until he retreated into a tall glass of iced tea.

"Okay. Tell us, Montez. Are you even *legal*? I mean, you look like you just came riding over the hill with Pancho Villa."

I was beginning to truly adore Lindsay. She had yet to pull a punch and had absolutely no guile.

Rafe smiled, a long, warm smile that made the hot sauce seem mild in comparison.

"Dallas, Texas, ma'am. I'm more native than the bunch of you. Not only did I grow up smack in the middle of Big D, I was born here."

I stared at him.

"You're kidding. Where did you go to school? Did you do shows around here? How did I miss meeting you before?"

"Jesuit High. Where, incidentally, I played more than my share of leads in theatrical extravaganzas. I don't know why we haven't met before, although you Arts Magnet types ignored the productions at Jesuit. As for college? I went to Notre Dame. Football scholarship. I did a few shows there as well."

Amazing. He did possess a great physique, but even college football players nowadays seem to be giants. Rafe was a shade less than six feet tall and wiry rather than big.

My mouth dropped lower.

"Football?"

"I happen to be a damn good kicker."

I laughed. "I thought those toes pointed right smartly for a villain when we were rehearsing the 'Business Is Bad' number."

He acknowledged the compliment with a slight tilt of his head.

"Remember I told you my mom danced with New York City Ballet? Blame it on her. My Dad moved down to Texas, she was only about eighteen when I was born, and she missed being out of the company. So I got the brunt of her frustration until she began performing with Dallas Ballet. She'd dance at home—with me. Actually, I was the only kicker in Notre Dame history ever to do *tours* in the air after the ball sailed through the goalpost."

We were all howling. For the first time, Rafe seemed to be relaxing. I wondered how long that would last. I couldn't stop myself from asking questions.

"What was your major?"

He lifted the right eyebrow at me.

"You are one nosy woman, you know that?"

I nodded. True. I've never denied it.

"So?"

"Art."

"You're joking."

"I'm absolutely serious."

The man looked like he could grind metal in his teeth and bench press three times his weight. Art. I knew I was thinking stereotypically, but still I was so astonished I couldn't even think of a clever quip. Fortunately the dessert platter of sopapillas arrived and everyone got busy pouring butter and honey over the pastries. My lack of any witty *bon mots* didn't seem to be noticed.

The conversation took a series of rapid turns, from college majors to football teams to who was dating whom and where. The last naturally launched us into a delightfully tacky discussion about Jason going off for lunch with three women we speculated had very clear designs on the man.

"So does Daisy."

This last came from Larry, the assistant costumer who had joined our group only moments before. I hadn't seen him at first, which was surprising because he was dressed in what I could only label as his Great Gatsby: vanilla ice cream suit with a pink shirt and mauve tie with dots of white and pink. How he could wear something like that when the temperature was well over ninety outdoors was a tribute either to the deodorant industry or a clear conscience. He wasn't eating, just visiting. He informed Lida Rose that he was on his way to the Garland Summer Musicals to look at old slut costumes he thought might work for the dancehall girls.

We stared at him after he made his astonishing revelation about Daisy Haltom. He threw his hands into the air in a gesture of "Yo! You gotta problem?"

"Well, *pardonez moi*, y'all, but I'm not making it up. She follows him around like a puppy. And she was crying in the costume shop the other day after he'd been flirting with Macy all afternoon. Daisy's always coming up with excuses for him to check her car or offering to help him learn his songs. The man's an ass, but he is a good musician. He no more needs help learning that music from Miss Spinster than I need a wife."

Since Larry made no bones about being gay, this last statement was a firm indicator of just how desperate Daisy Haltom had gotten.

Lida Rose smiled a bit too sweetly.

"Well, golly gee. I never knew Miss Daisy even recognized differences in the sexes. This is truly an eye-opener."

Lindsay shook her head. "She's in for some serious hurt. Jason likes 'em young and pretty. Let's face it, she's neither."

"The man's a snake."

"What?" We turned as a unit to the *older* twin, Ham.

"He goes after every poor girl in every cast. Love 'em and leave 'em. I've counseled more broken hearts in the years I've done shows with Jason. I should be paid analyst fees."

"Ah, you're just jealous cause you're passionately in love with Amber and she's not interested. Yet."

Ham blushed as his brother stated this embarrassing fact.

So Ham (and doubtless Hank, since the pair seemed

joined at the hip) disliked Jason Sharkey with a passion. And Daisy, the spinster wren with the grace of an ox, had a passionate crush on Jason. Jason was passionately chasing both Macy and Amber. I was passionately trying to finish my dances while not giving in to the passion rising in my body for a certain disbeliever of the paranormal. The passion level at the theater for the next few months could prove interesting.

Lida Rose started gathering up her troops to shepherd us back to rehearsal. I swallowed the last of my *sopapilla*, hurriedly chugged down a glass of iced tea, and tried to get my mind back on the show.

Jed was howling behind the kitchen doors. As soon as I let him out of his prison, he hurled all sixty-five pounds at me and began to lick my nose. We went through the little dance ritual practiced by dog lovers and their pups around the world upon reuniting after an absence. No matter if that absence is two minutes or two weeks. Thelma Lou walked in and laughed at the sight of Jed's paws gripping my shoulders.

"That mutt wasn't left alone for more'n a minute while you were gone. I just now stepped out to go to the little girl's room. He's nuts about you. He was good the whole time, but he had that lost look in his eyes like he was afraid he'd been deserted forever."

Jed stopped licking long enough for me to gasp out, "Thanks!

"I love him, too. I don't know what I'm going to do when Ted and Margaret come back. I may have to ask them to adopt me so I can live with them and this damn dog."

She grinned, started to leave, then turned and asked in a completely different tone, "By the way, didja hear about the folks comin' back for the show?"

I nodded.

"Yeah. Lida Rose told us this morning. I hope we can do justice to their performances from years ago. I keep hearing how wonderful they all were."

Thelma Lou sniffed.

"Honey, *all* of 'em weren't that wonderful. Of course, Don was. And some of the others. But don't you fret about it none. From what I've seen so far, this production is much better."

"Well, thanks. That's sweet of you to say."

I disentangled the dog from my body and started out of the kitchen with the elderly wardrobe mistress. She stayed silent until we reached the stage area.

"Kiely? I gotta wonder how Don feels about all those folks comin' back. And Cyrus Boone? How's he gonna react when he watches Lance Lamar shoot Nick Nefarious? I hate to be shoutin' doom and gloom, but I told Lida Rose when she invited 'em. This is just askin' for trouble."

Chapter 7

Coming in early to choreograph had worked so well the previous day (except for that short unscheduled chat with Rafe), I decided I'd give it another try this morning.

For once, the front doors were locked. I whipped out the key Lida Rose had provided and prayed for it to work. She's been known on occasion to hand me keys that open either one of her kids' lockers at school, or the safety deposit box at her bank. But with an easy twist, the door gave and I was in.

I smelled coffee. Thelma Lou was a saint. I needed to find a fun good-show gift for her for opening night. Perhaps some brightly colored sports memorabilia earrings to match one of her team caps.

I grabbed a mug; filled it with coffee, cream, and sweetener; held it in my right hand; then grabbed a wad of paper napkins with my left. I had to use my butt to open the doors leading into the theater from the lobby entrance.

Half of a body was sticking out of the top of the old upright piano. A pair of jeans encasing muscular legs was all that could be seen. I screamed and promptly spilled my coffee all over the floor. It appeared as though the piano had swallowed its victim, rather like a scene from an old horror movie, like *Attack of the Hungry Piano.*

Sounds were emanating from the keys, though, so apparently this piano hadn't quite devoured whoever was inside. A living being quickly brought the top half up when I yelled, "Who's there?"

"Kiely? Is that you?"

"Rafe?"

Sure enough. The man disentangled himself from the innards of the piano. The scowl on the face could only belong to Rafe Montez, noted art historian and kicker of footballs.

"What in hell are you doing? You scared the living fool out of me. I thought someone had stuffed a body into the piano."

He quickly made his way down the aisle of the theater, knelt down, and began mopping up the coffee.

"Sorry. Daisy told me yesterday she thought something might be stuck in the piano. Said the keyboard action didn't feel right. Wasn't springing back the way it's supposed to. She didn't have time to check it out, so I thought I'd do it for her this morning."

I glared at him.

"How did you get in? The doors were locked."

He looked wickedly innocent, rather like a choirboy explaining to his priest why that copy of *Playboy* had been passed around the loft during services.

"Hey, they were open when I got here. I locked them while I was working on the piano. Wouldn't want a break-in, would we?"

He smiled at me. Intuition said he was lying, but there didn't seem to be a motive for it. I had no idea what to say or how to call him on it.

We finished cleaning the spilled coffee with the

wad of napkins I'd thoughtfully juggled in. Jed helped by lapping up this new treat. I prayed that caffeine mixed with cream and chemical sweetener wasn't a harmful substance to canines.

Rafe gently took the empty mug from my hand.

"You need to get to work, don't you? I'll get you some more coffee, since it seems I was responsible for you losing that first cup."

I looked at him. He seemed sincere.

"Thanks. I'll let you do just that. I must admit I'm still shaking. I thought someone had joined our resident ghost by means of piano vivisection."

His laughter filled the theater with a rich baritone sound.

"You *do* have quite an imagination, Miss Davlin. Believe me, there was no violence being perpetrated by either the piano or myself."

"Mmmm."

He turned to go.

"Rafe? Cream and fake sugar. The pink stuff, please, not the blue. Teaspoon each."

He didn't even turn. "I know."

I didn't want to ask how he knew how I liked my coffee. I was just glad he was going after another cup. After the scare of seeing him inside the piano, I needed a serious jolt of java.

I set up my tape player and notebook on the stage, then dug out a toy for Jed from my bag. Ted and Margaret had thoughtfully supplied a seemingly endless accumulation of chew toys, but Jed had been eliminating them at an awesome rate.

I was about to ease into my usual warm-up routine when Rafe came back laden with a mug of freshly brewed coffee. I took a sip. Pink stuff and cream, in just the right amounts. I was feeling much more kindly about Mr. Montez, but I waved him away almost rudely.

"I have work to do. Thanks for the coffee. Where you off to now?"

"I have props to search for. And lines to learn. And dances to go over. I shall leave you to your creative processes."

I watched as he headed toward the lobby doors. Nice view. I couldn't resist calling as he opened them, "Watch out for the ghost! He's up and around today."

He did not respond.

I cranked up the music. I needed to concentrate on the steps for the "Brazos Shuffle," a crazy little number performed by the villain and his sidekick in Act Two. I decided to add a high kick. Mr. Football Scholarship with the ballerina mom could doubtless execute a flawless one with pointed toes, straight back and all. I giggled. I began imagining Rafe kicking vigorously and continuously over the head of Ben Collins, who played Jackson Wild, while the man squirmed on the floor ducking flying feet. I liked it.

Someone applauded. Apparently my efforts were appreciated.

I glanced into the audience. A figure wearing a black tux with tails, black pants, black stovepipe hat, and white sneakers stood near the back row. Had Rafe changed into the villain costume again and come back to bug me? I called out to him. He had vanished. Into nothingness. I breathed quickly and heavily. That had not been a shadow. No trick of the morning light had conjured up that vision. Fifty-years-deceased Don Mueller had just appeared and clapped his ghostly hands hard enough to be heard.

I sat down on the edge of the stage and took a large

swallow of the now-tepid coffee. Jed rested his soft head on my dance bag and snored. The darned mutt hadn't even looked up.

I tried to assimilate what I'd seen and heard. I'd been right in telling Rafe our ghost was up and around. I had no doubt that this was the spirit of the murdered actor. I stared into the audience where I'd seen him. Nothing. Then a movement up by the light booth caught my eye. I craned my neck and squinted. My villain casually leaned next to the railing and waved at me. Without even thinking, I waved back.

"Who you waving at?"

"Him. Don Mueller." I'd answered without a pause. Then I realized who'd asked the question. Rafe strode up and hovered over me.

"Kiely. Go home. Have you eaten today?"

My response was immediate and indignant. "Power drink, fruit, omelet, bagels, and peanut butter for breakfast. I am not hallucinating from hunger, if that's what you're suggesting."

He sat down beside me and shook his head.

"It crossed my mind. But damn, girl, how do you eat like a linebacker and stay skinny?"

"I am not skinny. I am a dancer! I dance all day and I jog back and forth from the theater in this heat with my new four-footed roomie."

He put his hands up to defend himself. "Hey, I wasn't being insulting. I thought women liked being called skinny."

I stuck my tongue out at him. "'Thin' is nice. 'Lean and stacked' is nice. 'Skinny' sounds like a crone spinster with fifty cats at home who hasn't had a date in forty years."

He stifled a laugh. "I'll remember that. You are definitely not in the skinny class. Lean, stacked, and thin would be okay to say? Wouldn't get me hauled off for sexual harassment or sicced on by your rabid beast there?"

Jedidiah was lying on his back, tongue hanging out, paws dangling, oblivious to the world outside of bunny-filled dreams.

Rafe's tone grew more serious.

"I'm worried about you. Bonding with nonexistent spirits."

I drew myself up like one of those fifty cats.

"Look. I'm not usually into psychic stuff. And I normally discount half of what Lida Rose says outside of when she's directing. But she swears Thelma Lou has seen Don, too. So it's not just me."

"Kiely, Lida Rose has an imagination that would make George Lucas, J.R.R. Tolkien, and Steven Spielberg green with envy. And Thelma Lou? Jeez, woman! Don't get me wrong. The lady is a terrific person and she was apparently one hell of a great costumer in her day. But she's about a hundred years old. Who knows what memories she has that may be expressing themselves as ghost sightings?"

I refused to listen to rational thinking or logic.

"Fine. Then would you care to explain why I just heard hands clapping, and saw a man dressed in the villain costume standing here no more than ten minutes ago? You'll note, please, that you're in jeans today, not the black outfit, so it's not you. No one else is here. It looked exactly like his picture. And he was waving at me up by the light booth."

Rafe looked troubled.

"I don't know what's going on. The only theory halfway plausible is that Lida Rose and Thelma Lou have got you so worked up about this guy, you're dreaming him out of thin air. Or someone's playing tricks."

I stood up.

"That's one lousy theory. Actually, that's two lousy theories. Now, I have to get back to work. Excuse me."

"Look, Kiely. Don't get so caught up in your spooky beliefs that you lose sight of reality, okay?"

"Yeah, right."

He sighed and left the stage. I started to rewind the tape player. I supposed he had been trying to be nice. I couldn't fault him for not believing in psychic phenomenon. Up until a few days ago, I hadn't bought into it, either.

"Rafe?"

He turned. I waved my hand at him.

"Change of subject. I wanted you to know before we start rehearsals. In honor of your mother's past career and your own days imitating the Rockettes with Notre Dame, I've added a few little things to the 'Brazos Shuffle.'"

He looked skeptical and slightly worried.

"Why is it you're saying that with far too much enjoyment? What did you do?"

I showed him the kick sequence at the end of his soon-to-be-learned dance. He burst out laughing.

"I love it. My mom would be so proud. Just watch, my lean, mean, stacked choreographer. I'll do that dance so well, the audience will forget to throw popcorn."

I was delighted. I could like this man, if he'd quit sneaking up on me, sticking his butt out of pianos, and being such a naysayer about my ghost. That got me thinking about Don Mueller again.

Had I truly been visited by a dead man? If so, why

me? Thelma Lou did seem like a psychically connected soul. But Lida Rose was the one who should be seeing him. She firmly believed in six impossible things before breakfast, read palms and tea leaves, was highly sensitive to anything eerie, and probably had a subscription to *Paranormal Times*. But I was just a dancer who'd seldom experienced more than one moment of déjà vu in my whole life. How did I get the honor of visitations by a dead villain?

I had no answers. I nudged Jed, who yawned, showing a cavernous mouth and every one of his teeth. He promptly fell asleep again.

"Uh-uh. Don't think so. Come on, mutt. I need fresh air. We've got fifteen minutes 'til rehearsals start, and I'd like to get out and breathe a little before the hordes arrive."

Jed heard the magic word. Out. He leaped up and bounded toward the door enthusiastically. I chased after, with no hope of overtaking him. I do love this dog.

We strolled slowly around the grounds. The theater was situated between two vacant lots and had a sizeable parking area as well. This area was part of the Deep Ellum community that was just beginning to enjoy a return to businesses and restaurants. From the lot behind El Diablo's I could see a boutique that looked as though the main attraction was body piercing and tattooing, and a small art gallery. On either side of the lot were old businesses that had been closed for more than thirty years. One, an import-export shop on the order of a Pier One, had at least stayed in good shape. I squinted. There was a new sign proclaiming this to be MiaMaya Imports. I immediately began to plan a shopping expedition there for junky good-show gifts to give the cast on opening night.

A Woolworth's-style department store stood next door to MiaMaya, its broken sign swinging from an awning looked long decayed: HENRY'S FIVE AND DIME. Hopefully with the reopening of East Ellum Theatre, this area would enjoy new prosperity, although I doubted that Henry's would ever make a comeback.

Maybe if there'd been people around, Joe Hernandez wouldn't have been run down in the street. I shivered under the midday sun.

I'd reached the back of the theater and was yelling at Jed to get away from the dumpster—he was trying to jump inside after watering the corner—when I noticed a pair of jeans standing by the loading dock of the scene shop. The owner hadn't heard me because his head and upper body were buried in an old steamer trunk. I recognized the butt. It was a decidedly sexy butt.

"Yo! Rafe. What's up!"

I heard the sound of his head as it hit the top of the trunk. Ouch. This would not make him happy.

"Kiely! What are you doing back here?"

"I'm walking Jed. Actually, he's walking me. What are *you* doing back here? Why are you immersed hip deep into iron luggage?"

"I was seeing how large it was and whether it might work for that bit in Act three when Nick Nefarious is looking for a place to hide."

It sounded *almost* plausible. As had his piano operation earlier this morning. I didn't believe a word. I was getting mighty suspicious of Rafe Montez and his omnipresent appearances and prying at the East Ellum Theatre.

I smiled sweetly at the man.

"Why don't you simply talk to Charlie, our resident tech genius, about making a trunk? He's very creative. Not to discourage you, but that thing looks way too real. Doesn't appear to have an abundance of air holes."

Rafe escorted me back to Jed, who had succeeded in pulling a large garbage bag out of the dumpster and was now blissfully rooting through it.

"I think the trunk *is* a bit too solid. It looked like it might have been the one they used the first time they did this melodrama. About a hundred years ago. In which case the props people would have neatly provided spaces in order for the actor to be able to breathe. Guess this was used for a different show as a real trunk."

I was engaging in a tug-of-war with the mutt over the garbage bag and only half heard this semilogical reason for Rafe's behind turning up in an odd place. The man himself nodded in my direction.

"So, are you and the canine trash machine ready to go back in?"

I picked up my watch, which had fallen to the ground during my struggle to free a paper sack full of chicken bones from Jed's eager grasp.

"Yeah. It's almost ten. Rehearsal time. Yo, Jedster. Are you through with your business?"

The dog trotted good-naturedly ahead of Rafe and me as we headed toward the door of the theater nearest the loading dock.

Just before we entered, something made me glance back. Don Mueller was sitting quietly on top of the trunk. He waved at me. Apparently his territory extended to the theater grounds as well. Perhaps even ghosts need a bit of sunshine.

Chapter 8

The cast members were seated in the first two rows of the theater. Daisy slumped at the piano to their left. Lida Rose faced the group with her back leaned up against the orchestra pit railing. Everyone was quiet and on time. Something must be wrong.

Rafe and I hastily joined the others and grabbed two chairs in the second row. I sat on the outside so Jed could lie in the aisle and rest his head on my feet. He circled three times, performing the doggie-must-find-the-best-spot dance, flung himself to the floor, and immediately went to sleep, obviously worn out by our stroll around the theater.

Lida Rose nodded to both Rafe and me.

"Thanks, everybody, for being here on time. Now then. There have been rumors going around that the playwright of *Bad Business* withdrew our rights to perform it. Since he died about eighty years ago, I don't think that's a problem. What *is* true is that the composer from the show done fifty years ago wants to join us at rehearsals this week. There are several changes to Act Two that should have been implemented back then. We're doing them now."

A hand shot up. Macy Mihalik's. "Excuse me, Lida Rose. This doesn't even make sense. Who the hell is this old coot who wants to come in and monkey with a show that doesn't need it?"

"I am."

Heads whipped around fast enough to make a chiropractor smile. As one unit we stared at the tiny woman marching determinedly down the aisle in tandem with a man who matched her size. They made a cute couple. Neither was over five-foot three. They were dressed in identical khaki trousers with blue golf shirts the exact color of their eyes. Each had been blessed with an abundance of white hair. She was neat and natty, chin-length bob in place, trim, wiry, and tough. The gentleman reminded me of an aging Cary Grant or Sean Connery. Much shorter, but suave and handsome with that air of "I'm just now coming into my own."

Lida Rose stepped forward to greet the pair.

"Cast, meet Billie and Cyrus Boone. Billie was the composer of *Bad Business on the Brazos* when it was turned into a complete musical fifty years ago. The gentleman with her played the original Lance Lamar."

I couldn't help but grin. Billie Boone looked bright, fun, and more than capable of making changes to the score. I rose to shake her hand but was stopped by the strident sound of Jason Sharkey's voice.

"Billie Boone? I thought you were a guy."

The lady in question smiled. "That was the point. When I began composing, most producers wanted music or a script by a man. I knew my work was as good as anything I heard sung or played, but I couldn't get anyone to listen. I decided to send the songs for *Bad Business* to this theater fifty-one years ago. I mailed it to the producer under my nickname, Billie. My given name is Amelia."

Billie nodded at Jason. "I got a call shortly after they received the music. They were about to produce the show, and wanted some changes in the script and music from the original of one hundred years ago. They planned to use my work for the gala anniversary of the theater. I was thrilled. Then I sent Cyrus over to audition and he got the part of Lance Lamar."

Jason stared at the couple. "Mrs. Boone, I'm Jason Sharkey. The *current* Lance Lamar. Do you mind explaining exactly why you want to play havoc with these songs fifty years later, after this cast has memorized both music and script? This isn't some cheesy community theater moseying around with a summer's worth of rehearsals. We had a total of three weeks to put up this show. Eight days now. We'd like to be perfecting; not relearning."

Billie crossed to Jason. She looked up into the man's hard blue eyes. Jason was at least a foot taller and about forty years younger, yet Billie had by far the more formidable presence.

"I'm changing the music and with it part of the script because I always felt Act Two ended with a whimper. It's boring. I dislike boring. So I rewrote a scene and added a song or two."

"Well, no offense, ma'am, but *I* think the idea of changing something now stinks. Especially since it will probably affect what I do in that scene. Am I right in that assumption?"

Billie rejoined her husband, then turned to face Jason again. Two sets of blue eyes pierced through the man.

"Yes, Mr. Sharkey, it will indeed affect your scene. However, we felt that your character ending that act in a love duet with the ingenue was just a bit too *Ok-*

lahoma! It was sweet and lovely and ultimately wrong for this show."

Jason began speaking in a rapid clip. I could tell he was furious. "You're taking my number? Oh, this is just terrific. I don't have that many good songs in this production anyway and now I lose the best one. Since they're the resident minorities here, doubtless Theo or Lindsay or Rafe will have wonderful solos instead of me. What's next, kill the hero instead of the villain?"

Lida Rose picked up my dance bag, which was full of heavy tapes, character shoes, and dog treats. The look in her eye suggested Jason was about to be bonked right on his tactless skull.

I guess I've lived too long in Manhattan. I think nothing of yelling at cab drivers, or kneeing perverts in delicate areas when they get overly frisky on the subway. I even chased a pickpocket down Columbus Avenue one afternoon, then tackled him by executing what I must say was a spectacular leap into the air. Before Lida Rose could move more than an inch with my bag, I marched up to Jason Sharkey and glared directly into his far too pretty face.

"You, Jason, are one stupid, arrogant swine, ya know that? This is not about *your* career. It's about making the show better and if that means changing, then it means we work at getting it done in time. And by the way, I think you owe a huge apology to the Boones— and to Theo and Lindsay and Rafe. You know, those 'resident minorities' you've maligned. And if you don't care to give one, I will personally take this opportunity to kick your expensively perfect teeth in."

I could hear gurgling behind me. Rafe was either choking or stifling a laugh. I didn't turn around to see. Jason looked stunned that anyone would speak to him this way. The ever-adoring Macy looked stunned that anyone had dared challenge her man. Daisy Haltom looked stunned for the same reasons as Macy. All stunning emotions were aimed at me.

After an excruciatingly long moment of silence, Jason drew himself up to his full six-foot four inches, turned around, and faced the cast. "I'm sorry. I have to admit I'm not thrilled with changing this scene and my song, but I didn't mean any offense to anyone. Including Lindsay, Theo, and Rafe."

The Humble twins and Theo surrounded him. Ham gestured to our director who had stayed silent for the last few minutes. An amazing feat in itself.

"Lida Rose? Want us to take this boy behind the woodshed and open up a serious can of whup-ass?"

She chortled.

"I don't think that will be necessary. Yet. Now, then. Jason? Behave. I've worked with you in what, five shows now, and you've become steadily more obnoxious. I think it's time you just concentrate on giving the best performance you know how and not annoying these folks—or me—any more than is possible for you. Holy Henry. We've just wasted about half of the time it takes to perform the entire act Mr. Sharkey is so worried about. Enough, okay. Everybody? Places. Daisy? Are you at the piano?"

Jason took a breath. Rafe stood up and strolled to where Jason and I still stood facing each other in the aisle. Rafe stared for a second at Jason, then quietly took my arm.

"Leave it, Sharkey. Not another word. Your apology, inept as it was, is accepted."

He glanced at Theo and Lindsay, who both nodded. I was still furious. I thumped Jason in the arm with my index finger.

"*They* might accept it, but I don't. Honestly, Jason, you need lessons in sensitivity. And I'd be more than happy to provide them."

Rafe lifted a different eyebrow. "I'd watch my step, Jason. Our feisty red-haired choreographer here is more than capable of taking you down. I, for one, would love to be there for the fight. And my money would be on Kiely."

Cheers rang out from Theo, Lindsay, and the Humble brothers.

I blushed. "Sorry, everyone. I know Rafe and Theo and Lindsay are more than capable of fighting their own battles. As is Ms. Boone. I'll just retire quietly to my corner now and try to stay out. At least 'til the next round. Ring the bell if you want me."

Cyrus and Billie were still standing, but remained silent. Billie motioned for Jason to sit. He did. Billie looked around at the cast and continued explaining the changes in Act Two as though Jason's interruption had never happened.

"I think most of you will be very pleased with what we've done. There was always a lot of humor in *Bad Business* and we're adding even more. Like having the villain held at gunpoint by heroine Polly Sue Primrose while Lance Lamar literally hog-ties him," she said.

Rafe's left eyebrow lifted. Then it dropped and the right one came up. "Hog-tie?"

Billie laughed. "Think calf roping at the rodeo. With you as the calf. Feet and hands trussed up. The twins will lift you and it will appear they're about to throw you into the orchestra pit. Instead, they'll cart you out like they're on their way to a barbeque.

Which they will be. We've added some lines about having Nick Nefarious roasting over hot coals and a low spit."

Billie looked at the cast, the majority of whom were now smiling. She began waving her hands to explain.

"At the end of the act, Polly and Lance will embrace, not sing. Nick will enter, accompanied by Jackson Wild. Nick shakes his hat out, and sauce comes dripping down. Jackson runs his finger down Nick's coat and says, 'Hey, Nick, you're tastin' better'n a steak at the Cattlebaron's ball. We should bottle you and sell it at the county fair next year.' Nick will start to strike Jackson, but will twirl his moustache instead, then pull out a handful of papers from his coat. His last line is, 'I've got patent papers right here. Nick Nefarious's Barbeque Sauce. Hot and spicy like the man himself. We'll make a million.' He'll give an evil laugh and the audience will roundly boo."

I loved it. It seemed that most of the cast did, too, because immediate applause came from everyone but Jason, Macy, and Daisy. I did see Jason nodding as if he privately liked the idea of getting to lasso Rafe on stage.

Ham and Hank Humble jumped up from their seats and began advancing on Rafe. They lifted him up by his hands and feet and pretended to swing him into the orchestra pit. Rafe took it calmly, sighing occasionally as he swayed in the air. Then he laughed 'til he began to cough. The twins put him down none too gently.

Lida Rose had regained her equilibrium and good humor. She beamed at all of us as though she'd written the script and songs herself. "Isn't Billie wonderful? I knew y'all would love the idea."

Everyone began chattering at once. Pandemonium reigned until a loud chord sounded. We all turned toward the piano.

"Well, excuse me for interrupting this gaiety, but does this mean we're cutting the song Lance and Polly sing just before he shoots the villain? It's Jason's—I mean Lance's—best number, you know. And I guess I have to learn to play a bunch of new songs?"

The words attempted to be fierce, but they came out of Daisy's mouth like a whiny mouse griping about the cheese being gone. Apparently she was deaf as well as stupid. I *almost* felt sorry for her. Her single-minded devotion to Jason Sharkey was fast reaching the point of embarrassment for him as well as for her and the rest of the company. Lida Rose walked over to the piano and patted Daisy on the shoulder. I knew she was dying to thwack the girl in the jaw, but she stifled the impulse.

"It's okay, Daisy. The ending to Act Three stays the same. We're discussing Act Two. Act Three still ends with the villain being shot. Lance and Polly will perform the song they originally did in Act Two just before the final kiss. It's actually a better place for a song. It'll stay in the audience's mind that way. And yes, there will be a few new tunes. I'm sure you can handle them."

The cast began talking again. I took the opportunity to approach the Boones. "Hi. I'm Kiely Davlin. The choreographer. And playing Delilah Delight."

Two pairs of bright blue eyes with bevies of crow's-feet circling them crinkled at me.

"We know. Lida Rose has told me all about you. Her description was quite solid, I might add."

"Uh-oh. Dare I ask what she said?"

Billie smiled. So did Cyrus, who still hadn't said a

word. I remembered Thelma Lou's comment about Cyrus "not being the same since Don's death. Too quiet." I shivered. Billie must have thought I was honestly worried about what Lida Rose had said about me, because she immediately jumped in with, "It was very complimentary. Along the lines of, 'You'll like Kiely. She's an Irish beauty with grit in her soul, fire in her eyes, and too much sensitivity for her own good.' I'd say she was dead on."

I turned redder than the lipstick Thelma Lou was sporting today.

"That's sweet of you to say."

Cyrus stared at me, then nudged his wife.

"She looks familiar. Why does she look familiar? And the boy playing the villain."

Billie shook her head.

"I don't know, sweetheart. It'll come to you."

She turned back to me.

"You want to ask me about Don Mueller, don't you?"

"What is it with you people? First Thelma Lou, and now you. Are all of you mind readers? I wasn't going to just jump up and start a cross-examination, but I must admit, he intrigues me."

"He was an intriguing man. Charming, with a devilish sense of humor and smart as a whip. I remember he adored a young woman named Naomi. No, wait, make that Noemi. Different spelling, different pronunciation. Anyway, they planned to get married. Then she disappeared. I've never seen a man so brokenhearted. He was on the phone every minute he wasn't rehearsing trying to track her down. He almost left the show, but felt duty-bound to the cast."

Billie smiled wryly. "Funny. More than one of the

women in the cast seemed more than willing to help him get over her. But Don wasn't interested. He *did* attract the women, though. They'd be offering to cook for him and he'd get more invitations for the holidays than a millionaire with a dozen heirs."

"But he loved Noemi."

"Yes, indeed. You know, it was barely a week before we opened the show when she disappeared. I always wondered if she knew Don died. To this day I have no idea what happened to her. Sweet lady. But no one could ever figure out why she jilted him like that, either."

Billie glanced quickly at her husband, then continued. "Much as I'd love to see Noemi again, I hope she doesn't just pop in opening night. It's like stirring up a big pot of very hot chili. There were high emotions felt at this theater fifty years ago. I can't help but wonder if bringing all these people back won't cause that pot to explode. I'll tell you something. While I'm glad I get to work the show again, I'm also glad Cyrus isn't on that stage."

I looked intently at Cyrus and Billie. "I understand about the pot exploding, but maybe that's a good thing? Maybe those emotions were suppressed too early, long ago? Maybe this is the only way to give Don Mueller some peace."

Rafe strolled toward our threesome as I made that last statement.

"Don't discuss Mr. Mueller with this one, Mrs. Boone. She's got a thing for him as is. Apparently, the man's charm outlived him."

Rafe stood by my chair. He was smiling but there seemed to be an edge to his tone. I just hoped he'd keep quiet about my sightings of Mr. Mueller in front of Cyrus Boone.

Billie grabbed my hand. "You've *seen* Don? I thought all this haunting the theater stuff was just drivel."

Rafe snorted. I glared at him.

"Well, I could sure swear I have. Of course, Rafe here doesn't believe in ghosts and thinks I'm obsessed with shadows."

Billie winked at me.

"Could be just as well. Wouldn't do for the current villain to be jealous of the last actor to play the role. An actor, I might add, who had a phenomenal talent."

She eyed Rafe the same way I eye the menu at El Diablo's.

"You remind me of Don a bit."

Rafe seemed stuck on her previous words.

"Me, jealous? Of a ghost?"

Billie tried to hide her grin. She was not successful. "Well, yes. After all, the ladies adored Don. Seems Kiely could be the start of another generation that's just waiting to succumb to that quirky little smile and funny charm."

Rafe pursed his lips together and narrowed his eyes.

"Well, if any of *this* generation cares to succumb, I guess that's their own foolish business. It's not mine."

He walked away. Billie laughed.

"That young man is crazy about you. It's all over him. When he gets through denying it to himself, there's gonna be more than popcorn flying around this theater."

I'd just taken a sip from my water bottle and I nearly spat it out. Mrs. Boone was a sweetheart, but obviously a poor judge of romance. Cyrus nodded in agreement with his spouse. I shook my head vigorously.

"I think the only thing flying around here will be the curtains, but it's very sweet of you to say, anyway. Rafe could care less about me other than as a choreographer. Half the time he thinks I'm nuts. And please, whatever you do, don't mention that idea to Lida Rose. She's enough of a matchmaking busybody as is. I keep telling her I'm not interested in her efforts, but in twelve years, she has yet to hear me."

Billie sighed, "I'm a hopeless romantic. Fortunately, I'm also quite intuitive about people. You just wait."

Before I could respond, Lida Rose started shepherding the wayward cast back to their seats.

"Okay, cast. We need to get going. Daisy, can you give them a speedy vocal warm-up? I didn't mean to take so long, but I wanted everyone to meet Billie and hear about the changes. I'm going to start today with Act Two while Billie and Cyrus are here."

Daisy nodded to Lida Rose, tripped over a bag someone had left in the aisle, got to her feet, and finally made it back to the piano without further incident. When she started playing I noticed no problems with the sounds. Since Rafe hadn't seemed to come up with any impediments to the piano strings from his early morning dip, inside my curiosity soared as to exactly why the man had been waist-deep in the Steinway.

I glanced over at him. He was singing loudly. He smiled sweetly back at me. Too sweetly.

We finished vocalizing in less than ten minutes, then I took the cast through a short body warm-up as well. *Bad Business on the Brazos* was a very physical show—lots of dancing and lots of fighting. I got everyone stretched and ready to go, then nodded at Lida Rose to begin.

I took a moment first to glance down and see if Jed was comfortable in the partially raised orchestra pit. He sensed my interest and immediately began to whine with excitement. His paws grabbed the sides of the pit, but he wasn't quite able to jump out. Which was precisely why this was now his spot. None of the musicians' chairs were up, so he couldn't destroy the legs, and I kept a steady supply of toys coming his way so he wouldn't start trying to eat the pit itself. It was proving to be a good arrangement for both the puppy and me.

The cast worked steadily for the next few hours with breaks only for beverages and bathroom. We finished blocking out the entire act up to the changes. I was interested to see what Billie Boone had in mind for my character. Delilah Delight, dancehall girl, had originally interrupted the big love scene in the old Act Two ending. Now she would be struggling with the heroine, Polly Sue Primrose, for the gun as Nick Nefarious was being roped and tied. I looked down at Lida Rose, who was seated on the front row with the Boones.

She stood. She motioned to me. I sensed it coming. Trouble.

"Kiely? This is perfect! Billie wants to add a song and dance number for the cast just before Polly Sue gets a hold of the gun. After Nick Nefarious wins another hand from the poker game, Delilah will start a dance to get everyone's attention off of his cheating. Gradually, the whole cast will join in and Polly Sue will manage to steal Nick's gun from him and the dance will end with her pointing it at him and Lance pulling out his rope."

I stared at her. That sounded like half the scene. I

tried to keep my voice casual and even. "And approximately how long will this number be?"

She fluttered her eyelashes at me. Serious trouble. "About twelve minutes."

I nearly fell into the orchestra pit. I sat heavily on the edge and moaned. Jed tried to jump up and throw himself onto my lap but he was too far down. I considered joining him, lowering the lift to the bottom, and staying there for the next year or so. We opened in eight days. I still had four numbers to choreograph and teach. I also had to finish learning my own lines and songs.

Lida Rose wore an expression of total innocence. She smiled winningly at me. I smiled back. I, too, can act when the occasion arises. Right now I was acting like I wasn't plotting revenge on my best friend.

Chapter 9

Someone was rhythmically whipping my damp face. I checked the clock. Ten in the evening. I'd been asleep for three hours. I wondered if I'd been having pornographic dreams. Or memories of the trashy novel I'd been reading before taking this nap.

Neither. The whip turned out to be a furry black-and-white tail. I owed my wet face to the ten-inch tongue slurping lovingly over my cheeks and chin. Tail and tongue belonged to Jedidiah. I hoisted the dog off my chest and sat up.

I hadn't intended on napping before actually going to bed for the night. But I'd been so exhausted after the end of the day's rehearsal that I'd flopped on the couch and conked out before feeding myself or the dog. Jed hadn't seemed to mind. He loves sleeping, with or without me. But I guess hunger finally woke him. Smart dog. I, too, was starving. I rolled off the couch and headed for the kitchen with the eager puppy at my heels. Ten minutes later he was content-edly chomping on puppy chow and I was spooning chili over tortilla chips.

Another five minutes and a feeling of severe restlessness overtook me. One should never nap at night unless one is sick. I was healthy. Too healthy. Healthy and bored. It was Friday night, Saturday rehearsals didn't start until one-thirty in the afternoon, and I was in the mood to do anything that didn't involve learning lines, songs, or choreography.

Lida Rose had taken the Boones out to dinner after rehearsal. Doubtless she was still chatting and devising ways to stir up more mischief for her choreographer. I had not been invited and I was miffed. George Rizokowsky, Lida Rose's spouse, had picked all of them up at the theater.

I looked at Jed. He attempted to lick my face again, but I was too fast and now completely awake. I ducked.

"I love you, puppy, but I'm bored. I'm also stir-crazy. I've either been at home or at the theater for a week. I need to get out."

Ted and Margaret Wyler had not only provided me with a house, they'd kept their subscription to the *Dallas Morning News* going, which included the *Guide* weekend section. I opened it. Maybe there was a movie in seminear walking distance. The newspaper fell open to "Nightclubs." I brightened. Why not? I hadn't been honky-tonkin' for a good three years. County and western music, men in tight jeans whirling women across smoky floors as the background scents of booze and beer fill the air. I could consider this research. After all, the twelve-minute number Billie Boone and Lida Rose had dumped on me sounded like a C&W hoedown. I could check out the latest steps on the dance floors of Dallas.

With this absurd rationalization in mind, I showered, then pulled on a pair of jeans, a hot-pink silk shirt, and my comfy boots with the two-inch heels. I added enough eye makeup to do a dancehall girl proud. After scouring the apartment to see if anything enticingly destructible was lying in reach of Jed's eager teeth, I hurried downstairs to wait for the cab. I'd called one the minute I saw the name *Sweet Ruby's* listed in the *Guide*.

The honky tonk looked like every Western bar I'd been in since first dancing with my older brother, Sean, back in high school. How he'd snuck me inside without proper ID was something I'd never questioned and never abused. I never drank anything alcoholic at these places out of fear of that driver's license being carefully scrutinized, resulting in me (and Sean) getting thrown out.

Sweet Ruby's had once been a huge old warehouse. Years ago someone converted it into a nightspot with wonderful wood floors, a stage currently holding a five-piece band, six bars within easy walking distance to the dance floor, and enough tables so that folks not aerobically engaged could "set for a spell" and talk.

I found a small table and checked to see if any purses, jackets, or half-filled glasses were in sight. Two empty beer bottles were all that remained from the previous occupants. I sank into a chair just as a waitress sporting a long braid, tank top, and impossibly tight black jeans efficiently scooped up the empty longnecks, asked for my drink order, then took off. I sat back and prepared to enjoy the music and the dancers.

I immediately sat up again. Rafe Montez was twirling a trampy-looking bleached blonde in a series of spins around the dance floor. He saw me the same time I saw him and waved cheerfully at me. I waved a bit less enthusiastically back. I felt unreasonably ticked off. The man had a perfect right to go out on a Friday evening with whomever he chose as his companion. None of my business.

The song ended. The blonde smiled seductively at Rafe. He said something to her that must have been funny because she laughed. She headed to the north end of the ballroom and, oh lordy, he headed south. Right to my table.

"Kiely."

"Hi, Rafe."

He sat down on the other chair. I hadn't extended an invitation, but he didn't seem to notice.

"So, whadja think of rehearsal today? Billie is quite an imaginative lady. You okay with the extra work?"

He was being entirely too nice. I went along. "I'm fine. Just needed a night to relax before I try choreographing that marathon last number Lida Rose dumped on my creative little toes. I felt like we got a heck of a lot done, though. And I *do* like the changes to the second act. Especially the hog-tying. Cheered me up no end seeing you upside down and swinging."

He snorted.

"Thank you so much. I might have known you'd enjoy watching me get lassoed. I'm sure Jason will be all too pleased to be the one actually doing the lassoing. I'm surprised he hasn't suggested tar and feathers to go along."

"He's a pain, isn't he? But he seems to really dislike *you* in particular. Is it this WASP versus Hispanic thing or have you stolen some roles he wanted?"

His head tilted back as he laughed louder than the guitars wailing on stage.

"Well, that's blunt. Where did that come from?"

"Audition survival techniques. One has to learn to stand up for oneself or one doesn't get the job.

Sometimes that includes just coming out and saying what you're thinking. Although perhaps I have taken it to a fine art."

I wriggled my shoulders flirtatiously.

"I've inhibited more than my share of muggers by telling them exactly where they're going to feel the pain when my foot connects with their anatomy. My kicks can be aimed at any level."

He shook his head. "Remind me not to get you riled, Miss Davlin. You're a force to be reckoned with."

I acknowledged what I supposed was a compliment. "You didn't answer me. What's up with Jason?"

"Other than that he's a jerk? Well, let's start with the fact that he's resented me ever since we were in high school. The football thing."

I stared. "You're kidding."

"Nope. He was at Dallas Carter; I was at Jesuit. We never played against them. But he was Dallas's resident bigot even then. Ignored all blacks and Hispanics on the team as much as possible. I used to play sandlot baseball with some of the guys from Dallas Carter and they did not have a high opinion of Mr. Sharkey."

Rafe grimaced. "He was already off at whatever dinky college he ended up at when he found out I was offered a scholarship to Notre Dame. Apparently the man was livid. I gather going to the Big Irish U was his dream. I truly believe he's hated me ever since. As for my feelings? I don't care for him. I try to ignore him. To be honest, I never thought he should be cast, although I will acknowledge he's a decent actor. But he's a negative influence on the cast and we don't have time for his womanizing and his sarcastic little comments. He also has a tendency to upstage everyone in every scene he can. I won't let him get away with it and he knows it."

"I hadn't really considered that. I mean, I'm always over in the corner with the other dancehall girls waiting to do a number, or hanging over the gamblers when they're at the table."

Rafe grinned, flashing white teeth.

"Believe me, the gamblers are *very* aware of the dancehall girls leaning across the table."

He paused as if to add something, then extended his hand to me.

"Forget Mr. Sharkey for the night. Care to take a turn around the ballroom? They're playing a nice western waltz."

"Won't your little blonde be upset?"

He looked puzzled. "What little blonde?"

I'd started it. Now I had to finish it. With both feet in my mouth. "The one you were dancing with just a moment ago. Gee, how quickly they forget."

"You mean Candy? Oh hell, Candy's the daughter of Ruby Sweet, who's a good friend of mine. I've known Candy since she was a kid. She's married. Got two kids. Her husband is that fiddle player up there with Hog Heaven and the Mutant Fleas."

He waved to an impossibly gigantic man on stage now flailing a bow back in Rafe's direction while I prayed for the floor to swallow me up. I didn't have time to stay embarrassed, though, because Rafe was spinning me around that ballroom with the ease of years of practice. I looked into his brown eyes as we turned.

"You're an enigma, Mr. Montez."

"I am? How?"

"An art historian who looks like Cortez conquering

Mexico, sings with perfect pitch, dances like a champion, and hangs out in a place that might easily be termed a redneck bar."

Rafe shrugged. "I was brought up to like people for who they are; not what they do or who their folks were. And I like trying to become a well-rounded Renaissance man. I also simply like different kinds of people."

"Well, there I totally agree with you."

We didn't talk for a while, just kept dancing as the music changed from waltzes to rowdy swings to two-steps. Rafe ordered more club sodas for us both and asked the braided waitress to bring huge bowls of popcorn to his table also. The latter made me remember Billie Boone's comment that Rafe was crazy about me and more stuff would be "flying around the theater than popcorn." I still didn't buy it, but at least Mr. Montez and I were on better speaking terms. We danced like we'd been partners for years.

The fiddle player announced a ballad by Garth Brooks I hadn't heard in a while, appropriately entitled "The Dance." Rafe extended his hand to me and we took the floor again. He held me close as we swayed to the music. I could smell the musky, masculine scent of him. No splash-on, just the real Montez. I felt his heart beating against my chest and his soft breath against my cheek. He started softly singing in my ear and I didn't make a move to stop him.

The song ended. The band started another waltz. Rafe pulled away. Hank Humble, the twin playing Billy Joe Bob Travis, stood behind him, tapping his shoulder.

"Mind if I cut in?"

Rafe allowed the strapping redhead to lead me off

to the strains of some Clint Black number I didn't recognize. Hank was not the dancer Rafe was. Hell, Hank
wasn't even the dancer Jedidiah was. At rehearsals I'd
been trying to teach Hank and his brother Ham their
dance numbers, but had had little success. Both of
them had huge feet and both of those feet were left.
Since they were twins, that made a total of four left feet
stuck on the bottoms of Howdy Doody look-alikes
standing at pro basketball-player heights. More than
once I'd shut my eyes to avoid witnessing what I knew
was bound to be a painful descent into the orchestra
pit after a crash into a gaming table or another cast
member.

As I was musing about the clutziness of the man, his
clone appeared and whisked me off with him. I looked
way, way up into Ham Humble's grinning countenance.

"Do you guys ever go anywhere without each other?"

Ham considered his answer quite seriously for at
least a minute.

"No. I think last time we *weren't* together was about
six months ago. Hank had to take off work to drive
Daddy to the hospital. I had to stay."

"Y'all work together, too?"

He seemed surprised at the question.

"Sure. Humble Home, Hunting, and Hardware.
Been in the family for generations back in San Augustine. Hank and I opened a branch in Dallas when
we decided we wanted to work in theater, too. We've
turned it more into a contracting business than a
store. Gives us less regular hours so we can act."

I was trying to assimilate this picture of the Humble
twins playing contractor in their spare time, while
gracing the stages of Dallas theaters, when Rafe took
over again.

"Theo, Lindsay, Amber, and Macy just arrived. Take a look."

I did. He was right. He then acknowledged that this cast get-together might be partially his fault.

"Originally started out as the Humbles and me. We grabbed some dinner after rehearsal today and talked about meeting up here later to unwind. They got on the phone after that. By the way, did you know no one has your number?"

I wondered if this was a sneaky way of asking for it. Then he spun me out again. I couldn't have answered if I'd wanted to.

I spent the rest of the evening with the group from *Bad Business*. I hadn't planned on seeing these people quite so soon after rehearsal, but it turned out to be fun. Often the best way for a company to bond and truly form an ensemble is to forget the show and party together. I looked around the table and wondered how hard Hank and Ham had tried to contact Jason Sharkey. Or Daisy. The surprise of the evening came when a tiny figure dressed in a yellow rhinestone-studded shirt and tight black jeans approached our table.

"Mind if I join y'all? Seen ya from the other side of the ballroom and you looked like you was havin' a damn good time."

Rafe pulled out a chair as Thelma Lou thanked him, then jumped into theater talk without preamble.

"Did you kids know you were gettin' some more visitors tomorrow afternoon?"

We looked at the lady with some trepidation. Billie Boone's additions had proved welcome, but we weren't sure we wanted to endure more changes before this melodrama opened. Amber looked distressed.

"Who's coming?"

"The rest of the original cast of *Bad Business.*"

I looked at Thelma Lou, surprised. "What gives? I thought they weren't due 'til opening night. . . ."

"Just before Lida Rose left the theater this afternoon, she got a call from Fran Watkins. 'Pparently, Miz Watkins has been talkin' to the other folks and they're all excited about seeing the show in rehearsals. She didn't so much as *ask* Lida Rose, as *tell* her they was comin'. In a clump."

Hank muttered softly, "Sounds like a seniors field trip."

We all chuckled at the image of a minibus pulling up to the theater letting a troupe of camera-toting elderly tourists out to roam the grounds.

Thelma Lou continued, "Don't know if you know it or not, but Miz Watkins and Miz Kincaid are the owners of *East Ellum.* Lida Rose didn't have much choice once they wanted things their way."

I snorted. "Are you kidding? Lida Rose is probably delighted. The crazier rehearsals can be, the happier she is. She'll probably have them on stage with us showing us how it was originally done. I'm amazed she hasn't double-cast *Bad Business* with any of the originals still around."

The instant I said it, I had a premonition that indeed the old cast members might end up exactly there. And that could very well bode nothing but trouble for all concerned.

Everyone nodded. They'd all worked with Lida Rose on more than one production and Theo, the only one who hadn't, had seen enough to be convinced he was dealing with a serious, shall we politely say, eccentric. Rafe had a pensive look on his face. I threw a piece of popcorn at him. He popped it in his mouth and chewed. I threw another piece.

"What?"

"What do you mean, what?"

I hate it when someone answers a question with a question. Fine. I'd do the same. "Care to share?"

He blew out a long breath of air. "I'm really wondering how bringing in all these people will change the dynamic at the theater. This could easily raise tension to an uncomfortable level. And let's face it, there's somewhat of a strain there now."

Macy opened her eyes as wide as she could.

"Why? It's just a bunch of old people coming to sit in and feel like they're part of things again. I'll bet most of them haven't been on a stage in years. So they sit there and watch and, really. . .what's the problem?"

He looked up into the rafters of Sweet Ruby's as he spoke. "Think about it. We're already nuts with extra scenes and songs. And now we're about to be rehearsing in front of the person who might well be responsible for sending Don Mueller to an early grave."

Chapter 10

I'd planned on sleeping in very late after my night of revelry at Sweet Ruby's, but my companion had other ideas. Seven A.M. on the nose was the wake-up call. I say on the nose, because that's where the contact was made—nose to nose. I opened my eyes to find Jedidiah's cross-eyed adoring gaze and wet snout inches from my face. Having gotten to sleep only three hours ago, I wasn't really in any mood to get up. Jed, however, had an anxious look that told me I'd better have the leash on and be out the door within the next five minutes or I'd have a mop job on my hands.

Dog-walking chores dispensed with, I was about to head back to bed when the phone rang.

"Yo?"

"Kiely? You up, awake, and around yet?"

It was a debatable issue since I'd been around the block but hadn't had coffee. I decided to cut Lida Rose a break.

"Pretty much. Why are you calling at the ungodly hour of eight?"

"Field trip. I want to go visit Joe Hernandez. And I know you've wanted to see him, so I thought I'd be nice and give you a ride. We never manage later in the day, what with rehearsals and all."

"Where are you?"

"Just turned off from Central onto Bennett."

I groaned. The woman was at the most thirty seconds from the apartment. I heard the squeal of brakes. Make that in the driveway.

I sighed as she bounded up the stairs leading to my back door.

"Do I get to shower or anything, oh chauffeur mine? I partied last night. I'm pretty ripe here."

"I know. About the partying. Not about you being ripe—although you do have a scent of Eau de Jose Cuervo about you."

Lida Rose dug into her bag and pulled out six miniature chocolate bars. She gave me one that was nut-filled, then popped a dark chocolate morsel into her mouth. It inhibited the clarity of her voice but not the intensity of her interrogation.

"How was Sweet Ruby's last night? Good band? Hog Heaven? Did you have fun?"

I stared at her.

"How did you know I was at Sweet Ruby's? I didn't even know I was going myself until ten last night when I found the place listed in the *Guide.*"

She brushed this off. "We always go to Sweet Ruby's. Why do you think I didn't invite you to come with George and me last night? You'd've been stuck with two old couples instead of partying with the rest of the kids."

"I still don't see how. . . ."

I stopped. Pointless to ask. Even if she'd been sure I'd be bored sitting alone at the apartment last night, she had no way of knowing I'd end up at the Dallas theater crowd hangout. She smiled at me like a cherub waiting for St. Peter to applaud her last mission. She poked another miniature chocolate bar (krispy this time) into my hand.

"You and Rafe seem to be getting along rather well."

"Don't start with me, you meddling psychic witch. I'll have you know that I danced with *all* the men from the cast who happened to be at Sweet Ruby's. Which is why my toes and shin are bruised purple today. Holy tamale, but those Humble brothers are the most terpsichorean-challenged beings I've come across since I had to teach Fred Myers to Charleston in *Grand Hotel*. Remember me telling you about him? He had the rhythm of a squirrel dodging a pickup truck."

I was about to continue my tirade when Lida Rose put a chocolate-scented hand over my mouth, leaving a trail of chocolate across my chin.

"Get that hand away from my face! What do you want, anyway? I'm going to take a shower now, so you can just wait 'til I'm through to tell me what devious schemes you're devising."

"You're avoiding the subject."

I turned on the water, but continued to yell at Lida Rose. "I am not. I was talking about dancing with the guys. By the way, Rafe danced with all the girls who were there last night, too. Assuming you can call Thelma Lou a girl at age ninety-something. Lindsay is nuts about Theo. But I think Macy may like Rafe, too. Especially if Jason is going after Daisy. Or Amber."

Lida Rose began making choking sounds. I stuck my head out from behind the shower curtain. "Are you okay? Do I need to Heimlich you?"

Her eyes were filled with tears but she managed to gasp out, "No!" I returned to my shampoo bottle just in time to hear her say, "Macy and *Rafe*? Don't think so, honey. She's still dating Jason and he her. Hmmm. Is that 'him her'?"

I brushed aside the grammatical concerns and called out, "I thought Jason had dumped her for Daisy. I figured that's why she was there in all her painted glory last night batting her lashes at Rafe. Incidentally, I want the brand of her mascara. Not a flake, smear, smudge, or part."

"She's married, you know."

"Daisy?"

"No. Macy. We were talking about Macy, remember? You got sidetracked on eye makeup."

I stepped out of the shower, grabbed a giant bath sheet, wrapped it around me, then stared at Lida Rose.

"You're kidding, right? About Macy being married? Hell, she's barely eighteen!" I choked out.

"You okay? Can you breathe?"

I nodded and began drying my hair. Lida Rose's voice bellowed above the eighteen hundred watts of air.

"She's spent five years of wedded discord with an idiot named Stan or Steve or Stew or some kind of name that starts with an *St*. And she's actually twenty-four."

"Damn. Well, shut my mouth and take me for a fool. The way she and Jason had been acting I thought their next step would be hip surgery to attach themselves permanently. Until he started paying attention to Amber. And then to Daisy. Does Jason know Macy's married? Is that why he's been flirting with the piano player and the ingenue?"

Lida threw me a look of sheer pity. "Kiely, my sweet Irish innocent, you are the most naive female I've ever known outside of a convent in Uzbekistan. Of course

Jason knows. That's why he's been chasing her as much as she's chasing him. Haven't you wondered why he's not been hotly pursuing you? Lindsay doesn't count since she's the wrong color for our supremacist bigot. Jason *likes* 'em married. I don't know if it's the challenge or the danger at being caught, but that's been his m.o. since I've known him, and I've done a good four shows with the man. He's had affairs with at least twelve women I know of and every one of them has been married."

I sank weakly back against the bathroom vanity. Lida Rose patted my cheek, then handed me my mascara.

"Kiely Davlin. You've lived in Manhattan for what, nine years or so? You've toured around the country doing four different musicals. You've been engaged at least three times since I've known you and you have somehow retained this belief that adultery and sin don't exist. The nuns would be proud of you. Even if you do play a great slut."

She smiled then. It was an evil smile.

"You and Rafe are so perfect for each other."

"Where is that coming from? Because I don't date married men and he doesn't date married women? And don't say 'perfect' around me again or I'll swat you."

"Because he's as straight as you are. I'm surprised the good brothers at Notre Dame didn't manage to press him into the priesthood."

I calmly applied the rest of my makeup and mumbled back at her, "I wonder just how clean and pure he is. Did you know he's been prowling around the theater at all hours, poking about into—well—everything. There's something fishy there. He's always got some excuse so stupid I feel like I need to believe him, but I'm telling you, something's not kosher."

Lida Rose waved her hand in the air. "He's helpful, that's all. Kiely, you know I'm a wonderful judge of character. So is my dear husband. He was Rafe's history teacher years ago when George taught at Jesuit. He says Rafe's beyond smart, and a good person, too. I adore Mr. Montez. And if you'd quit being such a stubborn, pigheaded dunce out of some notion of showing me my matchmaking talents are out of whack, well, you'd adore him, too. So. You ready to go visit Joe? You look gorgeous. Joe will be so pleased. Assuming he's conscious."

I've been lucky enough in all my years of dancing never to have sustained an injury requiring hospitalization. I break a toe now and then, tear a tendon, sprain an ankle, but all those mishaps usually mean trips to the podiatrist or a sports medicine center. I hadn't actually been inside a hospital since my sister-in-law, Katie, gave birth to my nephew about five years ago.

Maternity wards are fun. Smiles generally grace the visages of those visiting new mamas and cheery chatter can be heard up and down halls and coming from inside rooms.

Not so Intensive Care. Lida Rose and I were both wearing rubber-soled sandals and neither of us is exactly a heavy walker, yet I could hear our footsteps echoing down the bright white corridor as though we were the entire chorus tapping the closing number from *42nd Street*. A grim-faced nurse receptionist, who'd reluctantly told us on which floor and in which room Joe Hernandez was currently residing, glared at the two of us in our pastel sundresses.

"I thought she was going to ask us to don an insulated suit or something! Damn, L. R. How can Joe recover in this place? The tension alone would send me into a coma or begging for a transfer to the psych ward!"

I was about to expand further on my distaste for the entire wing of the building and its wardens when my mouth literally dropped to my chest. I poked Lida Rose in her ribs.

"Oh my Great-Aunt Hermoine! What in holy hell?"

We stared at the apparition floating down the hallway toward us.

"It's The Mummy. Returning. Or the Dread Pirate Roberts come to open the gates to the castle. Wow."

Whatever it was, it was wrapped in a full-body cast. Arms extended like a cross. Feet, encased in plaster, had been planted firmly atop some sort of rolling platform. Wrapped gauze bandages neatly hid whatever visage might be below them. Atop the head was a cap. The letters spelled out "Notre Dame."

I pounded on the wall next to me, trying to stop my laughter. Futile. Lida Rose joined me. A familiar voice echoed down the corridor. "Don't you two know it's not nice to make fun of the walking wounded?"

"Rafe! What are you doing?"

Mr. Montez peeked out from behind the moving statue.

"Taking Cousin Joe here out for his daily stroll. What's it look like?"

Before I could answer, a mouth nearly hidden behind the gauze moved. "Kiely Davlin? Is that you? Rafe told me you were in town. I can't believe the two of you hadn't met before this, as many times as you've been in every damn restaurant I ever worked in and him popping in whenever he was in town, too."

I helped Lida Rose to her feet, then hurried down the hall to greet the mummy.

"Joe Hernandez! It *is* you, isn't it? Hard to tell in that Halloween getup."

Brown eyes twinkled at me. Those were intact.

"Halloween getup, huh? I'm sure the docs who patched me up would be pleased to hear their work has not gone unnoticed."

How it could have escaped my notice that Joe and Rafe were indeed related amazed me. The same speech pattern. The same rich, darkly colored hair. Not that I could see Joe's today under the rolls of white cloth and the college logo cap.

Rafe interrupted our reunion with, "I'm wheeling him down to what is euphemistically called the 'sun room.' Figured if a crowd showed up we'd be less likely to attract attention. By the way, do y'all like the hat?"

"Your gift, I suppose?" I asked.

Rafe nodded gleefully as Lida Rose and I followed the men down the hall to a fairly large room that boasted three windows and two plants. Since this is Dallas, the sun was indeed shining through the glass. Rafe found a spot close enough to the window for Joe to be able to see outside but not be in direct sunlight. I imagined our plaster-cast-dressed cook might be feeling more than a bit warm inside that shell.

The four of us chatted for a few minutes about how great the East Ellum neighborhood would be once the theater was up and running again, and how El Diablo's business should soar. After Joe had made the comment that he was so proud of Christa and his staff for keeping the restaurant going, I jumped in with both feet.

"Okay. How in hell did this happen, anyway? Were you soused on your own margaritas and not watching where you were walking?"

Joe managed what appeared to be a smile. "Sober as the proverbial judge. Although, knowing some of the judges in Dallas County, let me change that to 'saint.' What happened? I'm still not sure. One minute I was crossing the street holding car keys in one hand, and the box that carries the receipts for the day in the other. I heard this screeching sound and the next thing I knew I was on the ground feeling like a used tire at a drag race. Then I passed out, and woke up here in this giant cannoli suit."

Lida Rose jumped into the interrogation.

"Have the cops found out what nitwit drunk did this? Any leads?"

Rafe spoke for his cousin.

"Not a one. It was past midnight and there just aren't that many people still on the street at that hour. The cops questioned some of the regulars at the gay bar down the street from El Diablo's, but that was prime drinking time. A couple of guys were just leaving and did see a car speed away, but they didn't have much of a description."

I had to grin. "Don't tell me. Let me guess. A dark-colored sedan. Sans license plates."

Three sets of eyebrows shot up. (At least, I think Joe's did. It's hard to tell when a huge white cloth is draped over a person's forehead.)

"What?"

Rafe frowned. "How did you know that?"

"Jeez, don't you people watch cop shows on TV? Or read mysteries? Every hit-and-run that's not caused by a stoned professional athlete in a Porsche is caused by an unidentifiable dark-colored sedan! Without plates. No exceptions."

Silence. Finally Rafe shook his head and addressed Lida Rose. "She's right, you know. Obviously she has lousy taste in entertainment, but she's more than correct on this one. That's the description the gentlemen gave the police."

Lida Rose sighed. "In other words, no help, and we'll never know who did this."

Rafe nodded. "Pretty much. It's nasty, it's scummy, it's eerie, but it's probably going to remain an unsolved crime."

Lida Rose brightened. "Eerie, you said. Do you think we can loop this onto the curse of *Bad Business*?"

Rafe, Joe, and I all screamed (softly—we were in a hospital), "No!"

Lida Rose settled back into a wicker chair and sulked for the next ten seconds. "You all are no fun. I mean, think about it. El Diablo's opens one week before we started rehearsals. The owner is mysteriously run down in the street. Inside East Ellum a ghost watches the activities in the theater. Gotta be a connection somewhere. Work with me on this, children. It's great for publicity. For the show and the restaurant. Hey! Do you suppose Don Mueller liked Mexican food?"

I closed my eyes and wondered where I could hire a dark-colored sedan with no plates and a driver with no scruples.

Chapter 11

Lida Rose and I ran a few errands, then she dropped me off back at the apartment to pick up Jed and my notes for choreographing the "Hog-tie Hoedown." She was even kind enough to dump me at the theater. I had about two hours before the cast was due to show up for this afternoon's rehearsal.

I opened the doors from the lobby and trudged up the aisle to the stage. The first thing I noticed was Rafe Montez lying under one of the set pieces, a gaming table. I didn't even blanch. I wasn't surprised to see him digging his conquistadorian nose into another inanimate object. Piano, trunk, gaming tables? What next? Floorboards leading into the pit? What the heck was he doing? Looking for buried treasure?

"Hi, Rafe!"

He obviously hadn't heard me enter, and Jed hadn't bounded up all the steps to the stage yet. I heard a loud thwack. Rafe's head cautiously emerged from under the table.

"Kiely . . . how'd you get here from the hospital so fast?"

"I might ask the same of you. I won't, however. What I will ask is why you're intently studying the underside of a set piece that's older than either of us?"

"Gum."

"Excuse me?"

"Gum. There are wads of gum under here from years of use. I was scraping them off before we got to today's rehearsal. It's really for your benefit. After all, you have that bit in Act Three where you're hiding under this piece. Wouldn't you prefer not being on intimate terms with decades of old Wrigley's?"

I didn't even bother to answer. Too much dancing the night before, then seeing Cousin Joe encased in white and in pain had obviously turned the man's brain to oatmeal. I deposited my stuff on the corner of the stage.

"I have to choreograph the last dance for that same Act Three. If you want to stay under the table and dig away at goo, be my guest. If you want to sleep under the table, feel free to do that also. I'll try and dance around you."

He nodded. "I'm finished. I'm going to go up to the Kismet prop room and see if I can locate those huge cards we seem to keep losing. See you later."

He left. I spent the next several hours creating what I hoped would be funny steps to the "Hog-tie Hoe-down." At some point, Rafe came back in and marched down the aisle to the tape player. He stood by it until I noticed him. (Which happened to be immediately, but I preferred he not know that.) When I looked directly at him he pointed to his watch.

"It's twelve-thirty. Want some lunch? We can run over to *El Diablo's* before everyone gets here this afternoon."

"Sounds good. Let me give Jed a quick run outside, then I'll be ready."

"I'll join you."

Twenty minutes later, the dog was happy, we were seated at the cafe, and I was debating whether to question the man as to what he'd *really* been doing for the last hour or so. Searching for prop cards is not a huge task, especially since the theater has a drawer full of them. If we lose one set, we get another.

I had opened my mouth to ask what constituted thrills and excitement in the prop room, when he took the initiative and started his own interrogation.

"So, how long have you lived in New York?"

It would be rude not to answer. I was brought up by Mom and eight years of elementary school nuns to be polite.

"Nine years."

"So you took off, what? Right from college?"

"Actually, no. I graduated in three years from North Texas, stayed in Dallas for another two years, earned my Equity card here, then packed five suitcases filled with dance clothes and headshots and boarded a plane for Manhattan. And if you're fishing, I just turned thirty-two this past May."

"You look younger."

"Mmmm." There was no other response I could give to this. I wasn't old enough to consider it a compliment or young enough to resent it.

"You live in Manhattan. Where?"

I didn't know if he was truly interested or just trying to make conversation before the enchilada special arrived. I decided to give him the benefit of the doubt and assume he was being nice.

"Are you at all familiar with the city?"

"I am, yes. I've lived there off and on myself for years. Wonderful museums, you know. And my mother was raised there."

Oh, yeah. Mr. Art Historian probably had lifetime passes to the Guggenheim, the Whitney, the Cloisters, and the Metropolitan, and was on intimate terms with every female guard and tour guide.

"I've been to a few, believe or not. I don't spend my whole life on stage."

He looked slightly distressed. "I'm sorry. Did it sound like I was implying you did?"

"I guess not. I may be a bit too sensitive. A guy I used to date accused me more than once of not being aware there was life beyond theater. Which was absolutely false. I just wasn't able to get overly excited about his job and probably did spend every waking hour rehearsing, in class, or performing."

Rafe looked curious.

"And his job?"

"Accountant for the section of the police department that handles traffic tickets."

He roared, then tried to sober his countenance. He failed.

"I'm so sorry. I didn't mean to laugh."

I joined him. "It's okay. I got the same reaction from both of my brothers, my roommate at the time, and my landlord when the guy came to pick me up. I chuckled myself whenever I thought about it. It's a perfectly respectable job. It's just . . . just . . ."

Rafe leaned forward and wiped a tear of sheer mirth from my eye with his napkin.

"I can't see you with someone in that line of work."

I grabbed a hot tortilla and began to butter it.

"I couldn't, either. Not a good start to a relationship. We didn't date long. About three weeks, if I remember correctly."

Rafe was buttering his own platter of the corn tortillas.

"Did he at least manage to fix tickets for you before you dumped him?"

I swallowed a too-large bite and shook my head.

"I don't have a car. At least not in the city. So I didn't need his help. I might have dated him at least twice more if I'd brought my old Chevy with me."

"What kind of Chevy?"

I stated stoically but with a trace of wickedness.

"Corvette. Nineteen sixty-six. I love that car. My baby brother Pat took it when he went off to college, then kept it when he moved to Kerrville about three years ago. He's the only person I ever trusted with it."

"Does he still have it?"

"Oh, yeah. It's hidden in his garage. He and my sister-in-law have a total of three cars between them, not including the Corvette, because she has full use of a company car, but the only one that has the honor of residing *in* the garage in Kerrville is the Chevy. My older brother Sean makes a yearly pilgrimage, on his motorcycle no less, to worship at the shrine. I think when Pat dies, he's going to refuse to enter the pearly gates unless they let the 'Vette in, too."

Rafe was laughing again. I felt the same heat swirling around my body as last night when we'd been dancing. I blamed it on the hot sauce. *El Diabo's* makes a mean bowl and I'd been liberally pouring it over every inch of my plate.

We talked about cars and my family. He knew I had two brothers, one older, one younger; knew my parents now also lived in Kerrville; knew every show I'd done since moving to New York, including the stints on television cop shows where I always seemed to play a hooker. I knew nothing about him short of what I'd discovered the previous day—that is, he was a helluva kicker, his mom had been a dancer, and he knew oodles about art.

"So, Rafe . . . you still have family in Manhattan? Or is everybody in Texas?"

"No. My mom was adopted and her parents died before I was born. So no one's up there I can call family."

"I'm sorry."

I smiled at him. "I need to introduce you to Eugenia Grace and William James Worthington, Lida Rose's folks. They're my in loco parentis duo when I'm in the city. They're still in shock they ever birthed Lida Rose and they seem to think I'm normal."

He inclined his head toward me.

"I'll take you up on that offer. Uh-oh."

"What?"

Rafe had just glanced at his watch. "It's one twenty-eight. We have two minutes to get back to the theater."

We hastily paid the check (split right down the middle) and ran back to the theater.

We barely made it into the lobby when Lida Rose pounced and grabbed my arm. She smiled at Rafe.

"I need her. Excuse us, won't you?"

She dragged me into the kitchen. I engaged in a reunion for a full minute with Jed and ignored Lida Rose's efforts to quiz me about my lunch with Mr. Montez.

"I'm telling you, Kiely, you two are made for each other. Think of the kids you'd have! Some black-haired, some red, all with brains and talent, and I'd immediately hire them for productions of *Annie* and *Oliver*."

The future father-to-be strode into the kitchen before I could come up with a withering comment to curb Lida Rose's enthusiasm.

I slithered off the counter and grabbed the strap of my bag off the floor, slinging it over my shoulder.

"Rafe? What's up? Are we needed?"

"I just thought you ladies would like to know. The senior contingent has arrived. We have in our lobby the remainder of the original cast of *Bad Business on the Brazos*. They look rested and ready for action."

Chapter 12

Rafe was correct. The lobby was teeming with actors. Actors from the past, actors from the present, actors talking, actors sipping coffee. Actors everywhere. I've been to cattle-call auditions in New York with fewer members of the industry.

Lida Rose immediately went into her Auntie Mame persona. She hugged each one of the former cast members of *Bad Business* so hard I prayed no one suffered from osteoporosis. Then she pulled me into the circle of chattering senior citizens.

"Kiely, I want you to meet everyone."

She gestured to a tall lady with iron-gray hair and an expression that matched.

"Fran Watkins. The counterpart of Bathsheba Bombshell from the cast fifty years ago. And of course, part owner of the theater."

This was no one's sultry vixen. I wondered how she'd come across on stage years ago. Maybe when she was young she hadn't had such a grim expression and icy countenance. Lida Rose moved on.

"Shirley Kincaid. Sultry Salome. And our second owner."

Shirley would have never made the height requirement for the Rockettes. Maybe for the clowns that pop out of Volkswagens in the circus. She was perhaps five feet tall on a good day, with heels. Her soft, baby-fine hair had been badly dyed a severe platinum blond, and her round cheeks and expression put her closer to another Shirley, a certain Miss Temple around age five. Shirley hugged me as though we'd been friends for decades. How she had played a wicked dancehall girl had to have been a feat of amazing acting. She was speaking in a high-pitched childish tone.

"We don't have any of the twins from our show, you know. Not that they were real, anyway. The actor playing Bobby Joe Bob Travis when the other one played Billy Joe Bob was about half the size and twice the weight. But Billie Boone said that made it funnier. I can't even remember their names now. But one was that boy who went on to Hollywood. He became a stuntman for a bunch of marshal arts films."

She turned to me and beamed. "I can't remember his name, either, but my goodness, he could kick. He used to practice kung fooey or mai tai or whatever that was during breaks."

I hadn't opened my mouth. As Shirley Kincaid let loose her unique bits of malapropism, I couldn't speak at all, because I was wondering how anyone could be such a ditz and live to the ripe old age of— what? Seventy-two? I clenched my teeth together and stayed quiet.

After Shirley's last remark Rafe began to cough and immediately covered his mouth with his hand. I poked him in the ribs. Either Shirley hadn't noticed the pair of us bleeding from bit lips or she was used to this reaction. The rambling continued.

"Did you know Fran here still acts? She's done commercials and had roles in about every movie filmed in Dallas. And she's played Tennessee Wilson, too."

I nodded. I wasn't sure if that meant performing roles in plays written by Tennessee Williams or going a few sets on the tennis courts with her Wilson racket. I assumed it was the former. Fran sighed.

"Shirley has a tendency to get things, well, a tad off. It's not age. We've been friends for fifty-five years and she hasn't changed. No one could make sense of her when we first did this show, either."

Shirley smiled happily at this moniker, then gasped. "Fifty-five years. My gracious stars in Hades! I can't believe it's been that long. Frannie and I actually met working in my daddy's store. You can still see it from the theater, did you know? *Henry's*. The old five and dime. Although Daddy actually sold it to become an antique store soon after. I miss that place. Now they have all these tactless dollar stores that don't even sell things for a dollar. But my, ah, store just repopped a few weeks ago!"

A rich baritone voice came from behind me, addressing Shirley. "Shirley Kincaid, you still have the most alarming way with words of anyone I've ever known."

The gentleman teasing the elderly lady resembled an elderly version of Denzel Washington. He took the hand I extended.

"Nathaniel Bollinger. I played Ace Royale way back when."

"I wondered. With that voice you could sing Ace's gorgeous ballad from Act One with no warm-up. Are you still working as an actor, Mr. Bollinger?"

"Nathaniel. Please. No, I gave it up right after *Bad Business* closed. After Don's death. I moved to Austin and I've been teaching history at St. Edwards University ever since."

We stared at each other for a long moment. "I'm so sorry, Mr. . . . uh . . . Nathaniel. About Don Mueller, that is. It must have been devastating to lose a friend like that."

His eyes crinkled as he smiled down at me.

"You have a sweet soul, Miss Davlin. And thank you. It was hard. Still is even after all these years. Don was a good man, and a good friend. I miss him."

I almost told him he might have a chance to renew old acquaintances if Don decided to put in a spectral appearance, then decided to shelve that comment for the time being. After all, I still wasn't sure I hadn't been hallucinating the few times I'd seen his form wandering through the balcony. Shirley Kincaid bounded into the conversation before I had a chance to say another word. "I wonder where Noemi Trujillo is. Do you think she's dead? I wonder if she'll show up."

I was struggling to deal with Shirley's last remarks. I had an unnerving vision of a deceased Noemi Trujillo showing up for the opening night party. On Don's arm.

I'd barely noticed the rest of our current cast, who'd crowded around during introductions and were now gathering their belongings together to start rehearsals. At least Lida Rose wouldn't need to stop and introduce the former cast. It appeared everyone knew who was who. Jason kept looking at Nathaniel with raised eyebrows, but at least he'd kept his mouth shut about nontraditional casting from fifty years ago.

The Boones were already inside. Billie sat in a chair next to the piano talking with Daisy Haltom while

Cyrus snoozed in one of the seats in the front row. As we entered, he got up, stretched, and waved at me. I joined him down front and was quickly enveloped in a huge hug. Billie saw us and trotted over.

"Were your ears burning last night, Ms. Davlin?"

"Pardon me?"

Billie smiled. "We were discussing you and Rafe. Cyrus and I have been trying to figure out why you both look so familiar to us. Took us a pitcher of margaritas to finally figure it out. We saw you when you performed in *Pippin* a few years ago. You looked different then."

"I was wigged for that one. Brunette. I'm surprised you were able to recognize me at all."

"You were wonderful. That dance as Pippin's mother was just terrific."

"Thanks."

"Not him, though." Cyrus closed his eyes tightly as if he could call to mind whatever tenuous memory kept eluding him.

"Cyrus? What do you mean?"

He opened his eyes and stared at me. He shook his head.

"What about Rafe? Did either of you recall which show you'd seen him in?"

Neither Cyrus nor Billie got the chance to answer. Lida Rose grabbed me by the hand, then pushed me toward the stage.

"I hate to break up the love fest, but we need to get to work. Kiely, would you start a warm-up? I have to talk to Daisy for a few minutes."

I nodded, jumped onstage, gathered the cast together, and began our series of stretches. I glanced into the audience. Fran and Shirley had taken seats in a clump dead center of the theater. Billie sat next to the piano with Lida Rose and Daisy. Cyrus and Nathaniel stood at the back of the theater, then joined their companions in the center of the audience.

A flash of light drew my gaze to the balcony. Don Mueller's ghost was leaning on the railing. He was staring at the group of old cast members. The new group was onstage straining to touch heads to knees and feet to heads.

His form was very vague and shadowy, but it was definitely Don. I couldn't see his expression from where I stood, but I suddenly felt chilled. Cyrus had fired that gun. And any one of the elderly actors calmly watching rehearsal might have deliberately switched blanks with live ammunition. Cold sweat trickled down my back.

Don Mueller had been nothing but benign the few times I'd sensed his presence. If his murderer now sat in the audience, would he become a vengeful spirit seeking justice?

"Accident, Kiely. A tragic accident. That's all. Besides, we're missing at least six old cast members. It might have been one of them who'd switched bullets. Not any of this sparse group."

Rafe asked, peering far too intently into my face, "You're muttering to yourself, Kiely, are you all right?"

I scowled. "I'm fine. Just going over the steps I'm teaching."

"Since when are steps tragic accidents?"

Before I could respond, another voice entered the conversation.

"Since Hank and Ham Humble are attempting to do them."

Amber was giggling behind Rafe and me. We

laughed. The Humble twins heard and converged on the poor girl with fingers outstretched in tickling mode. She took off running. Warm-up was at an end.

Lida Rose waved at us.

"Calm down, children. Act Two. Take it from the top. Blocking only, no songs. Places."

"Lida Rose?"

"Kiely?"

"May I make a request from the actress playing Delilah and not the choreographer?"

"Go ahead."

"Can we change my blocking where I'm under the bar? I don't mind being behind the bar or on top of the bar or next to the bar. I'm just getting, well . . ."

She nodded. "Highly claustrophobic."

"You got it."

Lida Rose shook her head. "How you ever managed to play the gorilla when we did *Cabaret* is beyond me. I don't recall watching you freak out behind the gorilla head every night."

This was getting embarrassing. Both old and new cast members were listening to our discussion and seemed to be enjoying hearing about Kiely's phobia.

I sighed. "I didn't wear the full head. Remember? They created a special mask that kept most of my face open. Could we not go into this now? I just need to know if I can change my blocking."

She nodded. "Yeah. Try crouching next to the bar between the two gaming tables. Actually, that might work better, since the audience can see Delilah trying to get the rope untied."

"Thanks."

We worked solidly for the next two hours. The new

blocking worked perfectly for me except that I was forced to look up into the balcony area. Which meant trying to see if Don was still there.

He hadn't moved. Lida Rose caught me staring at the balcony longer than was necessary. She spun around to see what had drawn my attention. Then she slowly turned back and smiled at me. I wondered if she'd seen him too. It was apparent no one else had. No gasps, no squeals, no pointing, or fainting.

I pulled my focus back to the scene at hand. We finished the blocking rehearsal, then Lida Rose called for a five-minute break. I lowered myself into the orchestra pit to see if Jed had enough toys and water.

"Kiely?"

"Hi, Nathaniel."

His voice was too quiet for anyone else to hear.

"You saw him, didn't you? I couldn't help but notice your attention wasn't completely focused on the stage."

I wanted to say no, and avoid sounding crazy, but this man had been Don Mueller's friend. I felt like I owed him reassurance.

"Yes."

"Is this the first time Don, um, has made an appearance?"

"No. At least, I'm pretty sure I've seen him before this."

He sat down in a seat closest to the pit. He looked calm, but sad.

"Has he ever spoken?"

I smiled. "Not to me. But he likes my dances. He's applauded for them. The man obviously has taste."

Nathaniel mused, "Funny. I've heard rumors for years that his spirit haunts this theater. Never really

believed it. Never really believed in ghosts. But today
when I saw you staring into the balcony? Well. Guess
one is never too old to change one's mind."

I couldn't help but glance over at Rafe.

"Mind telling a few others that?"

Nathaniel smiled, then Lida Rose's voice called out,
"All right! Break's over. It's time to dance."

I climbed out of the pit with Nathaniel's able assistance, then hoisted myself onto the stage and waited
for the cast to gather.

"Okay, troops. Nothing new right now. I want to review the 'Gambler's We' number, then give the guys a
short break and work with the dancehall girls on the
'Headin'' up the Brazos' dance."

We danced for the next hour. I didn't get another
chance to check out the railing of the balcony. Nothing hinted of another presence, though, so I decided
Don had called it quits as to watching rehearsals. At
least for today.

I made it a point to ignore Rafe Montez as much as
I was able. That was not too difficult from the physical
standpoint, since I had to spend most of my time patiently teaching the Humble boys the steps they'd
learned the day before. Rafe, of course, caught the
moves the minute I showed them. From an emotional
standpoint, I was all too aware of his presence. Why the
heck had Billie gone on the other day about how Rafe
was crazy about me? It was like the old lawyer's trick
about getting a jury to think about what the attorney
wanted them to. Tell them *not* to think about ele-
phants, and guess what's the only thing on their minds?

I glanced down at Billie smiling serenely at me
from the audience. And knew there was an elephant
just behind my right shoulder.

Chapter 13

I'd managed to get a good night's sleep, and decided to get to the theater early. In the midst of inserting my key into the door of the theater, I stopped. Unlocked again. Thelma Lou tended to arrive around six A.M. Maybe instead of coming in by way of the scene shop, she'd decided to use the classy entrance. Or perhaps one of the techies had done the same. Any one of a dozen people could be roaming the theater at eight in the morning.

I herded Jed through the doors and walked slowly toward the stage. I intended to dump my bag there before making coffee in the kitchen. But I felt twitchy. There was no reason for apprehension, yet Jed felt it, too. He galloped up the stage, then kept going into the wings toward the stairs leading to the prop room.

"Jedidiah! Get back here. What's the matter, boy? Did some idiot from the light crew leave his burger and fries on the stairs? Jed! Come here."

He ignored me. I ran after him and found him crouched in front of the prop room door, which was securely shut. I couldn't see the remnants of anyone's lunch or dinner take-out anywhere, so I started to haul the dog away by his collar. And stepped neatly into the blood oozing out from underneath the prop room door. I shoved Jed to one side and told him to sit. Naturally he paid no attention. He took off down the stairs, howling.

I tried to open the door. Stuck. I checked the lock. Open. But something was keeping the door wedged closed from inside. I heard breathing behind me and turned in time to see Rafe coming up the stairs at a clip similar to my own.

"Are you okay? Jed came tearing past like the hounds of hell were after him. Are you hurt?"

"I'm fine. But I'm not sure I can say that about who's behind that door. Rafe? There's a lot of blood here. And I can't get this door to budge."

He put his arm around me and led me to the top of the stair where Jed sat in the stance of a serious guard dog.

"Take a deep breath. Okay. Let me think. There's another entrance into the prop room. From the balcony where the light booth is. I'll climb up the ladder to the booth and see if I can get in that way."

"I'm coming with you."

He shook his head.

"No you're not. Who knows what's happened here? Why don't you go downstairs and call nine one one. Then Lida Rose."

"But if someone's hurt, I can help. I took first aid when I was certified in CPR. Red Cross of Manhattan and all. Nice building on the Upper West Side."

He took my shoulders gently and made me face him.

"Kiely, somehow I don't think first aid is going to help. And, for what it's worth, I'm certified as well. Let's go."

He escorted me and the dog back down the stairs,

then headed over to the ladder that connected directly into the light booth. I watched him for a second, then pulled myself together and ran into the kitchen that houses the public phone. I called 911, then dialed Lida Rose's number. The only voice I heard was that of her answering machine singing a few bars of 'Lida Rose' before it told the caller to leave the message. I did just that.

"L. R. Big problems at the theater. Get over here. Now."

I hung up, and opened the door in the hallway leading to the stairs to the orchestra pit. I grabbed the dog and dragged him along, so he'd be out of the way of whatever was coming. Also, I just plain wanted his company.

I carefully opened the door into the orchestra pit, checking under my feet first to see if anything liquid and warm might be under them. Clean. I clicked on the light. The pit looked as it always did. The chairs for the musicians were stacked neatly along the wall. A few of Jed's toys I hadn't quite gotten to the day before were littered around the floor in various stages of chewed. I started to pick them up when I heard a voice screaming, "Kiely!"

It was Lida Rose. A frantic Lida Rose. She couldn't have gotten my message and driven over this fast. Either she'd been on her way, or was already here when I arrived and I simply hadn't seen her.

"I'm here!"

She leaned over the pit, which was still in the Down position. I turned the key from where I stood and raised the pit to the level of the audience floor.

"Do you know what's happened?"

"Yes and no. I found blood near the prop room.

Rafe is checking, 'cause we couldn't get in from the main entrance."

"I know. He waved at me from the balcony a few seconds ago. For a second I thought it was the ghost again. I figured he was mistaking me for you."

I almost told her the day anyone, even someone long dead, mistakes a five-foot-ten-inch black-haired, beyond voluptuous woman wearing colors of neon pastels, for a five-foot-eight-inch redhead who's straight up and down and dressed in black, would be the day the ghosts took over the theater.

When I'd seen Rafe he'd been dressed in the black tux and tails of the villain. I'd been so upset, I hadn't really noticed until Lida Rose brought up Don Mueller's ghost.

That made me look up at the balcony again. A man was standing near the prop room wearing that black costume. This time it *was* Don. He pointed to the pit where I was standing. Then he faded away as the doors to the theater burst open and two cops and two paramedics sped in.

"What's the problem? Someone called and said they'd spotted a pool of blood in the prom room?"

I sighed.

"That's prop room."

The cop, a kid of maybe twenty-five, looked embarrassed. "I thought that sounded wrong. Our dispatcher has a tendency to get things a bit mixed up, although she's excellent with exact addresses and with calming people who think they've surprised burglars."

Lida Rose glared, then hissed at the policeman.

"Thanks so much for that inane explanation, Officer, uh . . ." She peered at his nametag, "Carter."

His partner, a female of Amazon proportions who

looked like she could have modeled for *Vogue*, took over the conversation.

"Where is this prop room? Has anyone gone in?"

Rafe shouted from the balcony. "Up here. I managed to get in through another way. It's serious. One of the cast members. Um, there's a huge cabinet blocking the doorway from the stairs, so you'll need to come up by way of the lighting booth until we can move it."

As one, the police, the paramedics, and Lida Rose headed in that direction. I stayed a few steps behind them and hoped they wouldn't notice I was there.

Rafe had managed to shove the door open enough for people to squeeze through. I stood in the doorway between the prop room and the balcony, grabbed for the nearest person, and tried to ignore the tears flowing down my face.

Jason Sharkey lay in the middle of the wreckage of the huge cabinet where for years the theater had kept its medieval period props. A scimitar looked as if it had been neatly placed across Jason's neck. Whether the blow itself had done all the damage, or it had been the subsequent bleeding, didn't really make a difference. Jason was quite dead.

Rafe came over and put his arms around me.

"Kiely, I told you to stay downstairs. You don't need to see this."

He was right. Jason's perfect blond hair looked like he'd gotten a henna rinse. His throat was indescribable. I'd been in theater one way or another for over twenty years. I'd seen how makeup artists build latex wounds that are so realistic one has to touch them to believe they're really fake. I'd popped, then spit out blood capsules in scenes, and in fact had been prepared to chomp down on one in Act Three of *Bad Business*. But this was so obviously real and so obviously final. I shut my eyes and tried not to faint.

"Take a deep breath."

I did. It didn't help.

"Go downstairs, Kiely."

I slowly backed out and headed for the balcony. They didn't need me in there. Lida Rose wasn't needed, either. Rafe stayed with the cops and the paramedics. They didn't move the cabinet back to the wall. "Can't disturb the crime scene" kept running through my mind.

It hit me that this was indeed a crime scene. Was there any way that the cabinet could have toppled and spilled its lethal contents onto Jason without someone pushing it?

"What the hell was Jason Sharkey doing in the prop room bleeding to death at eight in the morning?"

Lida Rose shook her head as we sat in silence in the lighting booth. A third presence could be felt, but not seen. I knew Don Mueller was with us. It was the first comforting thought I'd had since I'd seen that blood this morning.

Lida Rose blew her nose into a giant-sized tissue and absently wiped off her lipstick immediately after.

"This is not good."

I looked at Lida Rose. She was as pale as Don Mueller.

"L. R. You have a talent for understatement. Damn. Did you ever imagine something like this?"

She shook her head.

"Kiely, what am I going to do?"

I hugged my friend. "You're going to wait to see what the police have to say. That's all you can do for a while. That and say a prayer for the man's soul."

We sat in silence for what seemed like hours. Rafe finally came in and told us the police had called in the Crime Scene Unit and we should just go on back down and wait for them in the lobby.

"What about you?"

He looked at me with one of those famous raised brows.

"What about me?"

"Don't the cops want you to vacate the premises with us? Or is it just women and children out of the way?"

"I found the man. They want me to stay right up here and answer any and all questions the detectives will have when they get here. Kiely, are you okay?"

He shook his head.

"Stupid question. Of course you're not."

Lida Rose was already climbing down to the stage. I stayed a moment longer.

"Rafe."

"Kiely. Just go on downstairs and get a cup of coffee. With real sugar, not that fake stuff. You've had a shock."

He tried to smile.

"I could use some coffee, too, and I'll bet the cops could. I know it sounds like it truly *is* women, kids, and dogs out of the way, but would you mind making a huge pot? It's going to be a long day."

He hugged me for a few moments. This was the second time I'd been comforted by a villain this morning.

I half slid down the ladder and nearly crashed into Lida Rose who was waiting at the bottom. She seemed unable to move.

"Coffee. They want coffee. And we need it, too," I blabbered.

She wasn't listening.

"What am I going to tell everyone when they get

here for rehearsal? And that means *everyone*. Damn it, Kiely, our cast, the original cast, the techies, Daisy, the rest of the orchestra, even Brett Barrett. Do you know him? He was bringing a photographer. The *News* was going to give us some nice publicity for the anniversary. Oh, this will read well. I can see the headlines. *"Bad Business at Bad Business! Headless Hero Murdered!"* Shit. I thought I'd cause a bit of trouble playing up that stupid curse business when I talked to Brett just yesterday. Only *that* was fun. This is not. Excuse me while I grab the first plane to Aruba or somewhere."

I steered her into the kitchen and started the process of making strong coffee for a mob.

"Lida Rose! Calm down. First, you call the paper and you cancel Barrett for today. I don't know a single reporter beyond the crime beat types who gets up at this hour of the morning. So there's no need for them to know anything until the police have made a preliminary investigation. Secondly, quit crying murder until you know for sure that's what it is. That damn cabinet was hanging from the ceiling with pins, isn't that right? Well, who knows how long it's been up there? Those pins could have rotted or rusted away, and bam! Down came the cabinet."

She almost brightened. "That's true. Let me think about this. It's well known that Jason used the *Kismet* prop room as his little love nest. Maybe he met Macy last night, and she left and he was checking to be sure they hadn't left anything nasty around—if you get my drift—and boom! Down comes the cabinet and that stupid scimitar was a crazy fluke landing in his neck like that. Isn't that a possibility?"

It sounded ridiculous even to me, but it was better

than the alternative theory—that someone had snuck in and knocked that cabinet on top of him.

I poured more water into the pot.

"As for everyone who's due in the next thirty minutes or whatever, you tell them the truth. That Jason was found in the prop room and he's dead. Let the cops do their jobs. Okay?"

She sat suddenly in one of the rickety old kitchen chairs.

"Kiely?"

"Yeah?"

"Why do you suppose someone murdered him?"

I sank next to her. I didn't repeat the accident theory. Neither of us believed it anyway.

"I don't know. I mean, Jason was not my favorite person. Let's face it. Jason was not anybody's favorite person except for maybe Daisy and Macy. Or Amber, once upon a time. He went through women like I go through M&M's, he was a bigot, he had a very high opinion of his own talent but not of others, and he was generally annoying. Ham told me he even cheated at cards. And really, any one of those girls might have gotten so jealous she lost control. But to kill *him*? I can see Daisy shooting Macy. But honestly, I can't see those girls as killers."

I continued to speculate, "Unless Macy's husband found out and went ballistic or something. Hey, that's a strong possibility, isn't it?"

Lida Rose let out a whoosh of air.

"Nope. I know Macy's husband. He's five-foot five and weighs one hundred and fifteen pounds on a good day after a large dinner. How could he knock a cabinet with stuff weighing hundreds of pounds onto a man Jason's size with biceps like Schwarzenegger?"

"Physics, hon, physics. I don't weight much more, but if something's at a proper angle, a heavy object can be easily toppled."

She shivered. Before she could respond, a male voice chimed in, "I wouldn't advise speculating. It could prove dangerous."

I looked up. Rafe was standing in the doorway of the kitchen. I scowled at him. "Did you take lessons from our theater ghost in sneaking around silently and appearing out of thin air? Or does it come naturally?"

He helped himself to a steaming cup of coffee, interrupting the flow of the machine. "Since there *is* no ghost, the answer to your first question is no. Which I guess means I was gifted at birth with the admirable ability to be sneaky. Thanks for the coffee, by the way."

Lida Rose, poured a cup for herself, then settled back down in the chair. She waved her spoon at Rafe. "Why can't we speculate? Why is that dangerous?"

He gave her a sharp look. "Jason Sharkey was murdered. You know it. I know it. But as yet, this is not an opinion shared by the local constabulary. If I am right, then a killer is very much at large and might be interested in knocking off anyone curious enough to wonder why Mr. Sharkey was ushered into the next world with undue haste."

I poured my own huge mug and added an extra spoonful of sugar. I craved sweets. I wondered if Lida Rose had brought her stash of miniature candy bars. Then again, it might not be considered in the best taste for the police to find associates of the deceased snarfing down crunchy and fruit-filled chocolates while said corpse was being carted off by a medical examiner.

I took an extra swig and asked Rafe directly, "Why don't the cops think it was murder?"

"They theorize that the cabinet fell when Jason might have been trying to get one of the cases of guns that were on the top, which, incidentally, is a damn stupid place to leave them. They think the cabinet was unbalanced and the cords rotten and it toppled on him and the scimitar just caught him at the wrong place, mainly his neck."

"But that's good, isn't it? It really *might* have been an accident?"

Rafe shook his head. "I've been in that prop room a lot in the weeks I've been here. That cabinet was no more unbalanced than I am. And why the hell would Jason be trying to get those cases anyway? He's not the propmaster. Doesn't make sense. Not to mention that the guns *we* use are in the new prop room next to the scene shop. Not in the *Kismet* room."

Lida Rose spilled coffee down the front of her blouse and didn't even notice. "You believe someone really managed to topple that case on him? That doesn't make sense, either. How would they do that with Jason standing there? Wouldn't he jump back?"

Rafe shrugged.

"I don't know. Hey, I'm an actor with a theory. What does that matter, right?"

Lida Rose looked at him for a long moment.

"It does matter. You're a very smart actor and we may very well have some lunatic running loose in our theater tossing cabinets."

Rafe and I raised a total of three eyebrows to that one. His left brow and both of mine. I patted her hand. "Lida Rose, I don't think a mad cabinet thrower is rampaging through the theater. Even if it was deliberate, much as I hate to mention it, we've said it before and it's true. Jason had a lot of folks angry at him."

Rafe took a swallow from a large mug of coffee.

"Kiely's right. Jason was not well loved by all."

I stood up.

"Crap. I'm about to be brilliant. Well, thanks to Don Mueller."

The other two looked at me like I was running naked down Central Expressway during rush hour.

"What the hell are you talking about?"

"I'm sorry. It just hit me. When I looked up and saw his ghost—yes, I did, Rafe, whether you believe me or not—he was making a swinging motion. I thought he was waving kind of funny. But maybe he was trying to suggest that someone *first* sliced Jason with the scimitar, then toppled that cabinet to make it look accidental. Given time and a ladder, even a little guy like Macy's husband, or hell, Macy or even Daisy could knock that sucker over. And if Jason was lying there bleeding, he or she would have all the time in the world to finish the job. I wonder when Jason actually died."

"I may be sick."

I looked at Lida Rose. She wasn't kidding. Her face was the same shade of green as the T-shirt I'd almost bought down in a vintage clothing store in Greenwich Village that specialized in sixties and seventies neon: a cross between lima bean and chartreuse. It was not a pretty color. I hugged her quickly.

"Hey, I'm sorry. Listen, I'm probably wrong. I mean, I really don't want to imagine someone wielding a scimitar at anyone's neck, not even a cad like Jason, then taking the time to casually toss a cabinet around."

We were interrupted when a shout came from inside

the theater. The casts, past and present, had arrived and were wondering why cop cars and ambulances were decorating the parking lot.

Lida Rose poured more coffee into her cup and threw open the door.

"Time to be the bearer of very bad tidings." She looked hopeful. "Unless the police beat me to it?"

Rafe gently guided her into the theater.

"No such luck, Mrs. Rizokowsky. They're still upstairs and not likely to come down for another hour at least. Didn't even leave anyone in the lobby to let the cast know. It's up to you, director lady."

The pair of them left the kitchen. I stayed. I didn't want to be there when Lida Rose announced that Jason Sharkey was dead. I didn't want to look at Macy's face or see Daisy's tears or wonder who in this group might have had a reason to kill the man. And I wanted to sit in silence for a second and try to figure out why Rafe Montez had been looking at the tops of cabinets in the prop room enough to know that was where the old gun cases were stored.

Chapter 14

Taking the time to gulp down several cups of coffee had been one of my better ideas. I felt a bit more ready to face the cast of *Bad Business*, now sitting in the audience section.

Macy was slumped down in middle of the front row. Tears had washed away every bit of mascara from her lashes, and black streaks now stained her white T-shirt. Daisy had curled up into a fetal position on the piano bench, and was rocking and holding her arms around her upper body. Tears trickled down Lindsay's cheeks, and Theo held her, but she at least seemed composed. The twins, Hank and Ham Humble, looked angry. Amber sobbed as Lida Rose tried to calm her by patting her.

Our older castmates looked just as perturbed. Shirley cried. Fran turned pale and clung to her friend for support. Nathaniel paced the far aisle. I didn't see the Boones.

Jed was whining down in the raised orchestra pit. He must have sensed I was back from the kitchen because he jumped out under the railing and galloped toward me. I hugged his warm body as he wriggled and licked and produced small yips of joy.

I looked around for Rafe and finally spotted him

standing by himself under the balcony at the very back of the theater, muttering to himself and shaking his head. Three more people entered—Thelma Lou and the Boones.

Billie spoke without preamble. "We've been talking. And we think we should close the theater for a few weeks, then open with a different production."

Lida Rose had been nearly distraught when she was in the kitchen. She doubtless had let her emotions show through when she had informed the cast of Jason's death. Perhaps this had registered as weakness. But Billie Boone did not know the real Lida Rose. Jason's death had devastated her. But this pronouncement brought the stiffness back into her spine. She straightened to her full height, marched toward the front of the orchestra pit, then stood next to me.

"Billie. I'm sorry, but this is neither the time nor place to discuss the future of this theater or this production. And excuse me if I sound rude or callous in the wake of a horrific tragedy, but any decisions made concerning this theater will be made by Fran Watkins, Shirley Kincaid, the board members, and myself, as managing director."

Billie appeared stunned, as did most of the people sitting in the theater. Fran had regained some of her normal grayish beige color in her cheeks. She patted Shirley on the back one more time, then stood and walked toward Lida Rose, back straight and head erect.

"Lida Rose is correct. As half owner of the East Ellum, I will be meeting as soon as I can with Shirley and the board. We will let you know what we intend to do when we ourselves know."

Shirley sniffed once and nodded. Rapid, unintelligible conversations burst forth from the crowd of actors.

Lida Rose yelled over the murmurs as best she could. "I believe the police may have some questions for all of us. Please stay in the theater until they're finished. You're welcome to go get coffee or soft drinks, but I suggest you bring any drinks back in here and stay close by."

The police responded to her statement faster than most actors respond to their cues. Officer Carter and his gorgeous lady partner looked sternly at the cast and crew and motioned for everyone to sit and stay silent.

That was when I finally noticed the female cop's nametag: "Melinda Krupke." I choked and tried to look anywhere else. Not the best last name for a cop having to interview a roomful of musical theater people. Even with all the horror I'd witnessed this morning, the lyrics to "Gee, Officer Krupke" came barreling through my mind as clearly as the last time I'd done *West Side Story.*

Rafe was staring at me. His mouth twisted to the side just enough for me to know instinctively that he was humming that tune as well. Doubtless each member of the cast was inwardly sniggering and praying not to break into song during interrogations.

Officers Krupke and Carter were quietly asking individuals what I assumed were the basic, "Where were you? When did you last see . . . ?" questions. I wandered to the back of the theater and sank down on the floor, resting my feet up on one of the seats. I fell asleep. I know this because I was awakened by Rafe nudging me none-too-gently, telling me I was snoring and suggesting that if I was planning on sleeping I probably needed to be on my side and not my back. Or buy a snoring aid. (I vowed to myself never to eat dairy products again. Except for the *queso* at El Diablo's.)

I glared at him, then cast a furtive look toward the front of the theater. Not much had changed.

"Was I loud?"

He smiled. "You weren't buzz-saw level, but you were distracting me from being able to eavesdrop on the interrogation techniques of the good officers."

I threw my water bottle at him. Fortunately for him, it was empty.

"Learn anything?"

"Only that since he's been killed, Jason Sharkey has become a saint in the eyes of many. Although, I must admit that the Humble twins, Theo, and Lindsay haven't changed their perceptions. They're just staying low-key about how much they really despised the man."

I nodded. I was about to ask Rafe whether he'd heard any more about how Jason had ended up decorated by a cabinet when Officer Melinda Krupke appeared.

"Do you two mind answering a few questions?"

Rafe answered for us both. "It's fine."

I had it pegged right. Basic questions. We gave her basic answers. Rafe had already explained the circumstances of finding Jason's body, and I added my bit about Jed sniffing something not quite right upstairs.

Then she asked the biggie. The one I dreaded.

"Did Mr. Sharkey have any problems with anyone

that you know of? Everyone I've asked so far has said—let me quote—he was a difficult man. Unquote."

I tried to stifle a fit of giggles. Rafe and the policewoman looked at me with varying degrees of surprise (from her), irony (from him), and not-so-hidden amusement (from both).

Thankfully, Rafe saved me from totally embarrassing myself. "Officer, Jason Sharkey had so many problems with so many people, you could start a Web site or therapy group. Frankly, the man could have been given the award for most despised actor of the year."

Her face registered amazement. Whether it was from Rafe's honesty or the fact that Jason had been a creep was not clear.

She gestured for the two of us to sit. "Tell me."

We did.

By the time we finished giving Officer Krupke the shortened version of the life and times of Jason Sharkey, I was more than ready to go home. It was eleven o'clock in the morning, rehearsals had been canceled indefinitely, and I was tired. Melinda Krupke must have sensed it.

"I think that's all I need for now. If either of you remembers anything you haven't told me, please give me a call."

She presented each of us with a nice business card. I stood up. I'd just flung my dance bag over my shoulder and was preparing to leave when I heard the new voice.

"The lovely Officer Krupke. And Kiely Davlin as I live and breathe! Plus the villain of *Bad Business*. Mr. Montez, isn't it? Well, well. Jackpot."

I knew that voice. I disliked that voice. It was the

sound of the reporter from the *Morning News*. Brett Barrett. He'd made it past the hapless rookie cop guarding the theater doors. Melinda Krupke gave the reporter a piercing look, then stalked off toward the rookie.

"Brett. How did you manage to slither in?"

He smiled. "Never reveal a source, Ms. Davlin. That includes never explaining the procedures a reporter undergoes to gain entrance to situations that are like candy to that reporter. As is this one. Wow! Jason Sharkey decapitated. Obviously, the curse of *Bad Business* lives. Aren't you afraid you'll be next? And you, Mr. Montez? Delilah Delight and the villain. Andy, get over here with that camera. I have the headline for tomorrow's story all planned and I need the shot to go with it."

I'd been too stunned at both Brett's appearance and too tired by the entire events of the morning to respond to anything the man was saying. Why should Rafe or I be next? What exactly had Lida Rose been saying to the press about a curse?

Rafe wasn't reticent or helpless. "Mr. Barrett. And, Andy? Let me say this once. If a photo of either Kiely or myself makes its way onto the pages of your paper without our permission, other than that cheery publicity photo you saw in the lobby on your way in, you'll have to deal with me personally. You don't want to deal with me, Barrett. You don't want me for an enemy. And I have no intention of being your ally. Believe me when I tell you I will find the means to sue you, disgrace you, get you fired from the *News*, and make it impossible for you to sire children in the future should you so care to engage in that activity."

Brett looked astonished. "How do you intend to accomplish all this?"

Rafe smiled. It was not a nice smile. I relished it with my entire being. "I know your boss. He happens to be my godfather. He and my Dad were college roommates. Enough said?"

Chapter 15

The days since Jason Sharkey had been found bleeding on the prop room floor had passed by with surprising speed. I'd finished choreographing my songs. The cast knew their lines, their songs, and their dances. Most of the company seemed at peace with the fact that Jason Sharkey was no longer with us. Even Daisy had stopped bursting into tears every time her fingers crashed the opening chords of a Lance Lamar song and Macy had cut her trips to run to the dressing room during the middle of a scene then sob for ten minutes down to twice a day.

Police still roamed the theater, but with halfhearted interest. Apparently those in the cast with motive had great alibis, and those without alibis had no motive. Officer Carter was leaning toward the freak accidental death theory. Officer Krupke wasn't as certain, but I had a feeling the brass at the police station wanted closure and wanted it *before* the show opened.

The accidental death theory fit neatly with the board's plan to go on with the show. And of course, the media loved it. The bane of *Bad Business* buys tickets. Fran had made the announcement less than three days after Jason's death, and East Ellum had been besieged with enthusiastic reporters.

The official line was, "We feel it would be a slap in the face of Jason Sharkey's memory to close *Bad Business* just before the grand reopening. It's what Mr. Sharkey would no doubt have wished."

It was a bullshit line and we all knew it. The actors knew it, the original cast knew it, Lida Rose knew it, and Fran Watkins and Shirley Kincaid knew it, too.

Shirley, the ditz, had then made an astonishing decision following Fran's statement. Instead of letting Jason's capable but unknown twenty-five-year-old understudy take over the role of Lance Lamar, she wanted to put sixty-eight-year-old Cyrus Boone, the original hero, in the part. Hey, if you're surfing that wave of media coverage, why not ride it to the very end? The board bought off the understudy's contract and explained that there would be extra rehearsals (with extra pay) to bring Cyrus Boone up to speed in the role that had nearly destroyed his life fifty years ago.

I thought it was the nastiest, scummiest, most hideous thing to do to another human being other than slice a neck open with a scimitar. I was in the minority. Even Lida Rose thought it would be a great thing for Cyrus Boone: it would give him an opportunity to "redo" a wrong done in the past. Show him that lightning doesn't strike twice. All that trash.

Surprisingly, Rafe agreed with *me*. We'd spent fifteen minutes talking about it during a coffee break several days before. He'd been muttering and shaking his head as he watched me dunk a delicious-looking chocolate-glazed doughnut into my mug.

"She's nuts."

"Who?"

"Well, now that you mention it, all three of 'em.

Shirley Kincaid, Fran Watkins, and Lida Rose Worthington Rizokowsky. A triumvirate of tasteless tarts."

He grabbed the last doughnut in the box before I could drown it as well.

"Tarts?"

"I was trying to find a *t* word for nitwits, but couldn't. When I saw that doughnut disappear into your eager hands and considered the role you play in this show, tarts naturally followed."

I took a bite. "Yeah. Naturally. I could have told you that Lida Rose is crazy. I've known her to be certifiable for years. But label Fran and Shirley nuts? Well, Shirley, obviously. But Fran? Why?"

"Because she agrees that Cyrus Boone should play Lance Lamar."

"Oh."

I carefully took a sip of my coffee. Too hot. I stuffed a bite of doughnut into my mouth instead.

"N'agreewifyou."

"What?"

I chewed and swallowed. "I agree with you. I think it's a rotten idea. And I think Cyrus thinks it's a rotten idea. Did you see how pale he got when Shirley came out with her statement a few days ago? I personally would find it damned difficult to replay a role that caused the death of my best friend."

I continued to chew, then looked at the floor.

"Don doesn't like it, either."

"What?"

I lifted my chin defiantly. "When Shirley told Cyrus he was going on as Lance Lamar, I saw Don Mueller in the balcony shaking his head and pointing to Cyrus."

Rafe poured a second cup of coffee for himself and scowled at me.

"Thanks for ruining what was something we both agree on. Well, anyway, forget the opinion of your ghost. I think we should talk to Lida Rose and persuade the woman to let Jason's understudy handle this. I realize the theater might lose some of the rampant curse coverage in the papers, but I think it'd be safer all around."

"I'm with you."

We strolled, literally arm in arm, toward Lida Rose who was scrutinizing the programs to be sure everyone's name was spelled correctly. The stage manager should have been taking care of that little detail, but Lida Rose is a stickler for proper spelling and rechecks everything herself. Probably a result of having Rizokowsky mangled by every driver's license and social security bureau in the county.

"Lida Rose . . . Kiely and I have been chatting, and—"

"No. Cyrus is doing the role."

Rafe stared at her. "How the hell did you even know what we were going to ask?"

She smiled at him. "I know Kiely Davlin. I know you. I know you've been talking in the kitchen. Ergo, I knew what you were going to say. Now go away. The decision has been made. Cyrus Boone is in the program under Lance Lamar, hero, along with a brief history of the theater, including the tragedies the last two times the show was performed. Oh, and a nice little memorial to Jason Sharkey. He'd've loved it. It's full of lies about how wonderful he was. We're starting rehearsal in five minutes, kids. Go away."

We went away, both of us shaking our heads like dogs in the window of a pickup truck.

"Brain dead. All of em. She and the board members have truly lost what was left of their collective senses."

"Yep. Mark my words, Rafe, there's gonna be more trouble. Lida Rose. Trouble. The words go together like 'serial' and 'killer.' Like 'earth' and 'quake.' Like 'dis' and 'aster.'"

He smiled at me. I smiled back.

"So, is there anything two sane people, i.e., *us*, can do about this? Short of actually burning down the theater?"

"I don't think so, Kiely. Cops are still prowling around the theater, so that should deter anyone else from ideas of throwing more cabinets around. We open in a week and hopefully that's not enough time for anything else to go wrong."

I sighed and took back my last statement. "One week is a damn long time. Everything could wrong. And probably will."

"Break over! Places for Act Three."

The stage manager was yelling at the top of his lungs.

We set down our coffee cups and headed back onstage. Act Three, Scene Two. The "Hog-tie Hoedown." I'd originally enjoyed choreographing the dance but now I hated the whole scene. Cyrus didn't seem comfortable with tying Rafe up, the Humble brothers were tentative about swinging "Nick Nefarious," and Daisy had yet to keep the right tempo for the whole number because she was glaring at Cyrus as though it was his fault Jason had died.

Today wasn't any better. Cyrus fumbled with the ropes and "Billy Joe Bob and Bobby Joe Bob Travis" dropped Rafe dangerously close to the orchestra pit when those ropes gave too soon. Rafe landed on

Macy's foot. She squealed like a stuck pig and the apologies flowed.

"Hold it!"

We looked offstage. Lida Rose and Billie Boone were in deep conference.

"Take five, everyone. We may have some changes coming here."

I glanced at Rafe. He glanced back and the communication was instant. Lida Rose was about to undo several weeks of work. I could feel it.

"Kiely!"

I jumped down.

"Yo. Please don't tell me I'm redoing the choreography? Please, please?"

Lida Rose smiled. "No. Nothing that rash. We're just trying to figure out what the problem is here."

"Ask Rafe. He's the one entangled in rope. Ask Hank and Ham. They're the ones who have to carry him. Ask Cyrus. He's the one that ties the man up."

Lida Rose lowered her voice. "That's why I'm talking to you. Is Cyrus capable of making that lasso tight? Is he holding back for fear of hurting Rafe?"

I glared at her.

"*Now* you want to know? *Now* you're uneasy because you've stuck Cyrus into a rotten position? And we haven't even started rehearsing the gun scene. I can't wait to watch that poor man choke up when he has to shoot Rafe."

I turned to Billie. "He's your husband. Why in hell are you letting him do this?"

She closed her eyes for a second. "Believe me, Kiely, I've gone over and over whether I should have tried to talk him out of it. But he's suddenly adamant about going through with the show. He believes that once he fires that gun opening night and nothing bad happens, he'll be free of all that guilt he's carried for fifty years. I can't change his mind. So what am I supposed to do?"

I stayed silent for a minute.

"All right. If he's determined, then we'll help him out. We'll practice the stupid lasso trick until he feels comfortable. I'll change the beginning of the dance so Hank and Ham will have time to make sure those ropes don't loosen."

Lida Rose beamed at me. "Thanks, Kiely. I knew I could count on you."

I growled at her and turned to the cast.

"Yo. Crew. Slight change in the hoedown."

It took me only about thirty minutes to add the time needed for the rope check. For once the cast listened and did exactly as I asked. The stage manager called lunch after we had rehearsed the new sequence at least five times through. I was more than ready. It seemed to be a brown-bagging day. No one wanted to go out. The kitchen grew crowded, the "Green room" intolerable with chattering and munching, and the scene and costume shops were off-limits to food at this point. Lida Rose was meeting with a few media types in the lobby.

I finally took my crunchy peanut butter and jelly on twelve-grain toast outdoors and headed for the only tree that offered any shade. I devoured the sandwich, then curled up for a short nap. Jed was with me and didn't mind being used as a pillow.

"Kiely. Wake up."

"N't wanto. Go away. I was just getting the Tony Award for Best Choreography for next year's hit musical. Thank you, thank you."

Rafe nudged me. "Up, dreamer. Afternoon re-hearsals are starting in one minute."

I yawned, poked the dog, who was snoring (at least it wasn't me this time), then followed Rafe back inside.

"Hog-tie Hoedown. Places, everyone."

It started off well. The dance before the actual las-soing sequence went off without a hitch. Cyrus tossed the rope around Rafe and tied it exactly as he'd been shown. The Humble twins swooped up Rafe and began to swing him. And swing him. And swing . . .

The rope broke. Rafe tumbled to the edge of the orchestra pit, which happened to be in Down posi-tion. I dove and grabbed his legs before he could topple to the cement floor twenty feet below. The music stopped. Screams came from every direction. I held onto to Rafe's legs until he could hoist himself to a sitting position. We stared at each other.

"Thanks."

"Don't mention it."

Lida Rose, the stage manager, and Charlie Baines were on stage faster than Jed normally goes through a chew toy.

"Crap."

"Charlie?" Lida Rose asked.

"This is the wrong rope. It was supposed to be thrown out with the rest of the garbage. How the hell did it get onto the prop table instead of the good rope? This thing is torn in so many places it's no wonder it snapped."

Everyone looked at everyone else. No one even breathed.

"Charlie?"

"Yeah. What?"

One of the other techies stood next to the prop

table in the wings near stage left. "There's about three ropes on the floor here. Somehow this one got mixed up with the good ones. I have no idea how, except that this whole table is a mess. Don't you people take care and check your props?"

The company nodded as a unit. I was furious.

"The table was not like that before lunch," I said, "and we don't normally check to see if the props have been mixed up while we're gone for one hour when no one is supposed to touch them. How'd everything get so screwed up?"

"Probably the media's fault."

"What?"

We turned as a solid unit and looked at Daisy.

She nodded vigorously. "They've been all over this theater today. Interrogating everybody they can find who'll talk. I found three cups of coffee on the piano after lunch. Can you imagine? Pigs. One of them probably got nosy and started messing with stuff onstage, too."

I hated to admit it, but it was a plausible explanation. Maybe Daisy had a brain lurking under the mousy brown hair after all. The reporters had taken the opportunity to stick their noses into every nook and cranny in the theater each time they got an invite to enter. Lida Rose *had* given a minipress conference during lunch. So one of them might easily have dug through the props looking for a loaded weapon, or a big sign saying, THIS WAY TO THE ORIGIN OF THE CURSE.

"Rafe? You okay?"

He nodded. "Just a bit shaken. I'll be fine, thanks to that flying tackle by Ms. Davlin."

He glanced at me with admiration. "Notre Dame could have used you. I don't remember a superwoman dive in the play books, but I'll suggest one at the next alumni function for my ex-teammates."

"Glad to be of service. No charge. Well, except for the Band-Aids. I've now got skinned knees no dance-hall girl would bare."

Lida Rose looked at both of us with concern. I had a feeling she'd've liked to stop rehearsals, but the stage manager was already calling places. We went back to work.

It was less than a week before we were going to open. The intercom system was still sputtering. The prop crew was being chewed out for allowing any of the press anywhere backstage. Daisy was carefully wiping coffee stains from the piano top. This grand reopening had more glitches than a lightboard from the 1920s. Our leading man was dead. We'd come close to losing Rafe because of a frayed rope. Cyrus would now be even more terrified to perform, but very soon *Bad Business on the Brazos* would play to standing-room-only crowds.

Chapter 16

"Fire! Fire! We're going to die! We've got to get out!"

Daisy Haltom, the mousy accompanist, was shrieking and waving, and pointing upstairs toward the old prop room, the one known as "Kismet." I tend to dismiss anything Daisy says other than her notes on our singing, but when music stops and an accompanist screams in an unholy and shrill manner, I pay attention. Along with every other member of the cast, I stopped dancing and tilted my head upward.

Sure enough, smoke was oozing out of the doorway of the prop room.

"Oh, crap! A fire in the theater is not what I need today."

Lida Rose's tone held more irritation than fear. Rafe, Ham, Hank, and Theo had already started running toward the stairs, ready to do their manly duty and destroy any possible blaze. I've seen speed skaters with less velocity and more politeness. The bruises every one of them would bear trying to elbow one another out of the way could well reach lethal proportions. Each man was hell-bent on crossing the finish line of the smoking door ahead of his peers.

Rafe won. The other three slid and crashed right behind him. Then all four looked at the door, now slightly ablaze, then back at each other with mixed expressions of admiration, credulity, fear, and stupidity. Not a one of the stalwart warriors had thought to bring any of the six fire extinguishers from anywhere in the theater.

Lida Rose and I stayed onstage and contemplated our fellow castmates and elderly audience with concern. Most were yelling incoherently and inanely.

"Theo, watch out! Be careful! You could get burned! You dimwit!" came from Lindsay.

"Oh hell, this'll mess up the theater's insurance," was Fran Watkins's practical statement.

"Run away for your lives!" Not surprisingly, Shirley Kincaid had resorted to cliche. A mangled one.

The only rational remark came from Thelma Lou. Along with her words came a solution. She entered the stage with the portable kitchen fire extinguisher in hand.

"Kiely? You're in better shape'n me. A' course, you're sixty years younger. Now, get this up to those morons before one of 'em gets hisself hurt."

I grabbed it and started running toward the ladder in the back of the theater that led to the balcony area. Two rungs from the top, I was able to fling the extinguisher to the heroes. By this time someone had managed to do the reasonable thing and beat out the flames with a tarp they'd found in front of the light booth. The blaze was dead.

Undeterred by this fact, Rafe bravely sprayed white foam over the door, over the other men, over me, and over half the balcony, including the ladder. I ducked and missed the worst of it.

"Rafe! Rafe! Yo! Stop already! Hey! Montez! It's out.

It's *been* out for five minutes. Halt. Cease. Desist. Look.
We're safe."

His gorgeous features became slightly sheepish.

"Uh-oh. Did I get a bit carried away?"

"I believe the word you're looking for is 'overkill.'"

"Well, I have this rabid fear of fire in theaters. With
or without an audience present. Too much flammable
stuff, too many people panicking. Even a little one
like this can suddenly turn nasty. It's that Boy Scout
thing of being prepared."

He acknowledged, "Maybe taken to the extreme?"

Lida Rose had made it to the barely charred door
by this time. She'd taken the regular stairs and was
eyeing my soaked ladder and sodden hair with a mixture of amusement and disdain.

"Okay. Let's see the damage."

She kicked bits of white foam off her feet.

"Well. My, my. Thanks, gentlemen, for dousing the
blaze. Although, I do believe you may have been
overly enthusiastic with the fire extinguisher, Rafe.
Considering the fact that from where I stood there
was barely a flicker of flame. Oh, I like that. Flicker of
flame. Has such nice alliteration. Flicker of flame.
Flicker of flame! What a great idea for a song!"

"Lida Rose? A request from those of us who are currently soaked in white goo and not really up for your
wiseass comments? Shut up!"

Rafe smiled sweetly at me. "It was kind of fun, spray-
ing that thing. Gives one a feeling of power. Of
manliness."

I snorted, then sneezed as white foam dripped too
near my nose. "Reminds me of attacking one's best
friend in grade school with Cheez Whiz. A favorite
sport of mine and obviously one of yours?"

He ignored me. "Let's survey the damage to Kismet. A room I admit I hadn't wanted to enter for a while."

Lida Rose stood back to let Rafe and Theo kick in the door. Stupid, really. We had no idea where the fire had started and I'd seen movies with back-draft blazes engulfing stuntmen. A vision of a roaring flame bursting through and knocking us all down onto the stage as we screamed in anguish flashed before my eyes. I shivered as I tried to forget that a real death had taken place in this very room less than two weeks ago.

We were blessed. A wisp or two of smoke remained. That was all. Apparently the door was the only object to have actually been burned. Rafe gently pushed me behind him with the comment, "Women and children to the rear," and started looking through the room for what might have ignited the small blaze. I debated about hitting him over the head with the discarded (and empty) fire extinguisher for that crack, but decided instead to stay at his shoulder for a few seconds. Then I began to wander through the old prop room on my own.

"Nothing," I grumbled. "I don't see one damn thing that could have started this fire. No cigarettes, no frayed wires, no cans of propellant, no candles burned to oblivion. No nothing."

Both of Rafe's eyebrows lifted. "What are you? The arson inspector? Could have been anything, Kiely."

"Mmmm."

I ignored him. I was busy exploring the space. Kismet. I'd never been up here before and the various props from shows half a century ago or older were distracting me from my new role as fire detective detector.

The sofa that was reputedly the spot for various lovers' enjoyment stood boldly in the middle of the room. I tried to avoid staring at it and realized I was blushing. "Spot" was the operative word. There were many. All over the sofa. I had no desire to find out if they'd been made from coffee, tea, or other organic substances. I caught Rafe eyeing me, his right brow lifted, so I quickly shifted my gaze to what was left of the huge cabinet in the corner closest to the door. The cabinet that had ended up on top of Jason Sharkey.

Weapons of all kinds were still scattered around the floor. Other scimitars from the show *Kismet*. Heavy swords and maces from *Camelot*. Huge lances from *Hamlet* or the Scottish play, or perhaps a 1960s production of *Man of La Mancha* were lying neatly beside bow-and-arrow sets (*Robin Hood*—the musical?). All the weapons looked real. I knew the scimitars were. I repressed a sudden desire to run screaming from the room.

The cabinet itself had once been a work of art. I'd been dragged to many antique stores in years past by my mother, a fanatic woodworker with a sharp eye and a desire to pass on knowledge to her daughter. This piece reminded me of wardrobes and curio stands from the 1880s. The large box that had originally perched on top of the cabinet now lay in pieces next to the bow-and-arrow set. Some enterprising props person had painted the word "guns" on the front of that box in calligraphic red letters.

I couldn't take looking at the weapons or the broken cabinet anymore. I turned my attention to the areas that were still intact despite Jason's accident and the fire.

A table bearing bottles of booze, cards, costume jewelry, birthday candles, and tin flowers more than hinted of *A Streetcar Named Desire*. Next to it stood a tiny curio cabinet filled with miniature crystal figurines. *The Glass Menagerie.* This must have been the repository for every Tennessee Williams play ever performed at East Ellum. A wire birdcage even held someone's discarded script from *Eccentricities of a Nightingale,* Williams's rewrite of his earlier work *Summer and Smoke.* The front page of the script bore the names of a Teresa Barrett and Alma, the lead character, in bold print. I let the small book remain in the cage.

Long ago these items had dressed the stage and provided a means to telling a story. Now they were nothing more than junk.

I crossed to the corner opposite the weapons cabinet and the Williams memorabilia.

"Rafe! Look at this!"

He whirled around as though I'd discovered a book of matches with the words, "Arsonist for Hire" on them.

"What's the matter?"

"Nothing. Jeez, you're jumpy. I just wanted you to take a look at some of this stuff."

He hurried over to join me in the corner.

"Rafe, do you think these could be props from the very first *Bad Business?* I mean, there's a ship's anchor that says "Brazos Belle" on it. It's all tangled up with fish netting but it really doesn't look bad. And that bar. That's gotta be a hundred years old. There's a steamer trunk, too. I'll bet that's the one they used in Act Two."

I squatted on the floor and dove into the props like a toddler making mud pies. I was oblivious to my foamy hair and general disarray. It took some doing, but I managed to open the old trunk and started tossing out items.

Take A Trip Into A Timeless World of Passion and Adventure with Kensington Choice Historical Romances!
—Absolutely FREE!

Enjoy the passion and adventure of another time with Kensington Choice Historical Romances. They are the finest novels of their kind, written by today's best-selling romance authors. Each Kensington Choice Historical Romance transports you to distant lands in a bygone age. Experience the adventure and share the delight as proud men and spirited women discover the wonder and passion of true love.

Get 4 FREE Books!

We created our convenient Home Subscription Service so you'll be sure to have the hottest new romances delivered each month right to your doorstep—usually before they are available in book stores. Just to show you how convenient the Zebra Home Subscription Service is, we would like to send you 4 FREE Kensington Choice Historical Romances. The books are worth up to $24.96, but you only pay $1.99 for shipping and handling. There's no obligation to buy additional books—ever!

Save Up To 30% With Home Delivery!

Accept your FREE books and each month we'll deliver 4 brand new titles as soon as they are published. They'll be yours to examine FREE for 10 days. Then if you decide to keep the books, you'll pay the preferred subscriber's price (up to 30% off the cover price!), plus shipping and handling. Remember, you are under no obligation to buy any of these books at any time! If you are not delighted with them, simply return them and owe nothing. But if you enjoy Kensington Choice Historical Romances as much as we think you will, pay the special preferred subscriber rate and save over $8.00 off the cover price!

We have **4 FREE BOOKS** for you as your
introduction to
KENSINGTON CHOICE!
To get your FREE BOOKS, worth up to $24.96, mail
the card below or call TOLL-FREE 1-800-770-1963.
Visit our website at www.kensingtonbooks.com.

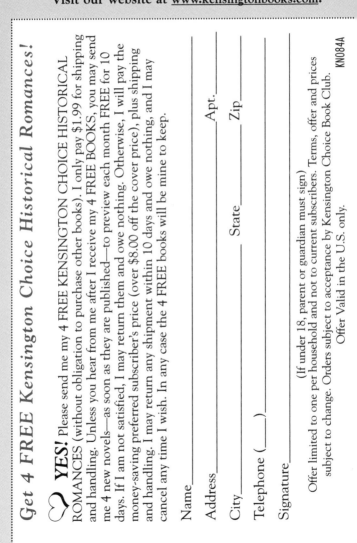

Get 4 FREE Kensington Choice Historical Romances!

YES! Please send me my 4 FREE KENSINGTON CHOICE HISTORICAL ROMANCES (without obligation to purchase other books). I only pay $1.99 for shipping and handling. Unless you hear from me after I receive my 4 FREE BOOKS, you may send me 4 new novels—as soon as they are published—to preview each month FREE for 10 days. If I am not satisfied, I may return them and owe nothing. Otherwise, I will pay the money-saving preferred subscriber's price (over $8.00 off the cover price), plus shipping and handling. I may return any shipment within 10 days and owe nothing, and I may cancel any time I wish. In any case the 4 FREE books will be mine to keep.

Name _____

Address _____ Apt. _____

City _____ State _____ Zip _____

Telephone (_____) _____

Signature _____

(If under 18, parent or guardian must sign)

Offer limited to one per household and not to current subscribers. Terms, offer and prices subject to change. Orders subject to acceptance by Kensington Choice Book Club.
Offer Valid in the U.S. only.

KN084A

"Oh my gosh! There's the deed to Polly Sue Primrose's property. How did it survive? Maybe these things aren't as old as I thought. Maybe from the production fifty years ago?"

Rafe peered over my shoulder at the paper used to represent what the villain intended to steal in *Bad Business*. The deed makes one appearance in the show, in the last act, during the card game.

"It's well preserved, but I think you were right the first time. All this stuff looks way over a century old. I'm surprised you didn't notice earlier—when Lida Rose gave you the tour."

I shook my head. "I didn't get the tour. Never had the time. If you remember, I came in late after Lida Rose lost her other dancer. Jason offered to show me around up here, but I figured he meant the couch only, so I declined."

Rafe squatted next to me and begin carefully lifting items out of the trunk. I waved at Lida Rose to come over.

"Hey! I wonder if anything really valuable is up here? You know. A first edition, hand-written copy of a Eugene O'Neill masterpiece. Even a first-edition, hand-written copy of *Bad Business*. That should be worth something to this company just in sentiment alone."

Lida Rose leaned over and let the netting from the ship's anchor glide through her fingers.

"Kiely? Forget it! I hate to crush your hopes of finding treasure, but this place is pretty much old junk."

"Party pooper. You have no imagination. In that case, if I do find anything, I'm hanging on to it and keeping it a secret. So there."

Lida Rose snorted, "Yeah, right. Like Miss Honesty-

Trained-by-the-Nuns was going to sneak out of here with the crowned jewels. Okay, folks. I think the excitement is over for a while. I don't see anything offhand that could be responsible for that paltry little fire, unless it's a cigarette butt that burned itself out before we got here. We'll never know. So . . . downstairs. Much as I'm enjoying this brief respite, we do need to rehearse. Kiely? You're having far too much fun. Up, girl, and prepare to dance. After you clean up. You look like you got stuck in a shaving cream container."

Rather in the manner of sheep following the shepherd, the boys and I lined up behind our director and began the march back down. I was bringing up the rear, so no one noticed when I tripped in the doorway over a very tiny object.

A piece of popped popcorn. One. It could have been left there days ago by Jason or one of his girls. It probably didn't mean a thing. Rafe hadn't been eating any—for a change—when he came bounding up the stairs, but he had been in this prop room looking for cards before Jason had died here. I picked up the bit of food, held on to it, then hurried to catch up with my fellow firefighters.

I stopped at the lighting booth. Don Mueller stood just inside, holding a bag of popcorn in his hand. He gestured at the prop room, shook his head, and disappeared.

Chapter 17

"Who's there? What's going on? Who's hiding under there?"

At the sound of the voice, I jumped and knocked my head on the edge of the couch, then screamed, "What the hell are you doing sneaking up on me like that? After everything that's happened here in the last two weeks! Are you looney?"

"Kiely?"

"Yes! Kiely. The dancer with the headache and probably a large bump on my forehead thanks to you."

"I saw a body on the floor under the sofa and naturally wanted to know who was up here after hours."

"Well, now you do. I should ask you the same thing. What brings you to Kismet this late in the evening?"

Rafe sat down on the floor next to me and peered at my forehead. "You're not bleeding. That's good."

"Thanks for the concern. So—why are you snooping around scaring me into probably premature white hair?"

"Same as you. I'm curious as to what started that fire earlier. I'd like to know if something in the wiring is about to short out and cause the whole theater to go up in flames."

"Mmm."

Rafe looked sharply at me.

"What does that mean? Do you know something you're not telling?"

I did, but he'd never believe me. The popcorn pointed directly to my ghost. A ghost who, as far as I knew, had no good reason to play arsonist in his off-hours. I shook my head and avoided Rafe's question.

"I'm not looking for faulty electrics. I wouldn't know one if it reached out and bit me. To be honest, I wanted another look at that stuff from the original *Bad Business.* Something kept nagging at me to come up and poke around. I thought perhaps some of the pieces from the old show might have been kicked under the sofa through the years. And since the romantically inclined who use the sofa aren't exactly interested in historical research, they stay on the top, so to speak. I was trying to check underneath!"

"So?"

My head hurt and I didn't feel like being social.

"So, nothing. I'd barely gotten started in this corner when Rafe, the resident snoop, barged in on me."

"I told you I wasn't snooping; just trying to make sure things stay safe around here. I got a bit too close to those flames today to be nonchalant about the theater burning down. Not to mention, this might not be the safest place to be right now, even without flames bursting forth."

"So why isn't our tech director or stage manager or even Lida Rose taking on this chore? How did you get elected? Are you now the resident hero?"

His brows were set. I knew I was pushing, but I really wanted an explanation for Rafe's odd habit of diving headfirst (literally) into everything in the theater.

"None of the people you've mentioned feel there's

a problem. They think the fire was a fluke. I do not agree. Is that clear enough for you? As to that, your explanation for whatever lured you to the prop room after hours to hunt for buried treasure or first folios seems a trifle thin as to a sane reason for you being here, too."

We glared at each other for at least thirty seconds. Then I began to laugh.

"Kiss or kill?"

"What?"

"Didn't you ever take Directing 101? 'Kiss or kill.' When two characters are in a tense scene and they get closer than two feet to each other, one of two things has to happen."

His expression softened for the first time since he'd surprised me under the sofa.

"I get it."

He did, too. He grabbed me, put his lips to mine, and began the more pleasurable of the two choices. Lips were exploring lips, tongues getting entangled, arms were clenched around bodies, and hands were starting to roam. I was giving back as good as I was getting and enjoying the whole process far too much. Lida Rose would be proud.

Rafe started to lift me up—perhaps heading for the top of the Kismet sofa?—when my foot got caught by the netting I'd seen this afternoon next to the *Brazos Belle* anchor.

"Rafe!"

"Mmmm?"

"Put me down. There's something clinging to my foot and it's not pleasant."

He reluctantly complied, then knelt down to free me from the rope.

"Damn, Kiely. What a mess. This is actual fish netting. I'm surprised there's not a big mackerel or carp in among the ruins."

I finally managed to get my foot free. The two of us were now busily trying to untie the thick rope.

"Rafe! There's some old jewelry mixed up in this netting. I wonder why the costume crew didn't end up with this?"

I held out my hands to show him the glass piece caught between rope strands.

"Kiely, it's really matted in there. Costumes probably didn't know anything was there. Assuming they even had a costume crew. From what I've heard about the original theater productions, they were pretty casual."

We worked at the netting until the piece came free. An earring. Garnet. My hand closed over the stone and I immediately wanted to run out of the room, which seemed to have grown very small and very dark, and very dusty. I was freezing. I closed my eyes and breathed in slowly. For an instant I could detect the presence of another being. Not Don. A female exuding a sadness I'd never experienced in my thirty-two years of life.

I heard the barest hint of a whisper. "Please, Elias. Please, don't. Let me have my life!"

Then it was gone.

Rafe's head was cocked to one side. He seemed to be waiting for me to say something.

Instead, I held the earring up for his inspection and nonchalantly asked, "Whatcha think? Real? Or literally, costume?"

He studied it. "Garnets aren't exactly my field, but this looks pure. We should take it to a jeweler and get it appraised."

I wasn't really listening. "I wonder who it belonged to."

I shivered again. Rafe glanced at me.

"Oh, no."

"What?"

"You've got that ghost-sighting look in your eye. I saw it the day you were trying to convince me our deceased villain was in the audience. I hate to tell you this, but I don't think Mr. Mueller was playing the part of Nick Nefarious fifty years ago with a garnet dangling from his ear under a stovepipe hat!"

I postulated, "The politically correct version? Nefarious was gay and just coming out to sidekick Jackson Wild? Well, maybe not."

I grew more serious.

"I'm sure this had nothing to do with Don Mueller. But one of the dancehall girls might have worn it. All of us now have similar pieces. Except ours are definitely fake. But this? I think it's real. Having it appraised is a good idea."

He was watching me closely. "You're not telling me something."

I looked up at him as he helped me stand again. "You won't believe me. I'd prefer not to have you scoffing at me, at least for a while."

He frowned. "Try me."

I quickly inhaled, then told him about the flash of that other presence, the incredible misery that had accompanied it, and the certainty that this earring had belonged to a lady who had been dead for perhaps a century. I didn't mention the voice. Rafe raised both eyebrows. (I was making progress. Two brows signified he was at least listening before making tacky comments.)

"Kiely, this is beyond my understanding. I have heard that what we call ghosts might be heightened emotions from people who've passed on and left some sort of chemical energy behind them."

"Is that a willingness to listen to another idea? Like it's more than just a feeling that stays behind? To be honest, I didn't buy any of this paranormal stuff until I began communing, if you will, with the spirit of Don Mueller, but I'm beginning to believe that ghosts hang out on this earthly plane for a reason. Usually things left undone."

"So what did Don leave undone?"

I set my jaw. "His murderer was never found. Never brought to justice. He also never got to be with the love of his life and maybe he doesn't know what happened to her, either . . . ?"

Rafe shook his head. "I'm sorry. The man was buried and given a nice funeral and should now be a beam of light somewhere above waiting to welcome the newly departed to his bosom. Dressing up in costumes and watching rehearsals waiting for revenge is just too much to swallow."

"I didn't say he was out for revenge. I said justice. Two different things. Or maybe that's not why he's here at all. Maybe there's some reason I haven't thought of yet."

Rafe looked at me, then around the room.

"And your other ghost? As if one wasn't enough. What's her *raison d'être*?"

"I don't know. Maybe I should be researching that first cast of *Bad Business*? Maybe more than one murder has been committed?"

Rafe suddenly smiled at me. "You're having way too much fun with this."

"I know. Wanna search the room and see if the other earring turns up? Got to have been part of a set, especially from a hundred years ago. People didn't wear just one unless they were pirates. Early rock stars?"

Rafe didn't hear me. He'd gone diving under a pile of drop cloths that should have been in the scene shop. Actually, they should have been tossed. Blue paint clung to the parts of the fabric that were still intact. On closer inspection, the paint turned out to be mildew. I wrinkled my nose.

"Rafe? Unless you want to gather this stuff for penicillin, I'd suggest avoiding it. Why on earth is this still here?"

He popped up and wiped his hands together in disgust. "Sheer laziness on someone's part. This is truly gross. There's about three trunks underneath all these cloths, but I'm not touching 'em even if every one is loaded with real garnets, not to mention diamonds and pieces of eight from your heavy-metal pirates."

I helped him dislodge a piece of cloth that had managed to attach itself to his shoulder.

"It's past midnight anyway. Perhaps it's time to leave Kismet and let the techies come up here with disinfectant and a few large garbage bags."

He smiled at me. "Maybe we shouldn't have stopped the fire. Let the place burn to the ground."

I looked at the birdcage, the old scripts, and the anchor.

"No. There's too much really great stuff up here. Look at this. There's a stack of programs under the 'Alma' birdcage. Someone really needs to go through and separate the treasures from the trash."

"Volunteering?"

I let out a deep breath. "Nope."

He held out his hand and we started to leave. Another voice filled the space.

"Kiely? Rafe? My goodness, you're both filthy. Have you been sampling the sofa? It's about damn time."

We faced our accuser. Lida Rose stood in the doorway. A huge grin spread over her entire face.

"Lida Rose? I thought you'd gone home. And, *no*, we weren't sampling the sofa."

"I did go home. I came back after worrying for the last hour that the theater would burn down before I got back on Monday unless I found out what started that fire. So? What *are* you doing here?"

The grin grew even larger.

"As if I couldn't guess. I've heard King Arthur's throne chair is quite comfortable, too."

I sighed and took her by her chubby hand.

"Lida Rose. There are no burning bushes up here. No smoldering cigarettes. No frayed wires and no blown circuits. You need sleep. I need sleep. Rafe needs sleep. It is way past time to go home."

She ignored me. "What have you got in that hot little hand?"

"Oh! Programs. I just found them. Haven't had a chance to look at them yet."

"Neat. I'd love to see them, but not in this light and not in this room. You children coming?"

We followed her out of the prop room, even though I was itching to continue my search, with or without Rafe and our director. The three of us headed directly for the kitchen where the light was strong and the surprising smell of freshly brewed coffee stronger.

Thelma Lou smiled at us from her stool nearest the coffeepot. "Find anything interesting?"

I handed her the programs. "I haven't had a

chance to look at them but they look really, really old."

Thelma Lou plopped them onto the counter and spread them out like a fan. She immediately pointed to the middle program. The worst kept of the lot.

"My God," I breathed out. "It's *Bad Business on the Brazos*. The absolute original. From a hundred years ago."

Lida Rose nearly knocked me to the ground to see the cover. Rafe peered over her shoulder. Both stared for a good minute while I patiently waited my turn. Then they turned and stared at me. And stared.

"What?"

"It's you."

"What? What's me?"

Rafe shook his head. "Lida Rose. It's not. Not really. It's just an impression. Nothing else. Don't get Kiely all wrought up here over nothing."

I wanted to scream. "Will you tell me what you're both jabbering about?"

Neither answered. Lida Rose handed me the faded, torn program and pointed to the photograph on the cover.

Our current cast of *Bad Business* had posed for a photo quite similar to this only days before Jason's death. Villain, hero, card sharks, and Polly Sue Primrose, the heroine, were all seated at a round table. Behind them, in various provocative stances stood the dancehall girls Sultry Salome and Bathsheba Bombshell. Plus the actress obviously playing Delilah Delight. I could have been looking in a mirror at a sepia-colored version of me.

Rafe was holding his breath. Lida Rose was grinning.

"It's uncanny. Kiely Davlin and—what the hell was the name of the girl who first played Delilah."

Thelma Lou quietly said, "Charity. Charity O'Sullivan. By all accounts a beautiful Irish redhead with great dance skills and a lovely voice to match."

She left.

Rafe shook his head. "Don't even start, ladies. Take another really hard look and you'll see there's only a superficial resemblance to our Kiely. Nothing more. Now then, I'm leaving. May I escort anyone home?"

I shook my head. I wasn't ready to be alone with Rafe Montez again.

Lida Rose waited until Rafe had gone, then she poked my side so hard I knew I'd have a bruise. Naturally she avoided any mention of Charity O'Sullivan. My clone.

"Damn, Kiely. If you and Mr. Montez are finally going to get it on, you could pick a much better spot than Kismet. It's so banal, so trite, so used. Not to mention the site of a very tragic death."

I glared at her.

"Mrs. Rizokowsky. Not that it's any of your nosy little affair. Wait. Make that your *business.* The word 'affair' will immediately strike chords of illicit sex in your mind and I'd prefer not to leave that impression, thank you."

She sighed. I pursed my lips together.

"Where was I?"

"Nosy. Business. Affair."

"Thanks. Anyway, I found the most incredible thing in Kismet under the sofa!"

She snickered. I rolled my eyes.

"Get your mind out of the gutter, wench. Look."

I showed her the garnet earring and explained that

it had been caught in the netting from the *Bad Business* prop anchor.

"Wow! Kiely. That's real. Not costume."

"I thought it might be. Listen. When I first touched it, it gave off the most intense feeling of pain. Sadness. It was frightening."

"Want me to keep it for you?"

"No. I want to hang on to it. I feel a strange link with whomever it belonged to. As if she's trying to tell me something."

Lida Rose patted me kindly on my back. "I'll betcha you'll be communing with the ghost of whomever wore it soon. Undoubtedly Charity O'Sullivan. This is great. Bonding with Don, empathizing with the wearer of garnets. Now if we can just get you and Rafe together, I'd be a happy woman."

"Lida Rose? Get your surgically altered prying little nose out of my love life!"

She nudged me. "Ha! This is the first time you've skipped the word 'pimping' from that statement. I'm wearing you down."

Chapter 18

Lida Rose kindly gave me a ride home since it was well past midnight. We spent the short drive from East Ellum to the apartment chatting about what we were planning to wear to the opening night bash once the show actually went on.

After walking Jed once around the block, I'd collapsed on the bed. I had no desire to go honky-tonking this late, eat, or even see what the Sci-Fi Channel had cooked up for the midsummer trashy movie even though we had no rehearsals the next day. My bed called, and I answered "yes."

Jed, the sweetheart, let me sleep 'til nine the next morning. Not bad. Steak bones were in the offing for that puppy.

I took him for a nice run, then decided I'd attend Mass at the old mission church at the edge of downtown. It was easy walking distance for any soul accustomed to Manhattan streets, so I left Jed on the bed taking his midmorning nap, then headed out. The service was short, probably because what air-conditioning there was in the ancient building was on the fritz. The heat wave continued.

There was a general rush to cool cars as soon as the priest gave the last blessing. I waited for the stampede to end, then sat down on a bench under a tree and tried to decide what to do for the rest of the day. I'd seen in the *Guide* that the museum at Fair Park was holding over a Mesoamerican exhibition and I really wanted to go, but wasn't sure if I was up for the bus ride to and from.

I pondered the extent of my desire to see the exhibit. Then I noticed a pickup truck, so old it was colorless, driving toward the church. It pulled up by the curb. Normally I ignore anyone in a vehicle I don't know (kidnapping is not on my list of favorite activities), but when a familiar face leaned out of the window, I waved.

"Rafe Montez. Whatever are you doing here?"

"Would you care for a lift somewhere?"

His handsome face peered out at me, then leaned back inside. I heard a series of curses from behind the driver's seat, then his door opened and he jumped out.

"I saw you at Mass. I remembered you didn't have a car so I thought I'd see if you were stuck waiting for the bus."

Rafe Montez in church. It fit. After all, Mr. Montez had probably forcibly converted Aztecs or Mayan warriors to Christianity in a previous incarnation as conquistador for Spain and Queen Isabella. Or at least several of his ancestors had. I smiled at the thought.

He didn't miss it. "Something tickling your funny bone?"

"I'll tell you later, when I know you better. Otherwise I might be in danger of being left to rot on my little bench."

"Hmmm. Okay. Need a hoist to the truck?"

"I'm fine, thanks. My knees are not so decrepit as to

flinch and buckle when faced with a ten-inch rise into a truck."

He looked solemn. "They're nice knees. Not decrepit at all."

"Speaking of various stages of decrepitness, what do you think of our old *Bad Business* counterparts?"

He smiled and let me get away with both the change of subject and the use of a word any Scrabble player would challenge.

"Interesting group. I've been talking a lot with Nathaniel. Very nice guy. Sharp."

"I like him, too."

Rafe's tone became a bit too light. "Nathaniel was a close friend of Don Mueller's?"

"Uh-huh."

I knew I was about to be teased again. I was right.

"And has Nathaniel had a chance to converse with his old buddy at rehearsals? If so, you didn't mention it last night while we were discussing ghosts and garnets."

I hit him, none too gently, on his shoulder.

"Just because you are not a highly enough evolved person to be granted the gift of psychic, uh, sightings, do not cast aspersions on those that have. And no, Nathaniel hasn't said anything to me."

I saw the trace of a smile cross his lips.

"I do enjoy tormenting you. You always have such wonderfully witty responses. Actually, if *anyone* really had the capabilities to see ghosts, I'd bet money on Nathaniel. Sensitive soul. Did he tell you I remind him of Don Mueller in my guise as the villain? I took it as a true compliment. I may not believe the man haunts the theater, but I do believe he was a phenomenal actor."

I stared at him. "I had no idea you even knew anything about Mr. Mueller as a person or his talent as an actor. You usually seem more interested in the scientific explanations for ghostly chemicals lingering on the earth."

"Chalk it up to being a lover of history. I'm fascinated by anyone or anything in the arts that has this much of an effect on people for so many years."

I suddenly realized we weren't heading toward my apartment.

"Not to change the subject, Mr. Montez, but you're going southwest instead of northeast. Ahem, ahem. Do you need directions or do you have that annoying male habit of not asking where you're going?"

He continued to stare ahead as he asked, "Weren't you planning a trip to Fair Park before returning to your pal, the dog?"

I stared at him. "I don't know why you don't believe in paranormal activity, 'cause you're definitely psychic. Yes. I wanted to see the Mesoamerican art exhibit at Fair Park. I have no desire to sit at home and create dance steps today and brood about whether or not Jason Sharkey was murdered or why I look like Delilah Delight *numero uno*. Besides, it's too damn hot in the apartment. Fans. No air-conditioner. I was either going to go the exhibit or hit the old revival theater near S.M.U. for about eight hours of Hitchcock movies. Howdja know I wanted to go?"

"Call it a great hunch. The exhibit is well worth the time. I saw it when it first arrived in Dallas and since it's leaving next Friday, this is your last chance to get down there."

"Are you sure you don't mind playing chauffeur? I

wouldn't want to take you away from wherever you were headed."

"I was headed there as well. I wanted to see the darn thing again. I was going to kidnap you if you hadn't said yes."

We reached Fair Park and Rafe found a nice parking spot under a tree. I didn't see many cars around. It was rapidly turning into one of those Texas Sundays when intelligent people stay indoors with the air-conditioner running full tilt and nonstop.

Rafe gallantly offered to pay my way into the exhibit and I immediately began to argue. "I'm not poverty-stricken, Rafe. I'm living in an apartment free of charge and Lida Rose pays me for both choreographing and performing."

"I'd make the offer even if you owned half of Dallas. Now be quiet and allow me to be polite. You can get the next one."

I started to ask, "The next what?" but kept silent. He and Lida Rose shared several character traits. Stubbornness and a refusal to listen unless finally forced to were high on the list of personal flaws.

It was nice having Rafe as my guide. After all, he knew his art backward and forward and could explain such trivial facts as why the Mayans had chosen hairless dogs to worship. Or why everything was made out of feathers and jade.

"Rather like a Vegas showgirl's costume."

"Pardon me?"

"Sorry. Thinking aloud. All the feathers and foo-foo. Oh my sweet mama! Yikes! That is one nasty, uh, person!"

"Not your type, Ms. Davlin?"

I'd come face-to-face with the sculpture of a feath-

ered serpent that also seemed part human. And very
ugly.

"Remind me not to offend who or whatever this guy
is. He does not seem to be a happy fellow. Or happy
snake. Or . . ."

Rafe patted me kindly on my head.

"Kiely, meet a war serpent. Usually plastered onto a
candy-striped column surrounding what we think of
as a pyramid. Like a barber shop pole in front of a
silo. Anyway, this guy's just the pawn of one of the
higher gods. He's not a real deity."

"Thanks so much. Damn. These sculptures aren't
exactly Degas ballerinas, are they?"

He shook his head.

We entered a room filled with small ceramic pieces
and a few assorted jewelry items. I fell in love with a
small jade pendant made in the shape of jaguar.

"Do you know if they have replicas of these pieces
in the gift shop? This is just too neat. I'd probably
be offending some ancient Aztec god, but this would
be stunning with the white dress I was planning on
wearing to the opening night party."

Rafe nodded. "We'll make a detour through the gift
shop before we leave. There are a couple of prints I
saw last time I was sorry I hadn't bought."

We were raptly gazing at a feathered mosaic of
what appeared to be three women washing a hairless
Chihuahua when I heard a giggle behind me.

"Fran! Lookee here! It's those two charming children from the theater."

I turned. Rafe turned. Shirley Kincaid and Fran
Watkins, arm in arm, were beaming at us like second-
grade teachers passing out gold stars to students who
stayed together during fire drills. I blinked. Shirley's

hair had changed since just yesterday. The platinum-blond locks now resembled a ripe tomato on the verge of explosion.

"Hi, Ms. Kincaid. Ms. Watkins."

Shirley giggled again. "Please, honey, it's Shirley and Fran! We're theater people! We don't sit on testimonies."

I translated that last bit of confusion to mean "stand on ceremony" and wondered whether Ms. Kincaid was for real with her mangling of verbiage or if she was attempting to stay the cute ingenue she'd been fifty years before. Doubtless many men had found the grammatical boo-boos charming and even apropos from the tiny actress.

Rafe gave the ladies a devastating smile while I tried to form the word "Fran" on my lips as ordered. It was difficult. I couldn't imagine Fran Watkins being called anything besides "Ms. Watkins" even when she'd been in kindergarten. The woman had what can only be described as a forbidding countenance. Mrs. Danvers overseeing the burning of Mandalay was the first image that came to mind. I shook off the thought. Rafe had taken the conversational ball and was making for midfield with it. He was explaining the meaning behind the Calendar Stone, which is a favorite of souvenir shops in Central America, plastered on ashtrays and welded to key rings. In his best art history seminar voice he told us that the stone didn't really represent a calendar; it was more a catastrophic cosmic scene display. By this time both women were gazing at him with much the same expression as I'd given my first plate of enchiladas the day I arrived from New York.

Fran lowered her glasses to the edge of her nose and

peered over them at me. "Kiely? Are you interested in art?"

I almost shot out, "No, I'm just here for the air-conditioning" but I wasn't sure if Ms. Watkins had a sense of humor. Instead, I nodded politely.

"I've spent more Sundays in the Metropolitan Museum, the Cloisters, or the Guggenheim than I have in my apartment in the city. I'm interested in art for its own sake, and I've discovered that each century, each style, each period has unique movement. It's very good for a choreographer to study."

The ladies nodded. Rafe smiled at me. I don't know if he was pleased that I'd answered Fran Watkins without sarcasm or that I really did enjoy browsing through museums. Fran was staring at the two of us.

"It seems the casts of *Bad Business* are quite a cultured group."

Rafe threw her a sharp look. "How so?"

Shirley answered him with wide eyes.

"You two are the third or fourth sex of cast members we've seen today exhibiting. Including the Boones. We ran into the boy playing Ace Royale and the other dancehall girl what's her name, over at the potty section. And those two tall children, the twins? They're down the hall in the almanac ruins."

My brain was racing away from the image of Theo and Lindsay in what had to be old ceramics and not a bathroom, the Humble boys staring at Olmec artifacts, and what in creation were the third and fourth sexes? Rafe's eyebrows had gone up a good inch, but whether it was for the same reasons, or the mind-boggling thought of Hank and Ham hanging out in a museum in their Stetsons and boots discussing pre-Columbian symbols and fertility gods, I had no idea.

Shirley was grinning at Rafe and me with close to the same look Lida Rose gets when she utters "Kiely! This is perfect!" then points me toward the nearest available male. I began to get nervous. Shirley nudged me.

"So, are you two itemizing?"

"Itemizing?" Visions of tax forms with 1040 Schedule C ran through my head.

Fran lightly swatted her friend on the shoulder.

"Honestly, Shirley, learn to speak the language. She means, are you two an item? I must say, you look very sweet together."

Rafe knelt down as though preparing to tie his shoes. I prayed that the goddess Quetzalcoatl would come to life, trot down the hall, and lop off my head for the day's sacrifice. It would be less painful than continuing to stay and endure the interrogation. Shirley took the opportunity of the short silence to ask another question.

"Did you spend the night?"

I started to cough. Did she mean at the exhibit, or together? Either way I had no desire to explain my actions to the old ladies. I opened my eyes as wide as Shirley's had been.

"Rafe gave me a lift from church this morning. It's really hot out today, isn't it? I have no car and I swear the heat is so much worse than Manhattan this time of year. Oh my, what an interesting mask over there. Shirley, that would look lovely on you as a pendant or something. You should see if they have anything similar in the gift shop. Rafe, I hate to rush you but aren't they starting the lecture on Mayan tripod vessels in five minutes? And *way* at the other end of the building.

Shirley, Fran. So good to see you both. We'll talk later. At the party. So looking forward to that. Bye."

I grabbed a shaking Rafe and hustled him away from the matchmaking duo. His teeth were over his bottom lip as he tried to keep the laughter from erupting.

I swatted his shoulder at three times the force Fran had used on Shirley. "You wimp. Thanks for letting me squirm away from Busybodies-R-Us!"

He chuckled. "I think you did a very nice job of sidestepping and tangoing around their nosy little questions. Jeez, what a pair. Miss Danvers meets Betty Boop on acid."

"Now, now. Be nice. We wouldn't even have had this revival of *Bad Business* if Fran Watkins hadn't persuaded the other board members of the theater to do it. They are the very model of opposites attract, though, aren't they? I'm still amazed they've remained such good friends. Maybe Fran was more fun in her younger years or Shirley had a brain then."

I waved a hand at Cortez and the king.

"Relative of yours?"

Rafe smiled and ignored the question. I pointed out another statue that was the image of Nathaniel.

"Well, well. There's a lot of familiar faces here. Didn't the goddess in the other room remind you of our lovely accompanist? Miss Daisy. Flat face, expression of stone, and superior attitude. And those are the nicer characteristics. Believe me, there are many things I could say about Daisy that would be less than kind. I shall try and forego saying them, however. I keep telling myself she truly is a whiz at the piano, but even that is getting difficult to use as an excuse for her constant screw-ups and the fact that I have yet to receive all the music I need to choreograph. Sorry. Why am I even talking about her? I'm normally not this catty. And I don't have to deal with her today."

Rafe's voice lowered to almost a whisper. "I don't think you have a choice. Take a look behind the representation of the astronomy pyramid from Chichén Itzá."

I groaned, then cautiously peeked around. Daisy waved unenthusiastically from a few feet away.

"Hey, Daisy. What a . . . uh . . . surprise seeing you here."

Tears welled up in her eyes. "I was supposed to come with Jason. He knows—that is, he *knew*—all about these Olmec and totem pole people or whatever. So this is my pilgrimage."

Rafe stared at her.

"Jason was interested in Mesoamerican art?"

Daisy glared at him. "No one really appreciated how incredibly gifted Jason was," she sputtered.

And did *you* learn to be *appreciative*, sweetheart?

For a moment I thought I'd said it aloud. Two heads turned in my direction with looks of amazement. Rafe's eyes held more than a touch of amusement. I suddenly realized I was humming "Love is a Many Splendored Thing" clearly in the key of G.

"Kiely?"

"Hmm?"

"Isn't that Ham Humble underneath the sculpture of the feathered jaguar? Looks good over him, doesn't it? Like a deity descending."

I turned. It was and he did. I waved, whistled, and jumped up and down. Anything to attract his attention. He waved, whistled, and jumped up and down. We looked like two kids on a trampoline in separate backyards trying to coordinate dinner times.

"Kiely! Rafe! We had no idea y'all'd be here. Good to see you. Oh, hi, Daisy. What a, um, surprise. I didn't know you liked art."

Rafe began whistling "I Saw Her Standing There" to cover his laughter. Ham Humble's attitude replicated ours; he had just been more honest about showing it.

I searched the area where Ham had been standing. "Your brother around?"

"Last I saw him he was headed to the snack bar for a soft chocolate cone. Make that two. That was ten minutes ago. I think it's time to hunt him down since one of those cones was meant for me."

Rafe put his hand over my arm.

"We'll help you find him. We were just about to leave anyway. Daisy? See you later."

I politely smiled good-bye as the two men led me down a large hall filled with terrifying images of human sacrifice.

Ham was muttering under his breath with just enough volume for us to hear "Damn. Don't see enough of her at the theater. She hates me, you know, because I thought Sharkey was one stinkin' SOB. I know it's not nice to speak ill of the recently deceased, but I must admit the thought crossed my mind how nice it would have been if one of these Mayan deities had swooped down on the swine and swallowed him whole and thrown him in the nearest volcano long before rehearsals started."

"Ouch. Hey. Let it out, Ham. Don't you know it's not healthy to hide your feelings?"

He hung his head, then smiled bashfully at me.

"Sorry. I know that was an awful thing to say. But quite frankly, I'm still picking up the pieces of what he did to Amber and I can't find anything nice to say about him, dead or alive. Or his idiot floozy the accompanist."

Rafe punched his shoulder lightly.

"We can see that. And we appreciate your sentiments. Just think, ladies and gents, we get another chance to rub shoulders with lovely Miss Daisy this evening at the soiree."

"Yeah. What's up with that?" Ham's irritation had been diverted. "We've got a wagonload of rehearsals coming up this week and Miz Watkins suddenly decides we need a preopening cast party? Is this to hype Cyrus Boone and reassure everyone he'll be up to snuff before production?"

I nodded. "I gather we are about to be involved in a major publicity blitz. Fran has a lot of money tied up in *Bad Business* and she's determined to make a profit. Believe me, I'm not thrilled, either."

Rafe smiled at the two of us.

"What? Neither of you is enthused about having your picture taken with the *crème de la crème* of society? Think of it as a chance to impress the media with our greatness. Isn't that why we're in this show—to create a bit of Dallas theater history?"

I crinkled my nose at him. "Actually, I was thinking this party's a chance for free food. At least for me. I imagine Fran Watkins will be hosting quite a spread."

Hank joined us, holding two chocolate soft ice cream cones. They looked wonderful.

Rafe glanced at me and laughed. "You have this look of sheer lust on your face. Would you care for some ice cream before we go? After all, it's only a few hours 'til the party. You need sustenance, don't you?"

I didn't care whether he was being sarcastic or not. I wanted a cone and I wanted it now. He took my arm and steered me determinedly toward the snack bar while tossing good-byes over his shoulder.

"Humble and Humble? We'll see you tonight. Come along, Ms. Davlin."

I scurried along beside him and turned back to look at the twins.

They waved. I waved. I'd been having such a good time exploring the ruins of the Mayan in air-conditioned splendor I hadn't thought about it, but I'd seen that look of resolve in obtaining an ice cream cone on Rafe's face before. Specifically, when he'd been searching for whatever he'd been searching for in the piano, trunks, gaming tables, and prop room at East Ellum. I was with him on this one. Chocolate ice cream can soothe the fiercest gods. Or their conquerors.

Chapter 19

"Are they cool enough to eat?"

I blinked. I'd been home from the museum less than an hour. In that time I'd managed to bake a batch of brownies that now rested on the counter of the kitchen. Apparently my activities had not gone unnoticed. I glared at my intruder.

"Have you never heard of the age-old custom of knocking on one's door before barging in?"

"Fiddle-dee-dee. I see no point if the door is unlocked."

I shook my head. "How did your poor mother manage to survive the eighteen years you were raised in her lovely Manhattan home before she packed you off to college?"

Lida Rose fluttered her lashes at me. "Eugenia Grace made quite sure I was a proper New Yorker. I never answered the door unless I knew for certain who was there, and I never went into a neighbor's apartment without buzzing first. You still haven't gotten over your good Texas trust, I see. You really should lock your doors, Kiely. You never know who's going to walk in."

She plopped onto a kitchen stool, giving me the opportunity to fully appreciate her chosen costume for her day off from the theater. A vintage madras man's shirt hung loosely atop a pair of canary-yellow stretch capri pants. The toenails clearly visible under plastic sandals with rhinestone straps were painted yellow as well. Somehow, on Lida Rose, the ensemble looked trendy and dramatic.

"You never answered my question."

"I'm so sorry. Your outfit has blinded me to any other thoughts. What question?"

"The brownies. Are they cool enough to eat?"

I took a seat on another stool across from her and scooched it closer to the kitchen island that doubled as breakfast table and brownie bar.

"How did you know I'd made any?"

Lida Rose grabbed a knife and began slicing through the double batch I'd taken from the oven no more than five minutes before her arrival. She crammed a huge chunk into her mouth and mumbled, "It's a gift. The sweet scent of chocolate drew me all the way from White Rock Lake. I swear, Kiely, if you ever decide to give up dancing you could go into a whole new business. These are truly orgasmic. What did you add?"

"White chocolate chips and walnuts. Thank you for the compliment. By the way, aren't you a tad early to be picking me up for this bash tonight?"

Lida Rose had kindly offered to give me a lift to Fran Watkins's party. Fran lived in Highland Park, which was too far for even Kiely the Manhattan strider to deal with.

"I *am* early. Very early. Strictly speaking, I am not here to pick you up yet. George will come by for both us eventually. I just needed out for a while."

I didn't ask. Something was bothering The Madam.

I knew whatever it was would emerge in Lida Rose's own sweet time.

The two of us spent the next few minutes contentedly chewing away and washing down crumbs with iced cold milk and Diet Coke. After I'd downed at least six of the gooey cakes, I took a last swallow and pointed at my friend.

"Okay. Truth now. Why are you really here? You have an undeniably great nose for chocolate, not to mention trouble, but even you could not detect Kiely cooking from ten miles away. And we've got three hours before the party. What's up?"

"I'm getting twitchy."

This was not good. Twitchy to us both usually meant disaster. When Lida Rose had been audited three years ago by the IRS—"really, Kiely, he had no sense of humor about me deducting that bachelorette party at Wild Thing"—she'd been twitchy the day before the taxman called. When the neighbor's house two doors away from hers burned down, she'd been twitchy less than two hours before. I wasn't quite as adept, but I have to admit I'd been twitchy hours before finding Jason's body that day.

"Why are you twitchy? Aside from the fact that we're about to open way too soon and don't know our lines and songs? And that every other day we seem to have an accident."

She grabbed another brownie, slid off the stool, then began to pace around the kitchen.

"How can you even ask? Don't you feel it? The theater is a powder keg ready to blow. It's a dog about to be fixed. It's a virgin about to be knocked up. It's—"

"I got it, I got it. What specifically is bothering you?"

Lida Rose threw me a sharp look. "Let's start with

Jason's acci—oh, hell. Murder. The suspects are rang-
ing all over the theater. My bet is Daisy Haltom, but
that could be since I just don't like her."

"Daisy? Why on earth? Little Miz Milquetoast? I
know she was jealous that Jason was seeing Amber and
Macy, but really. Daisy?"

"Kiely, I swear you need to get out more. Daisy Haltom is the type of virginal obsessive female who would
have been panting to take a knife to Jason and give
him a free circumcision once it hit her that he wasn't
interested."

I winced. "Ouch. Thank you for that graphic picture.
Double ouch."

"Uh-huh. Anyway. Forget Jason. That's rude, isn't it?
You know what I mean. Back to the problem at hand.
Added to the general twitchiness is the announcement
I have yet to make. It's going to cause problems. For
you as well as the other cast members."

Now she was making me twitchy.

"What announcement? What problems? I thought
things were going well?"

"Fran Watkins called me late last night after I got
home. Are you ready for this? No, of course not. I'm
not ready, either."

I waved a brownie in front of her eyes.

"L. R. Focus. Tell me."

"Fran wants to use the surviving members of the
original cast of *Bad Business* in the show. *This* show.
Our show. The gala. She thinks it'll be a great publicity stunt. That's what this stinking party is about
tonight. She plans to have press and money people
sharing *paté* with the peasants before she makes her
big pronouncement to all."

I grabbed two more brownies and crammed them in my mouth before realizing I didn't want them.

"Lida Rose. Please tell me you're kidding. We open in less than a week. We're already dealing with teaching Cyrus. This could mean redoing blocking for *everything*. Does Fran expect these people to dance, too? Have lines? Songs?"

She shook her head. "We have been spared giving them lines and teaching dances. She just wants everyone on that stage. Like live scenery. Think of them as palm trees that breathe. She's already told the other cast members from the former *Bad Business* crowd. My arteries must be hardening so much the blood flow to my brain has shut down for me to have ever allowed this."

"Well, if you weren't scarfing down brownies like they were the last food you'd had in thirty-six hours, it might help those arteries. As for allowing? I don't think you had much choice, given Fran's position with the theater. What did partner number two say about this? Or don't you know?"

She ignored the first part of my statements. Lida Rose and I have long agreed that the major food groups consist of brownies, blintzes, and anything from Mexico or Italy.

Lida Rose choked on a chocolate chip. "Shirley? The nitwit who can't make a proper sentence? Actually, she's a total whiz at business. Can you believe it? Ran an antiques store for years at a profit. Has a financial brain beyond belief. I may go to her for stock tips next year. But as to what she thinks about joining the group onstage, I have no idea. Shirley lets Fran deal with the day-to-days. Fran is *also* offering suggestions about everything from the advertising to who's going to cater opening night to repainting the lobby to taking issue with my casting. Oh, have I mentioned the Boones? Cyrus has yet to utter a single word since Jason died, other than his lines onstage. I'm not sure he's capable of extemporaneous speech. Then we add your crazy boyfriend running around the theater at all hours poking his nose into pianos and trunks and Lord knows what else. And the two of you finding gems and ghosts in the prop room."

"Excuse me?"

She reached for another brownie and scooped up a few loose chips from the pan. She mumbled as she looked at me.

"What?"

"What crazy boyfriend?"

She gave a deep sigh.

"Rafe Montez. Who the hell else? I mean, *you're* the one who first mentioned he's been sneaking around like a bloodhound in a bacon factory. He told me you'd asked him why he was waist deep into Daisy's piano."

"He's not my boyfriend."

She snorted and started pulling various bottles out of my pantry.

"Crap, Kiely. Don't you keep anything stronger than vanilla extract around here?"

I patiently took my bottle of vanilla out of her pudgy hands, much as one takes a white lace blouse away from a child who has been building mud pies all day, then led her into the living room.

"Ted and Margaret have a well-stocked liquor cabinet here. Damn, woman, you *must* be upset. I've never known you to drink before the sun goes down."

She pulled open the doors to the cabinet and

grabbed a quart of Jack Daniels and two highball glasses.

"It's Daylight Savings Time in Texas. That means the sun stays up 'til ten or eleven. I'm not waiting."

"Lida Rose. Calm down. What else is going on? What is everyone doing to make you so nuts?"

She chugged down a good three swallows of her Jack and Coke before answering.

"Remember the night you went dancing at Sweet Ruby's? After Billie changed the songs in Act Two? I can't blame you. Any intelligent person would have known to go out and have a good time dancing with the cast. But, stupid me, I invited Billie and Cyrus out to dinner. Remember? I was kind enough not to include you in what turned out to be a production meeting dinner telling me how it was done in the old days. Okay. I can live with that. Billie is amazingly talented and I totally agree with the changes she's made. I didn't appreciate some of the comparisons she came up with from their cast to ours, but as I say, I can live with it. Then the second wave comes in with Fran and that moron Shirley in their capacity as old cast plus owners. Nathaniel was the only one *not* to tell me how badly I cast this show, and how badly I was directing this show, and how everyone of them could improve it if given the chance to direct. If I didn't love George so much, I'd divorce him and marry Nathaniel."

I was silent for a moment. Then I said, "I'm sorry. I had no idea you were getting so hassled by the oldies but goodies crowd."

I brightened. "I know one former cast member who likes the show."

She looked at me with an expression of hope dawning.

"Who?"

"Don Mueller. He was waving and giving me a thumbs-up sign the other day after we did Act One. Blew me a kiss."

She took another large swallow. "You're as loony as I am. Though I am glad our spectral ex-villain approves. From all accounts the man was a phenomenal actor. I'd take his opinion over certain live stiffs any day."

She finished the glass and held it up to me for more. I shook my head. "I hope you're not driving. You're going to be completely schnockered before we get to Fran's. I'll have to steer you away from any and all media types or you'll find yourself blushing when you read tomorrow's arts section with all the slanderous things you're just aching to say."

She glared at me. "First off, I'm so pissed at everyone I could stay sober even if I downed this entire bottle, but to assuage your fears, George dropped me off on his way to the health food store. He's due back in"—she checked her watch—"oh hell, right about now. Where's the friggin' bottle?"

"Don't bitch at me. I am trying to keep you from either getting arrested or crashing into parked cars on the street below. Listen. Yo! Madam. My buddy. You've had people bug you about shows before. Why is this so different?"

"Kiely, Fran Watkins and Shirley Kincaid own this theater. If they are not pleased with what goes on, they can and will shut it down. If Fran wants forty people onstage, she's got forty people onstage. Plus, she listens to *everyone*, and everyone has a different opinion. Even darling Nathaniel, who incidentally worships you. I'm almost glad Shirley doesn't listen to anybody.

Or maybe it's that nobody listens to her because she never makes sense. Where was I?"

"Nathaniel worshipping me."

"That was two sentences ago, but thanks anyway. Okay. Even darling Nathaniel, who has been so lovely about my direction—"

"You said that. Go on. What's the darling's suggestion?"

"That we redo Act Three so that Lance Lamar won't shoot Nick Nefarious at the end. He's afraid that it might freak out all the former cast members to see that scene done."

I pondered the idea for a bit. "Well, that's sort of understandable. I mean, that must have been really traumatic for them. After all, they watched a friend die right before their eyes. I know *I'm* still shaking over Jason and I saw his body for like fifteen seconds tops."

"I know. I know. I sympathize with them. But the idea was to do the hundredth anniversary of this melodrama, not to change it because of what happened fifty years ago. I've already added that nutty hoedown hog-tie thing, which admittedly is cute, but caused a pile of extra rehearsals and work for you and me. But change the ending? I mean, haven't people died down the years doing *Hamlet* from sword fights and poison? I don't see anyone changing the last act there."

I coughed and poured more liquid into her glass. "No offense, L.R., but let's face it, *Bad Business* ain't Shakespeare."

Lida Rose heaved a huge sigh that threatened to bust the buttons on her madras shirt. "Quite true. But it *is* a good show. And I hate the idea of mucking up a good show. There's one other thing. I don't want the bastards who murdered Don Mueller to think they've won. If I change the ending, it's like a signal saying 'okay, we're scared, we back off.'"

I nodded, then helped myself to some of the Jack Daniels, but added Diet Coke. For some reason this choice instantly set Lida Rose into a fit of hysterical laughter. I wrinkled my nose at her.

"Don't start with me. It has nothing to do with calories. I don't like it that sweet. That's all. Anyway, back to the murder, accident, whatever. You know I agree with you about this. Don Mueller's death was no accident, no matter what the official consensus was at the time. After all, don't ghosts only haunt places if they died too soon and have something to avenge? Rafe and I had a nice discussion about that last evening."

She beamed at me as though I had correctly answered the final jeopardy question. "Don't ghosts *also* hang out at the scene of their demises if those demises were strictly kosher?"

This worried me. I understood her. Nonetheless, I gently removed the glass from her fist.

"No more for you. The intent behind that statement was clear, but talk about murder. You just skewered the English language to the nth degree."

She glared me. "You're not doing much better. And I'm sober enough. I'm just twitchy."

We sat silently for a second, until she asked, "Aren't you?"

"Aren't I what?"

"Twitchy? Damn, Kiely, aren't you listening? The atmosphere at the 'double *e*' is ripe with spookiness. Jason's bizarre death. That weird fire in the prop room.

The rope breaking with Rafe on the end of it. Then that can of nails falling from the catwalk."

This had happened during the latter part of rehearsing the hoedown yesterday. Most of us had been too busy breathing hard and hadn't even noticed. I assumed that Charlie Baines, the tech director, who'd been balancing about six items including cans of nails, had dropped them. Apparently, Lida Rose had other ideas. She waited for me to agree with her. Naturally, I did so.

"Okay. Now that you bring it up, I am a bit twitchy. I've been trying to ignore it."

A horn sounded from outside the front window.

"It's George. I'm outta here. We'll be back in an hour to pick you up. Wear something gorgeous. By the way, how was the date with Rafe at the museum today?"

I sat down on the floor. The woman was a witch. "How in hell did you know I was at the museum today with Rafe?"

She smiled sweetly.

"I'd love to make you think I was truly psychic and had seen the two of you through some sort of haze in my mind, but it was sheer technology. Fran and Shirley used whichever's cell phone and rang me up. Talk about two old biddies with nothing to gossip about. Fran got on first and started right in on the fact that Delilah Delight was seeing Nick Nefarious and did I know that Don Mueller had been in love with that era's Delilah Delight. Then Shirley starts off on this tangent, and I quote, 'not to mention that the *very* first Delilah O'Sullivan had also had an affair with Nick Nefarious, and did I wonder if tragedy would repeat itself.'"

This called for another gulp of my drink. It possibly called for another shot of Jack in the drink. A large one.

I sighed, "Our two resident Delilah experts tried to grill both Rafe and me for a good fifteen minutes about our quote social relationship unquote, while we were standing in front of the Mayan god of Ping-Pong or somebody named Jose Hernandez or something."

I paused, then continued, "I wonder if that deity is any relation to our own Joe? Talk about recipes being in the family for generations. Hey. Did I tell you Christa called Rafe and told him Joe is getting out of the hospital for opening night? He's determined to see the show even standing on that nutty platform. Then he wants us all to come to El Diablo's for a Festiva. Uh. Fiesta. I wonder if he felt twitchy before the dark sedan ran him down?"

Lida rose grabbed my drink and set it firmly on top of the television. "Talk about me drinking and not making sense. Keily. Switch to iced tea immediately."

Lida Rose stuck her head out the living room window, barely missing a freshly watered ficus tree hiding most of the panes. She hollered down to her husband, who patiently waited in a Volkswagen beetle about the same color as her pants.

"Be there in a minute, hon!"

She turned back to me. "So?"

"So, what?"

"You are an annoying young woman, Kiely Davlin. What did you and Rafe say to Fran and Shirley? I swear you must have looked enamoured and guilty all at once, because they sounded ready to tack up the banns if you survive the curse of Act Three. I'm just glad they don't know about your little rendezvous in the prop room."

I chose not to respond to the last sentence.

"It *is* coming across like a curse, isn't it?" I mused. "Kiely."

"Oh, sorry. I told the ladies the absolute truth. Rafe saw me sitting on a bench after Mass trying to make up my mind whether to take the bus to the exhibit. He was planning on going to the museum, so gave me a ride there as well. That's all there was to it. Nothing else. Sheer chance. Coincidence. Nothing more. *Nada*. Got it?"

I was getting riled.

Lida rose smiled and patted the top of my head.

"That sounds so nice and logical, Kiely. Just one thing. I happen to know that when Rafe is in Dallas he sings in the choir of St. Bernard's Church over near White Rock Lake, not Sacred Heart Cathedral downtown. Think they needed an understudy?"

She carefully wrapped up four brownies from the pan "for George," then cheerfully waved good-bye as she headed toward the back stairs.

"See you in fifty-seven minutes. You really should try to sober up by then."

I stood, squished a brownie in one hand, and prayed that she'd forget to pick me up.

As soon as she'd gone I began tearing through the clothes I'd brought from New York. I had originally assumed that Fran Watkins's party was to be a simple, casual barbeque for old and new cast members to bond a bit. I had no idea it had become the theatrical social event of the summer. One good dress stared out at me from the closet. The one I'd planned to wear for the opening night party. Since I didn't want to show up in jeans at Fran's, this was the only option. Maybe I could hit my favorite little boutique in Highland Park Village sometime before the end of next week.

I showered, then put on a ton of makeup and the dress. It was a gorgeous white sundress, nearly backless with spaghetti straps and a nice swirly skirt. My hair, for the moment, was fluffy but not frizzy. Not to be too immodest, but I looked damn good.

I made myself a plate of nachos to go with the brownies and downed three glasses of iced tea. I was sober. And I still had at least thirty minutes to wait.

I was also twitchy. The fault of one Lida Rose. Nothing but trouble. Like battle and cry. Like cat and astrophe. Like doom and gloom. I redid my makeup and sang through all my songs for the show twice.

A horn honked below. I patted Jed good-bye, then scurried downstairs to catch my ride to the party.

Chapter 20

Fran Watkins's estate was exactly that. An estate. This was no little house carved out of any prairie. The mansion stood square in the middle of an entire city block in the Highland Park (read "old rich") section of Dallas. I am not ashamed to admit that when George dropped Lida Rose and me at the entrance gates I stared at the house in sheer awe. As did Mrs. Rizokowsky.

George wasn't staying. He had tests to grade for the kiddies taking his summer seminars. He waved cheerfully to us after suggesting we avoid getting too drunk to be able to call him.

We stood at the gate for five minutes, continuing to stare without exchanging a word. The architect who designed this house had either had a warped sense of humor or no humor at all. "Gothic" was the only word possible that summed up the turrets, the dark carvings, and the gargoyle sculpture in the middle of a fountain in the middle of the yard.

"Think Jane Eyre is in there partying with Mrs. Rochester and Cathy and Heathcliff? Burning down the house, perhaps?"

Lida Rose hit me on my shoulder.

"Now, now. We of the peasant class do not understand the workings of the minds of the aristocracy. Obviously there is a reason for a Cornish mausoleum to be slap in the middle of the Lone Star State."

I snorted. "How about atrocious taste?"

She laughed. "That'd do it."

I grabbed her arm. "I'm afraid to go in there. If it starts lightning and thundering I'm running like a bunny. I'm already set to jump out of my skin if someone I don't know says 'howdy.'"

We both looked heavenward. There was an ominous cast to the sky. Normally, Texans pray for rain in the summer but seldom get it. Tonight, it appeared that those prayers were to be answered. In a big way. At seven o'clock in the evening the darkness looked like midnight. I hissed into Lida Rose's ear.

"It was a dark and stormy night . . ."

"Kiely! Stop that."

"Remember that twitchy feeling we were discussing only an hour or so ago?"

She nodded.

"Well, my entire body feels like I've been in a poison ivy patch for a week. I am now seeing omens of disaster everywhere." I looked up. "But especially that house. I guess there's no hope for it. We have to attend. Maybe the inside is less threatening?"

"At least there'll be food. That's probably our problem. Nothing but brownies and bourbon. Our blood sugar has skyrocketed and we're filled with hypoglycemic forebodings."

"You're filled with something else, but my mother forbade me to use those words. Okay, L. R., let's make a splashy entrance."

We marched arm and arm up the long driveway. Before we could knock on the huge double doors, a man in full black tails with as gruesome a face as I've seen outside of Christopher Lee films pulled them open, then bowed.

"Mrs. Lida Rose Worthington Rizokowsky. Miss Kiely Davlin. Welcome."

I could feel Lida Rose shaking next to me. Whether it was from fear or laughter I couldn't tell, and was given no opportunity to ask.

"Please, ladies. Do come in. You may leave your purses with me. Most of the other guests are in the billiard room."

He disappeared with our purses around a dark corner. I clutched Lida rose's hand in mine.

"Did you hear that? Billiard room. Will we find Colonel Mustard standing over Miss Plum with a pipe in his hand? Miss Scarlet looping a noose around Mr. Brown?"

Lida Rose was starting to get a look I recognized as "I'm having far too much fun and am ready to sail off a bridge without a bungee cord."

She winked at me. "Do you suppose that horrid man actually works here or do you think we've just delivered our most precious belongings into the hand of a brilliant con man and purse snatcher?"

I shrugged. "Doesn't matter. George is still our chauffeur, the keys to the Wyler residence are under a brass bell on the sunporch, and I left the bathroom window open. I think other than an extra wand of mascara, two quarters, and three pieces of used gum in Kleenex, there's not a lot of value in that bag."

She wasn't listening. She was smiling.

"Kiely! This is perfect!"

My "uh-oh" antenna shot up faster than Jed's ears upon hearing, "Squirrel!" but with far less enthusiasm.

"Lida Rose? Leave me alone. Whatever you intend? Don't."

She snorted. "You always say that. Look! Heading in from behind that awful portrait of Fran's ancestor. It's Brett Barrett! From the *Morning News*."

I sighed. Lida Rose didn't know that Brett had snuck into the theater the day of Jason's death and tried to pump everyone who hadn't yet left for information. She also didn't know I was acquainted with Brett.

"Kiely. He's a hunk. And single. I think his divorce became final about two years ago. Long enough to be over it, and short enough not to get trapped into eternal bachelorhood."

She began hissing even though I hadn't said a word. "Be quiet. He's almost here."

"Almost" was not the operative word. All six-foot-five inches of Brett Barrett, including the coppery tanned skin and immaculate head of brown hair, loomed in front of us. He flashed his white teeth at us.

"Ms. Worthington. Kiely, my sweet. So nice to see you again."

Lida Rose shifted her gaze from him to me and back in a matter of milliseconds. "You two know each other? Kiely. You never told me."

I smiled. It was not a pleasant smile.

"You never asked. Yes, Mr. Barrett and I are quite well acquainted. He attended at least twenty-five performances of *Pippin* three years ago and kindly brought me roses after each one."

"Brett. You devil. I had no idea you were such a lover of the theater."

His smile grew broader. "Let's say I am a lover of beauty. And in my opinion Ms. Davlin definitely qualifies. But ladies, I'm not here to reminisce. I'm here to grab an early scoop on the excitement at the East Ellum Theatre. My nemesis, Jerry Klein, is currently engaged in hustling various theatrical types in a pool game. I haven't seen the idiot from the *Star-Telegram*, and Wilson from the *Observer* is in the kitchen devouring pastries. No one else matters. Cub reporters—wouldn't know a good story if they found the mayor of Dallas in their car boffing an alien."

I had to close my eyes to shut out that last picture. Lida Rose started giggling. I assume it was for the same reason.

"So, Lida Rose—is it true that supernatural events run rampant at East Ellum? And is Jason Sharkey's death part of the curse?"

My shameless best friend batted her lashes at him.

"They do indeed. And we believe Jason's death might have been caused by paranormal forces. Our costumer communes on a regular basis with the resident ghost, who incidentally seems to have a crush on Kiely."

I choked as Brett stared deeply into my eyes. "Can't say I blame him. Seems to be contagious."

"Stuff it, Brett."

He wisely chose to return to questioning Lida Rose.

"I've heard there have been some . . . let's call them 'incidents' at the theater since Mr. Sharkey's demise? Accidents? Is that correct?"

That did it. Lida Rose jumped in with both feet. "There have, indeed, been incidents. Beginning with the big fire. A roaring inferno in the prop room. Well, the old props room. We call it 'Kismet.'"

Her voice dropped its enthusiastic tone for a second. "Exactly where Jason was found. Rafe Montez, our wonderful villain, put the fire out before the theater could burn down, but we never discovered the cause of the blaze."

My mouth had gaped open to my chest during these last remarks and I didn't bother to close it. My best friend had been spouting the biggest pack of lies I'd heard since the mayor of Manhattan promised to roll back subway prices five years ago.

Brett was going to get carpal tunnel syndrome if he didn't loosen his hold on his pen. He wrote rapidly but kept his eye on Lida Rose the entire time. Transcribing those notes would be hell. A thought that made me smile. Brett looked up for a second.

"Lida Rose. Please. Go on."

"Okay. Yesterday in the middle of rehearsal nails started flying off the catwalk onto the stage. It was like a hailstorm of metal. We were running for our very lives!"

I coughed and poked Lida Rose in her ribs.

"Excuse me? Much as I hate to dampen the enthusiasm shown by my director, I have to point out that, A, the fire in the prop room consisted of one door smoking and becoming slightly charred, and B, that hailstorm happened to be *one*—get that?—*one* can of nails remaining capped and tumbling harmlessly to the floor."

Lida Rose and Brett turned equal looks of disappointment my way.

"Kiely has no imagination. Well, I take that back. She has a ton of imagination. She's just chicken. She's terrified that all these bizarre incidents are part of the curse of *Bad Business* and since that curse involves everyone who plays Delilah Delight, she'll be next."

That did it. I whirled around and literally ran away from the pair. Let Lida Rose deal with Brett Barrett for the entire party if she liked. Let the woman schmooze and lie her way into headlines and publicity. I wanted food and a drink and to be away from Mr. Perfection and his garrulous prevaricating source.

The butler with the features from a B-grade horror flick was nowhere in sight. He'd mentioned the billiard room as being the repository for most of the guests, but Lida Rose and I had been waylaid by Brett before I could ask directions, so I decided to wander and see if I could detect the sound of clanking pool balls.

I found the kitchen first, which was not a bad thing. Tray upon tray of delectable goodies hid every inch of counter space, not to mention the huge island in the center of the room.

"Kiely Davlin?"

"That's me."

I turned and tried to hide the gooey cream puff I'd snitched from the pastry tray.

"Wilson Carew. From the *Observer*."

"Hi, Wilson. How's it going over there? Circulation up?"

He ignored the question.

"I'm more interested in what's going on at the East Ellum Theatre. Word has it that there have been ghost sightings and fires and narrow misses with huge metal cans. Add that to the mysterious death of your leading man. And all these activities centering around you—aren't you afraid to be performing there?"

There was going to be another ghost sighting soon. I planned to kill Lida Rose as soon as I saw her again. I could easily persuade a lawyer to get me acquitted on the grounds of justifiable homicide.

"Wilson? In a word, no. Nothing bizarre is happening over at the East Ellum Theatre. We are redoing a nice old melodrama that unfortunately was the scene of some sad events fifty years ago. Yes, we had a horrible, freakish accident befall Jason Sharkey. But as I told Mr. Barrett, the fire was barely more than a puff of smoke and the raining metal cans consisted of one, mind you, *one* tiny little closed can that fell because a techie was overloaded and trying to balance. And none of it had anything to do with me more so than anyone else."

"Brett Barrett? Who's he talking to?"

Oh, good. Maybe I could sic Wilson on Brett and the two could duke it out over who'd get the scoop on the curse.

"Last I saw him, he was chatting up Lida Rose and getting some really great inside poop on everything and everybody. Um. I believe they were headed for the pool outside?"

"Thanks. I'll check it out."

I smiled as I piled a plate filled with everything I could find that had more than seven hundred calories per bite. I then wandered off in search of anyone who would not try and pump me for information or try to convince me the theater needed to change its name to "Spook Central Performing Arts Center."

The sound of clanking and "rack 'em" was coming from the room on my left. I headed that way. The billiard room. I only hoped Miss Scarlet hadn't bopped anyone over the head with the pipe. Unless it was Brett Barrett. Or perhaps Lida Rose.

Chapter 21

I glanced inside. Rafe was chalking a cue and gesturing to a corner pocket for his next shot. I looked to see if I knew the sad victim of his hustle. His features weren't familiar, but his looks were. Had to be a reporter. He had that undeniable air of superiority mixed with bloodhound. A very young reporter. It would be enjoyable watching Rafe Montez decimate him. I had no doubt that our resident art expert could, and would, do so. Only someone at ease with bars and poolrooms from many past experiences could wear that casual air that brooked ill for the poor challenger. I know this because I'm no slouch myself. Two brothers had thought nothing of dragging their sister to seedy dives on weekends and teaching her to destroy opponents three times her age and weight while she smiled a smile of pure innocence. I'd lost count of the money my Dad made us pay back to unsuspecting, thought-they-were-being-crafty sharks.

Rafe called his shots, made every one, then politely bowed to the young man who'd turned redder than the latest dye on Shirley Kincaid's hair. I waved to him. Rafe, not the humiliated and angry kid.

"Do you think it's wise to piss off the media before

we open? Could be the arts critic you just skewered with your stick there."

He lowered his voice to a whisper. "I know better than that. He's not from the newspaper. He's Shirley Kincaid's grandson. All of eighteen and a firm believer in his own greatness. When I came in he was trying to hustle Nathaniel. I thought it was time to teach him to respect his elders. I'll give him back the winnings later when he's had a chance to reflect on the error of his ways. I gather you haven't been by the box office or you'd've met him by now. So, you interested in playing a game?"

I nodded. He handed me a stick.

"I presume you know the basics?"

I fluttered my eyelashes at him as I began to apply chalk to the bottom of the cue. I nodded, then sweetly asked, "How's a short game of solids and stripes grab you? I only specify 'short' because I don't plan on this taking more than a few minutes of my valuable time."

A cheering section had formed in the corner of the room, away from jabbing sticks and flying cue balls. Lindsay and Theo placed nickel bets with each other on who'd be the winner. Hank and Ham Humble nodded intelligently whenever Rafe downed a solid. Nathaniel Bollinger and Cyrus Boone smiled knowingly at Rafe and me. I had the feeling the gentlemen were more interested in the subtext of the game than the actual moves.

I have no idea who would have been the ultimate victor in our pool match. We'd been playing for twenty minutes, exchanging shots and psych-each-other-out barbs, when Lida Rose burst into the room. She was balancing two large frozen margaritas; a plate filled with cheeses, cheese spreads, *queso* dip with assorted corn filled chips for scooping; and another plate overflowing with some sort of gooey cookies. Combined expressions of terror and glee were plastered across her face. I extended a hand to help with the plate and glasses.

"Yo! L. R.! Come join us. And share those goodies. Damn, woman, there's enough dairy on that plate to keep a Vermont farmer on skis in Switzerland for a year."

Rafe cocked his head at me. "What does that mean? How many margaritas have you imbibed?"

I set the plates down on a small table, carefully banked the nine ball into the corner pocket, then grabbed one of the drinks Lida Rose had extended.

"It means absolutely nothing and I am perfectly sober. So there. Game to me."

I took a sip. Lida Rose took a large gulp of hers, then pulled me toward her by grasping my hand quite painfully.

"Why were you so rude to Brett Barrett? The man is hot for you. And you didn't even *tell* me he's *been* hot for you. Roses and chocolates after *Pippin* on a nightly basis. That is just marvelous."

I chugged down half the margarita.

"Lida Rose. Back it up. Now. Think. You said it yourself. Brett Barrett has been divorced for two years. I did *Pippin* three years ago. Do the math, babe. The man was married when he was trying to get in my bloomers. I don't do married. You know that. Kiely's cardinal rule. Bikers, con artists, pathological liars I have dated. Married? No. Ixnay. Nada."

"Oh. Yeah. Well. You still needed to have stayed to back me up on spooky happenings at the theater. We want publicity, and quite honestly we don't care how we get it."

She licked her lips like a cat climbing out of the gold-fish bowl.

"I've now got Mr. Barrett convinced that we hold seances on an hourly basis and have communed with the spirits of the entire *Bad Business* cast from a hundred years ago asking their advice as to how to change that dreadful song in Act One."

Rafe sighed.

"Did the performing spooks have any suggestions?"

She ignored him and crashed her drink down on a table.

"Oh, crap! I forgot why I was looking for you. Kiely. Rafe. You have to come with me this minute. Trouble is brewing in the dining room."

Rafe turned from the cue holder cabinet on the wall where he'd been carefully replacing our sticks.

"What kind of trouble? Physical, mental, legal, deadly, or emotional?"

I do like this man. He hadn't rushed out of the room in a tizzy. He knew how to elicit a rational response from Mrs. Worthington-Rizokowsky. Something I've yet to have accomplished in twelve long years.

Lida Rose took a deep breath, a gulp of her drink, then one more. "Press trouble. I'm not sure where that follows in the troublesome list you just gave me, but I think it could end up as all of the above. Fran has been attempting to give a sane press conference, but the members of the Texas media who are still sober enough to ask questions don't seem interested in going where she's *trying* to steer them. I can't explain. It's easier if you guys just follow me."

I grabbed another piece of cheese off her tray, sucked down a few more swallows of my margarita, then obediently trotted off behind Lida Rose and

Rafe, the latter who had assumed the brave role of leader for this parade toward the dining room.

Fran had tried to set up the space rather on the order of a presidential Q and A, with chairs in rows reaching across the room and a podium (seriously) in front. She'd failed. Journalists were wandering the room scooching chairs close to food-laden tables and chowing down between questions. Most had micromini tape recorders and palm pilots. The fine art of note-taking apparently had gone the way of typewriters, except for Brett Barrett, who thought it looked more journalistic to write on a notepad. I recognized a friend of mine, Sherry Burt, the publicity director for the Garland Summer Musicals. I waved. She waved. Then she oozed through the hordes of food-obsessed writers to approach me. I was enveloped in a swift hug.

"Kiely! You look great. You involved in this curse business?"

I merely sighed. Deflecting the question was getting to be boring.

"Curse business? What curse business? Our resident costumer yelling at the Humble twins in language comparable to sailors on leave? Or have you been talking to Lida Rose about that stupid little fire and the big nail can tragedy?"

Sherry smiled.

"Don't be coy. The buzz around the press is that *Bad Business* has a deadly curse following it. You've had one death and several narrow escapes, right? Fran Watkins has been dodging the issue for the last ten minutes, trying to get everyone to focus on who's who in the cast and make some big pronouncement about the original cast joining the new, but the more sober and enterprising among us are not giving up."

She ran back to what must be her chair to salvage a huge slice of cake that was in danger of being absconded by a beefy, red-faced man dressed in the most elegant gray tux I've seen since brother Sean's wedding six years ago. Sherry won, wresting the pastry from his eager grasp with bare seconds to spare. I turned to Rafe, who had managed to sneak a plateful of Chinese-looking hors d'oeuvres. He graciously offered me a steamed dumpling.

"Yo. Rafe. Do we have a curse?"

"Probably not. But Lida Rose has been pushing for one for weeks. Thanks to Jason, perhaps she's finally convinced the media?"

"Come to think of it, now that I've found that spooky garnet earring and discovered I share my good looks with another Irish dancer who sends sad feelings my way, we may be headed in the right direction. Perhaps this whole curse thing warrants further investigation."

Rafe nodded toward a pack of journalists circling the podium near Fran.

"They appear to share your thirst for knowledge. Come on. By the way, what was that little *bon mot* about the original cast members joining us onstage? Did Fran mention anything to you?"

I told him what Lida Rose had told me this afternoon. He took it well, only downing an entire glass of what appeared to be straight bourbon. I wondered how the others had received the news. Or even if they had. I hadn't heard Macy's dulcet tones bellowing obscenities or Daisy's voice whining through the halls, so it was possible the current cast members were as yet unaware of the change.

Other, less dulcet tones were heard issuing from

the reporters. Brett Barrett bellowed from the middle of the room.

"What about the fire, Ms. Watkins? Or the nails? Do you believe these are merely coincidence, or proof of a paranormal being roaming the theater? What about the rumors that a ghost has been seen by your costume mistress? Or those antique jewels that were found in the prop room? The same room where your former leading man met with a very untimely accident?"

Fran and Shirley Kincaid both gasped and looked on the verge of collapse. When Fran handed the microphone to Shirley I nearly collapsed myself. All we needed were quotes from the bubble-tongued septuagenarian. Shirley looked as horrified as I felt.

Rafe and I pushed our way to the front of the throng just as the gray-tuxedoed bull stuck a microphone into Fran's face. Rude, but effective. It also conveniently cut out Shirley from talking.

"Miz Watkins. You've been tap-dancing around the issue. I'm Jerry Klein from the *Star-Telegram*. What can you tell us about the curse that clouds *Bad Business*? Without any more steps, shimmies, or twists, please."

I almost laughed. I had to admire his terminology. Fran gestured toward Lida Rose.

"Lida Rose Worthington, who is directing this production, will now answer all your questions."

"Like hell she will," I muttered. "The woman will make up some outrageous lie about falling bodies and spectral ectoplasm dripping from the coffeepot and have every one of those people camped out at the theater for the next week."

Rafe whispered, "Are you saying you don't trust dear Lida Rose to capably dispose of rumors and innuendo?"

I nudged him in the ribs.

"Definitely not. You are looking at the mistress of misdirection, the master of mania, the queen of crap, the—"

"I get it. Let's see what she says."

Lida Rose smiled at the crowd. Her countenance was one of serenity and honesty. Have I ever mentioned that in addition to being a fine director, she's a damn good actress?

"Ladies and gentlemen of the press. It is true that *Bad Business on the Brazos* has, shall we say, an interesting history."

I groaned audibly. Lida Rose narrowed her eyes at me and continued. "Fifty years ago, the illustrious actor Don Mueller was shot and killed onstage in a dreadful accident. You all know this. What you may not know is that the first time *Bad Business* was produced, one hundred years ago, three members of the cast died under mysterious circumstances. And it is true that our choreographer, who is playing Delilah Delight and who bears a striking resemblance to the original actress, even found a garnet earring belonging to that Delilah in the prop room."

I grabbed Rafe's arm and squeezed. "Holy tamale! This is improvising at its best! Or worst! We've been speculating as to where that earring came from but she's suddenly got this story cooked up and is spilling it to the press. 'Mysterious circumstances'? What the hell does that mean? Floodwaters from the Trinity engulfing East Ellum? A horde of killer bees from San Saba swarming through the theater and attacking at will? A rash of suicides? A rasher of bad bacon?"

Rafe was trying to hide a grin as he looked down at me. "You're good, you know that? I had no idea such a treasure of imagination and metaphor resided in that brain."

"Oh, shut up. Lida Rose is as drunk as a Grecian prostitute after shore leave and she has no idea what she's saying. We're going to spend the next week dealing with bored journalists trying to sniff out a story while we try and get some work done. Which includes adding four elderly thespians in every scene. If there's a curse on *Bad Business*, you're looking at her. Five-ten, dyed **black** hair, love of chocolate, Jack Daniels, and all."

Chapter 22

"Gentlemen. I believe that last hand was mine. Excuse me while take those chips."

"I don't think so, Hank Humble. Seems to me that four aces beat three of a kind every day including Sunday. So, I'll just take that pot."

"Not so fast, Mr. Montez. I'd say my royal flush makes those aces look pretty puny. Nothing personal, you understand. But *this* round goes to me."

"Hands off the table, Kincaid. If I remember the rules of five-card stud, a royal flush starts ace high. And since I've got four of the little darlings, you, sir, must be cheating."

Quoting Yogi Berra, it was "déjà vu all over again." The guys were engaging in a little impromptu rehearsal of the scene leading to the "Gamblers We" number. How Neil Kincaid knew all the dialogue when he spent his hours supposedly selling tickets in the box office eluded me, but this whole scene was right out of Act Two.

I wandered toward the card table placed dead center in Fran Watkins's spacious game room. Rafe, Neil, Hank, Nathaniel, and Cyrus sat upright, wearing identical expressions of concentration and mistrust. I peered over Hank's shoulder, but was careful to keep my own poker face even. The man was bluffing. A pair of fours. Nowhere near the park. Or even the garden.

I circled the table in turn. Nathaniel and Cyrus both had cards facedown in front of them. They'd wisely folded near the beginning of this hand. Rafe really did have four aces and Neil had a flush. Not a royal, just a straight, and not only from his cards. His face was a true crimson.

"I'm not cheating. I just had a momentary lapse in memory. I thought a royal flush went up to king, not ace."

Unintelligible murmurs were the only response from the other four. Rafe scooped up the pot and raised his right brow at me.

"My first win of the night. Can you believe it?"

He looked like he'd just been handed the blue ribbon at the county fair for his prize heifer.

"If this is your first win, perhaps you should have stuck to pool."

He shook his head. "No one will play with me. Word is out of my incredible prowess with chalk and stick."

Neil growled. "Would you just deal, Montez? That was the largest damn pot of the night and I don't plan on letting it stay in your greasy spic hands."

Apparently Jason Sharkey hadn't been the only person affiliated with East Ellum to have a few problems with bigotry. Rafe closed his eyes and took a deep breath. He kept his own poker face, though, so I couldn't tell if he planned to toss the chips in the kid's face, challenge him to a duel on the lawn, or just deal the cards and ignore the rudeness.

The latter. Rafe shuffled, shoved the deck toward Nathaniel to cut, then swiftly dealt the next hand. I left.

I had no desire to watch five testosterone-driven males playing the same game I must witness constantly during rehearsals.

Fran's guests were littering up the rooms in varying degrees of inebriation, gluttony, and lust. Lida Rose was schmoozing with at least three members of the Channel Eight news team in the dining area. The doorway to the kitchen was blocked by my friend from Garland and an unidentified male who was intently licking champagne from Sherry's neck. Theo and Lindsay were occupied in a similar manner on what appeared to be the most comfortable sofa in the downstairs area.

"Kiely. Lovely, talented Kiely. Please, come share a glass of champagne with me."

Brett Barrett. Great.

"Hey, Brett. Why aren't you down at the paper frantically getting your story in for tomorrow's issue? Don't you people have deadlines?"

He smiled. "You've been watching too many Spencer Tracy movies. Yes, we have deadlines and we also have cell phones and palm pilots. We poor reporters no longer have to tear out of parties and dodge traffic to end up chained to a desk."

"Mmm. Well, that's great. I'm glad to know the media is keeping up with modern technology. See ya."

He put his hand over mine.

"Wait. I promise I won't ask any questions about your ghost. I'd just like the chance to chat for a few minutes. For old time's sake."

I looked him squarely in the eye. "Why? You have your story, you've had your fill of food and drink, and yee, howdy! There are women here who might even be interested in one or more of your lines off-paper."

"Kiely, hasn't it occurred to you that this ghost nonsense could end up being dangerous? Especially to you?"

"What? Are you nuts?"

"I should ask you the same thing. Think about it. Jason dies under, well, kind of kinky circumstances. The cops say accident but this reporter isn't buying. Then there's a fire in the theater. Small, yes. I realize Lida Rose was, shall we say, *elaborating* more than a tiny bit for effect, but still, there was a fire. And a can of nails did fall from the catwalk. And didn't a rope break, placing your villain in a precarious situation over the orchestra pit? And you did find an earring that shouldn't have been embedded in the fibers of old fish netting last used, when? A hundred years ago."

"Damn. What did that woman do? Fill you in on the kind of coffee we drink and what we put in it as well? I swear, you're more up-to-date on the doings at East Ellum than I am."

He smiled. "Believe it or not, I'm very good at what I do. That includes getting people to talk. Not that Ms. Worthington is the silent type. I think she's so thrilled about this show and the publicity it's generating, she honestly doesn't see connections."

"Brett, Brett, Brett. You are indeed an ace reporter. And yes, my dearest friend is a blabbermouth when it comes to getting the theater's name in print, even if it's less than desirable press. But. No matter how sincere you are about the danger that envelopes me every time I set foot in East Ellum, which, incidentally, I think is a load of hooey, I am not about to add to your story. Now, then. I am off to face the perils of the dining room and dive into the carrot cake I've been holding back from all night. First, I'm going to go powder my nose. Ta."

I marched away from the reporter fully intent on doing just as I'd stated. After that stop in the ladies' room. Where I stayed for five minutes admiring the décor. The Watkins's bathroom was bigger than my entire bedroom. It even boasted a divan in the corner of the "nonfunctional" area. I lay down for a few minutes to test it out.

"Kiely. Get up. You're snoring."

I opened one eye.

"Hey, Lindsay. What's up?"

"Not much. Theo has decided to try and win back the money he's been losing all night and I came in to do what one does in powder rooms. I hated to wake you, but really, I was afraid everyone would hear you and call the cops for excessive noise."

I sighed. "I always snore if I sleep on my back. Especially after cheese. I love cheese. It just doesn't love me."

I sat up, began to literally and liberally powder my now shiny nose, then waited for Lindsay to finish her own business. We walked arm in arm back to the main room. Theo was standing by the bar, scowling as the bartender refilled his glass. Lindsay nudged me.

"Uh-oh. I think my man has bombed out of the poker game again. Cheering up time. Later, Kiely."

I nodded and watched as she grabbed Theo's hand and led him off to a dark corner for a bit of physical consolation.

I was bored. Bored, unloved, and in need of more food. I headed for the table in the dining room where I'd last seen the carrot cake. It was well hidden. Not only the cake, but the entire table. Every available space was crowded with remnants of drunken media and various cast and crew members diving into trays of food. I dodged reporters in need of stories and booze and slipped into the kitchen. The catering staff was knee-deep in cooking. All the platters were empty.

I smiled hopefully at a black-and-white-clad waiter who smiled wearily back.

"Anything ready to eat?"

"Try the Jarlsburg. It goes great with champagne."

The voice was not that of the waiter. Rafe Montez stood behind me holding a plateful of hors d'oeuvres. I grabbed a handful of calorie-laden goodies.

"Hey, Rafe. What? They kicked you out of the game?"

He snorted.

"It's not a game anymore. Neil has gone from pretending not to cheat to outright thievery. I've had it. Hank has had it. Theo left about ten minutes ago muttering names I've yet to hear in my twenty-seven years on this earth. Nathaniel and Cyrus are trying to impress upon the jerk—Neil, that is, not Theo—that cheating at cards is not considered kosher in the gentleman's rulebook of life and he's young enough to learn it now, but I don't think they're making much headway. Mr. Kincaid won't own up to it. Hank is still in there glaring and muttering he's going to tell Shirley that her grandson is a crook. I decided to seek a bit of sustenance, then find my car keys."

"What? The valet didn't park for you?"

He pursed his lips and tried not to laugh. "I thought about it. When I pulled up in the 'Ancient Mariner' I thought the poor guy was going to have a heart attack right there on Fran's driveway. I spared him the humiliation of driving it and trying to keep it parked at least six feet away from any other vehicle."

He chuckled. "I found a great spot at the next house down the block. Which, come to think of it, *is* the next block. Actually, I'll have an easier time leaving. No waiting behind cars parked too close together. See you tomorrow, Kiely. I'm off to get some sleep. Big day ahead."

He kissed me lightly on my forehead and was gone before I had a chance to wheedle a ride out of him. I noticed he hadn't offered one. Couldn't be pride. I'd ridden in that clunky old vehicle of his just this morning. Ancient Mariner. Cute. Maybe he was afraid he'd not end up driving me straight home? Maybe I hadn't asked for a ride for the same reason. I liked the man more and more, but couldn't figure him out. His actions at the theater were odd. I kept waiting to discover that he'd been casing the joint intending to rob everyone in the show, grab the box office receipts on opening night, then store them under the game tables, in the piano, or possibly in the prop room. Maybe he was a serial killer who'd been stashing bodies in steamer trunks and pianos. Or a bigamist finding hiding places for all his marriage certificates.

I felt sleepy. Obviously I needed more food. I started to ask the only caterer still in the kitchen if anything was ready, but stopped.

He looked harried.

"Problems?" I asked.

"Apparently the *queso* dip is the hit of the evening. Which is fine, except I'm out of spicy tomatoes and don't have time to hit the pantry for more. These darn cheese puffs have to be timed exactly, so I'm stuck in front of the oven."

"Where's the pantry and how many cans do you need?"

A whoosh of air whistled through his lips.

"You are a nice lady."

With a hand holding a huge stirring spoon, he motioned left, toward the swinging doors that led out of the kitchen into a hall.

"Down the hall to the end. Can't miss it. Dead end. Thanks. You've saved the cheese puffs."

I easily found the pantry and took a minute or two to admire the neat rows of canned goods, canisters filled with grains, jars of imported jellies, and one entire shelf devoted to tea cookies. I was tempted to open the box that said "Scottish Shortbread" but decided that would be rude.

The hot diced tomatoes were on the top shelf, easily reached by standing on the first rung of a stepladder. I grabbed a few, jumped down, then started to push open the door with my butt. Nothing. The door wouldn't budge. I thought my derriere was stronger than this. I set the cans down on the stepladder and pushed with my hands. Nothing. The door was not opening.

A wave of heat hit me, starting from my forehead and coursing to my feet. My hearing disappeared. There was no sound except the high volume pounding of my heart. My vision blurred. All normal brain activity stopped as panic set in. I first kicked off my shoes, then began to peel the sundress down off my shoulders. I stopped and tried to regain a sense of sanity. I had no desire to be found naked and quivering if the door miraculously opened. I needed logic and clear thought to get out.

I pounded on the door with both fists. When that didn't bring an immediate result, I began to howl, much like Jed whenever I left him in the apartment.

The door flung open so fast, I nearly fell onto my knees. A dozen or so people filled the hallway like a mosaic. I didn't stop to sort out who was who. I ran.

Chapter 23

The morning after Fran's party I wasn't able to crawl out of bed until nine-thirty. My head was throbbing and my eyes couldn't focus even with my contacts. I had barely a half an hour to shower, slap on some makeup, grab some food for Jed and a leftover bagel for myself, and literally run to the theater.

This was not a day to look forward to or mark down in the diary under pleasant events. This was the day Lida Rose and I had to carefully add the senior contingent to the show while attempting to stave off rabid journalists lurking around the theater in search of fresh fodder for the curse story. Lida Rose doubtless would be delighted to regale them with further tales of every disaster that had ever occurred on East Ellum soil. Oh yes, we also had to finish running Act One. A solitary leftover bagel was not going to suffice. Especially since that headache was threatening to become a major migraine.

Lida Rose and Thelma Lou were in the theater kitchen pouring coffee and distributing donuts and cinnamon rolls to any cast member who was interested. There are times when I want to lock Lida Rose into the nearest sanitarium—drug rehabilitation, criminal, mental, or fat farm. I don't care. As long as there are locks. Last evening I'd had more than one of those impulses. But the woman has a knack for finding carbohydrate treats on days when one needs one's serontonin levels high. A smell of hazelnut was emanating from the coffeepot. This was worthy of my forgiveness. Apple crumb fritters and flavored coffee in the same morning. I absently gave Jed a bite of doughnut and beamed at my friend.

"Bless you. I was going to ignore you all day and pretend you didn't exist, but this changes my mind. Are you sober yet?"

She grimaced at me. "Yes. I am sober. I am also in pain. My entire body feels as if the curse of *Bad Business* has taken over."

I shook my head. "Serves you right. Drinking like a first-time frat boy at a pledge party, then telling absurd lies to a mob of media. I tried to throw a dumpling at you when you so eagerly snatched the mike from Fran, but you were wound up and ready to fly. I think I hit the reporter from the *Observer* in the ear."

She laughed, then winced as the effects of numerous drinks caught up with her. "Ouch. My head. And stomach. Hey. I did *not* snatch the mike. Fran Watkins thrust it at me like a dead snake. I had to take over from the woman. She looked like a constipated turtle up there and Mr. Barrett, for one, was not letting up until he had a story. You're right. He's a toad."

"So you invented one wingding of a tale. And by the way, find some better metaphors than reptiles or I'm not going to last the day. My head hurts worse than yours and you're making me ill.

She smiled innocently. "If you hadn't had those last

four margaritas, you might not feel this way. Honestly, Kiely. If you have to be that violently claustrophobic you could at least learn to control it with something other than tequila. You shot out of that pantry and headed straight for the Jose Cuervo."

I hit her. Not enough to cause damage, unfortunately.

"I was upset. Someone locked me in there and I needed to calm down."

"You want to *think* someone locked you in. The door stuck. That's all. I think you let the curse story get to you. Delilah Delight going insane."

I was incensed. "Me? *Me?* Let that ridiculous tale get to me? Look who's talking, Miss Outrageous Lies Who's Going Straight to Purgatory for about a thousand years."

She grinned as she shoved half a jelly cruller in her mouth.

"Mmmph. Deednemaksho."

"'Scuse me?"

"I said, I did not make up a story. *Bad Business* did lose three cast members a hundred years ago. Week before they opened. Very tragic. Delilah Delight, Nick Nefarious, and Lance Lamar. Neat. You, Rafe, and— oh, my word. Jason. It really hadn't hit me before now."

I wriggled off the counter stool and grabbed two more pastries.

"Don't say 'neat' again. I never want to hear that word from your mouth. You realize now *I'm* going to be hounded and Cyrus will be hounded, and even Rafe the calm and stable will be hounded. They'll make comparisons between him and Don Mueller."

I started to leave the kitchen. Stopped. I had to know.

"What happened to them? The first group of actors?"

A look of innocence transformed Lida Rose's face. "They were shot. Well, actually, no one knows what happened to Delilah. But shots were heard and her body never found, so it's assumed she, too, was riddled with bullets. Or went mad."

I shivered. She looked overwhelmingly pleased with herself. She continued, "Some say there was a duel over Delilah, and the men shot each other. And she got in the way. Some say one of the men was the rejected suitor and he shot both Delilah and the other man, then committed suicide."

I groaned. "I don't want to hear this."

Thelma Lou had stayed silent throughout my conversation with Lida Rose. She now handed me a full cup of coffee and shook her head.

"The thing Lida Rose ain't mentioned is that the show done closed for the night and the ticket sales and a lot of jewelry and cash was missin'. And that there was a gang of what in those days was called 'outlaws' prowlin' through Dallas. Not to mention the fact that Delilah Delight was known to be quite a flirt and probably she ran off with one of them outlaws after the show. Guess they don't make for as spooky a tale. It's all in the newspapers from years ago if ya want to check."

I winked at Thelma Lou and sniffed at Lida Rose. My hungover friend got in one last comment before I made it to the door.

"A toad is not a reptile. It's an amphibian."

I didn't even turn. "Well you're welcome to go suck on a pond full."

I walked onstage and got my first glimpse of Rafe for the morning. He was lounging against the bar set piece. He stayed silent, but lifted up a paper. I asked tentatively, "What's this? *Morning News?* Do I want to read it?"

I shook my head. Mistake. "Not really."

Rafe firmly put the paper into my hand. I sighed. "Fine. I'll read it. Maybe they'll say a giant tornado is headed for the East Ellum Theatre and we're canceling the show. Or a hurricane. Are we at the *L*'s yet this summer for hurricanes? The weather service should name the next one Lida Rose."

Rafe smiled. It was a weary smile. He'd been the most sober of the partygoers and should have gotten at least three hours more sleep than I had. I'd last seen him heading for his truck at least thirty minutes before I'd been trapped in the pantry.

I turned my attention to the paper as he intoned, "Metropolitan Arts. Section C. Page two."

This did not bode well. If Rafe had taken the trouble to memorize the exact spot in the newspaper, that meant I wasn't going to like what was written there. I found Section C and opened with trepidation to page two.

"Bane of Bad Business," by Brett Barrett.

"Oh, boy. Alliteration and hexes in the same headline. I may need a *pot* of coffee for this one."

Rafe motioned for me to read on. I did. It was essentially the same story Lida Rose had told me in the kitchen, but fancied up to sound more ominous and enthralling. The deaths of both Don Mueller and Jason had been played up, along with the disappearance of Noemi Trujillo and her relationship to Don. Nothing had escaped Mr. Barrett's keen sense of the dramatic.

"Oh, sweet Saratoga. This idiot intimates that you, playing Nick Nefarious, and I, playing Delilah Delight, will doubtless meet a foul or mysterious end."

"My favorite bit was the part where Charity O'Sullivan was taking possession of the current Delilah, i.e., you. Lida Rose must have been rip-racing roaring drunk when she came up with that tidbit. Great for publicity, though. I checked in at the box office just before I arrived. Shirley's snotty, cheating little grandson told me ticket sales have doubled since eight this morning."

I sank to the floor of the stage, promptly followed by Jed who began licking my face. I pushed him gently away.

"I want to go back to Manhattan. I want to discourage perverts in the park and wait for five hours for my name to be called at an audition I have no hope of getting. I want to yell at the landlord for not recycling the garbage and letting it build up in the basement so I can't get to the laundry machines. I want to listen to overly made-up ladies with Bloomingdale's bags scream at bus drivers when they have to detour down side streets to avoid six alarm fires. I miss the calm and the sanity of it all."

Rafe started singing "Take Me Back to Manhattan" and I joined in during the second line. Cast members old and new jumped or crawled onstage and added harmony. The stagehands were buzzing around with hammers and noisy attachments; members of the lighting crew were riding the cherry picker up and down checking gels and leko lights.

Lida Rose stood by the orchestra pit waving her hands like a good conductor. I looked up in the middle of the phrase, "I miss the East Side" and saw Don Mueller in the balcony. He was swaying to the music. It occurred to me that if the curse held, Rafe or I might shortly be joining him in whatever hereafter ghosts inhabited.

Lida Rose clapped her hands together. "Okay! Hootenanny over. If everyone's warmed up, let's take places for Act One. We're going to add the other *Bad Business* cast, so I ask for patience today. With any luck and a lot of work we'll get out of here by dinnertime."

The company settled in as Lida Rose began the process of adding the older cast. She might be horribly hungover from too many margaritas and too much imagination, but at some point this past weekend, Lida Rose had done her homework. She knew precisely where to place the "new" actors so they could be seen and participate without unduly destroying several weeks worth of blocking.

It was going too well. Suddenly I heard a crash from the direction of our accompanist. A loud chord filled with fury.

We all turned. Daisy was sitting more upright than an Upright. An expression of intense indignation had given her face more energy than I'd ever seen in her.

Daisy repeated the discordant G chord. "You tell that trashy slut up there that her place is behind that bar! She gets there, then I'll start."

For a moment I thought she meant me. (I've played trashy sluts for too many years.) But since I was already behind the bar I didn't see how her words could apply. Then I realized she meant Macy Mihalik, and she didn't mean her onstage persona.

"Daisy. What's the problem? Why are you pissed off at Macy?"

"Didn't you read the papers? Didn't you see where Brett Barrett said Jason had been with *her* the night before he died? Doesn't anyone care that *she* probably was responsible for throwing that cabinet on him!"

I hadn't gotten to that part of the article. I'd been too pissed about the curse of Delilah et al. Why Daisy was bringing this up just now was beyond reason. Apparently she was still smarting from the fact that Jason had preferred Macy to her. And now the world knew it. At least the world who read the *Morning News* and Brett Barrett.

Lida Rose sighed. "Daisy. Just play the damn music. Macy. Places behind the bar with Kiely and Lindsay, please."

Macy threw a look of resignation at Lida Rose, and one of hatred at Daisy. I wondered whether it might not be a good idea to take a break. But when I raised eyebrows (both) at Lida Rose she looked at her watch, then shook her head. "Hog-Tie Hoedown" was coming up no matter how many tantrums got thrown.

I nudged Rafe, who happened to be in a spot next to me at the bar, and hissed in his ear: "What's with Miss Haltom? Has she just gone over the bend?"

Rafe kept a close eye on Lida Rose who'd run over to the piano to discuss some detail of the hoedown with the aforementioned lunatic.

He whispered, "She's trying to get Lida Rose and Fran to call off the production. She feels we're all being totally callous about Jason's death and she wants to shut down for the next year or so. She may have really loved the man. But she's losing it. By the way, speaking of losing it, what's this I hear about you pitching a major fit at the party after I left? What? Were you upset over discovering some serious cheating going on in the card game at Fran's?"

I smiled and drawled, "Honey, carrying aces is fightin' words. I believe Fran Watkins herself had to threaten Neil Kincaid with expulsion from the party. Nathaniel told me words were exchanged between Neil and that scary-looking butler who greeted us all at the door. As to 'pitching a fit,' as you call it? Had nothing to do with a card game. I didn't care who the hell was cheating. I cared about getting out of the pantry."

"What?"

"You didn't hear about that? Damn, Rafe, your sources are slipping."

I told him about my encounter down the hall from the kitchen.

"Lida Rose keeps telling me I wasn't trapped. She's probably right. I've been known to panic in airplane bathrooms if the door doesn't immediately open, and I assume someone has bolted it from outside. Don't tell Lida Rose I said that. I want her to worry that someone has it in for Delilah Delight after those ridiculous statements made to the press about the curse. She needs to feel a little guilty now and then. Not that she'll ever admit anything bad happening could be her fault for being such a publicity hound."

Rafe stared at me. "I hope you're right. About the pantry not being locked. I'd hate to think you—or any of us—are being harassed by some sick practical joker."

Lida Rose waved at us. "Hey, you two. Hush! We've

been ready to rehearse for the last five minutes. Everybody? Places for the hoedown. And for those of you who imbibed a bit too much last evening, just remember. The tech crew is working on the orchestra pit today and it's in Down position. I'd avoid heading too far off your marks if you don't want to land in on top of the Baby Grand."

Chapter 24

Rehearsals had gone smoothly for three hours. The elderly actors held up well throughout the morning, wisely staying silent during the arguments. Daisy had also wisely stayed silent, playing the piano with exceptional skill. Perhaps she needed a daily blow-up to release the talent within.

Then came the afternoon rehearsal.

Daisy and Macy had somehow gotten together during lunch, made up, and decided that the rest of us in the cast were not only responsible for Jason's death, but were continuing to show how unfeeling we were by not canceling the show or extolling the late Mr. Sharkey's virtues in casual conversation. They seemed to have been plotting how best to antagonize everyone. They arrived late, sat next to each other whispering while Lida Rose gave notes from the morning's rehearsal, and giggled when questions were asked by various members of the company concerning schedules, music, acting problems, and costume fittings.

Finally, Lida Rose had had enough. "Pardon me for interrupting what I'm certain is an important discussion, Ms. Mihalik and Ms. Haltom, but it really chaps my hide to give notes that are not heard or adhered to by cast members and musicians. So get your respective faces out of one another's, and pay attention."

Macy stood. She smiled. "We were discussing how best to save the show at this point," she said.

She looked around at the cast members sitting in chairs, on the floor, on the stage, leaning against the orchestra pit, and standing by the piano Emily had moved to the stage right audience.

"Because, let's face it. It's not working."

My first thought was, if anyone was possessed by a ghost around here, it was Macy. She sounded exactly like Jason.

Silence. Lida Rose stared up into her face.

"What's not working? Would you care to be specific?"

Oh, crap, L. R. Don't ask that. You're playing her game.

I feared my wordless thoughts had been heard. Rafe looked at me, smiled, and raised his left brow. I shifted my focus back to the debate.

Macy was answering Lida Rose's question. Actually, Macy was intoning as if she were at the microphone of a public address system.

"This oldies onstage trip is just not working. It looks stupid. I'm sure I'll offend the politically correct members of this group who believe old age is not a deterrent to talent, but it looks like a geriatric picnic up here and saps the energy from those of us actually hired to do this show. And Daisy agrees with me."

A buzz broke out all over the theater. I don't think there was anyone who wasn't arguing, agreeing, or trying to listen to others arguing or agreeing.

Except for me. I leaned against the railing by the orchestra pit, casually watched each group, and pondered the best way to end what was fast becoming chaos and possible mutiny.

The solution wasn't one I'd have thought of on my own, although it did end the ridiculous discussions. A light coming from the balcony caught my eye. I glanced up. Don Mueller was frantically pointing at me and shaking his head. At the same time, I felt the railing give way. I heard a crack and envisioned myself at the bottom with more than a bruised forehead. Life went into slow motion as I imagined the end of my career. The possible end of my life.

Gasps came from every direction. A strong hand grabbed my arm, then firmly pulled me away from the broken rail. I stood nose-to-nose with Rafe Montez, who'd just rescued me from what might have been the unhappy finish of the third Delilah Delight.

Lida Rose rushed over with a look of terror on a face paler than the white sundress I'd worn the night before.

"Oh, my God! What in bloody blue blazes is going on? Charlie! Charlie! Get your crew here. Now!"

The tech director poked his head out from behind the stage near the scene shop.

"What's the problem?"

"The problem is we nearly lost Kiely thanks to the railing giving way. I thought this damn theater had been renovated. This piece of wood looks like termites have been having a dinner party."

Charlie hurried across the stage and took a look. Two techies had followed him. Charlie looked as guilty as Jed had the day he'd eaten the bathroom mat.

"This is left over from years ago. It's ripped in so many places it's no wonder it gave way. Sorry, Kiely. I should have checked to see that a new railing was put in. There's supposed to be an iron one."

I was shaky, but couldn't stand to see him so miserable.

"Not your fault. Honest. I've seen that railing every day for the last few weeks when my dog has been cooped up there and I never noticed a thing wrong. I don't think any of us did."

Lida Rose nodded. She was calmer now that it was clear she hadn't lost one dancehall girl and best friend to the concrete below.

"I'm sorry if I seemed nasty. No one's to blame. I don't even know if plans for a new railing were part of the renovations. Well. Now they are. Kiely? You okay?"

I smiled. It was a shaky smile, but at least I hadn't burst into tears.

"I just need to sit for a minute or two. Maybe some coffee?"

"Here."

Thelma Lou appeared at my side with a steaming mug.

"How do you do that? Come up with just the right thing at the right time?" I asked.

She grunted. "I listen."

The coffee even had the right amount of cream and sugar. I'd been about to ask for the real stuff anyway. I'd always heard sugar's good for shock. I didn't care if it was true or not. It just tasted a lot better than chemicals. Lida Rose signaled for attention.

"Okay. Cast? Kiely's all right. And I think the excitement is over for a while. I hope. Now. Regardless of the fact that we wasted ten minutes arguing over Macy's theories on casting and directing, I hate to tell you, but theater is *not* a democracy. At least this one isn't. The other cast of *Bad Business* remains part of this company. Age or no age. Case closed. Back to work. Kiely? We'll start with scene two of Act One. You're not in that, so rest for a bit."

I did as asked. Rafe hadn't said a word other than "You're welcome" when I'd thanked him for the fast save before what could have been a fatal dive. Worry was etched all over his face, but he got onstage and flawlessly delivered his Act One, Scene Two lines.

I cautiously looked up into the balcony once the rehearsal was back in progress. Don stood next to the ladder leading to the catwalk. He waved and nodded his head in satisfaction that he'd been able to warn me of impending disaster with enough time for me to slightly readjust my weight forward into Rafe's firm grasp. I wished I had a way to repay him for the help.

The rest of the day ended up being far less traumatic than I'd feared. I was able to get up and sing and dance and go through the numbers with ease. I was even able to get the nagging feeling that the railing had been stronger yesterday than today out of my mind. Well, almost able.

Rehearsal ended at five o'clock. I was more than ready to get home, take a hot bath, and watch something mindless on TV. I grabbed Jed, looped his leash around his neck, and prepared for the walk home. I'd made it halfway across the parking lot when I was accosted by Brett Barrett, the reporter with the intuition of a bloodhound. Jed growled. I unwisely told him it was okay and advised him not to tear Mr. Barrett's trouser legs to shreds. Yet.

"Kiely! I heard you nearly took a header into the orchestra pit this afternoon."

I stared at him. That's all I needed. A psychic reporter.

"How did you know about that? And it wasn't a header. More like the other end."

He winked. "I'd love for you to believe the ghost told me, but since there isn't one, the truth will have to suffice."

I wanted to relay the fact that the ghost was more than capable of relaying the information (well, I hadn't heard Don talk, so maybe not) but I didn't want to get Brett started on paranormal possibilities.

"So? How did you hear?"

"I've been out here for the last hour waiting to catch whoever will fill me in on the latest concerning curses, jewels found, and general doings amongst the cast. I lucked out. Shirley Kincaid and the kid who works box office. Some relative of hers? Anyway, she gave me the scoop and he translated, since she is not the most, um, lucid person I know."

I had to agree with that assessment of Shirley Kincaid, while fuming over the fact that the woman didn't have the sense to keep quiet about what was really nobody's business.

Brett continued. "I was also able to gather from Ms. Kincaid's comments that she, unlike some people I could name, does indeed believe the theater has some sort of jinx associated with this show. Great scoop."

"Brett. Please don't print all this garbage. Shirley is as bad as Lida Rose about publicity. Worse, really. At least Lida Rose doesn't come out and say she gives the curse theory any credence. She just puts it out for the universe to decide. Anyway, you know it's all rot."

"Maybe to you, babe, but Shirley thinks the show

should close before it starts. She's willing to be onstage but said she's nervous about the whole thing now."

I shook my head. "She's a sweet, rattled ditz. And she's pulling your chain. She knows quite well the amount of revenue that's being generated with the anniversary showing of this melodrama. No way would she want to shut it down. And she could. She and Fran discussed doing just that after Jason died. Shirley's known Fran long enough to convince her if she had a mind to do so. Bottom line, Barrett? You're giving this theater exactly what they're asking for. Just don't hassle *me* about it all. I've got enough to do. I can't worry about what I say to the press corps."

"Come on, Kiely, just one quote. You almost took a twenty-foot drop into an orchestra pit today. How does that make you feel?"

I smiled and pointed to the expensive Italian shoe on Mr. Barrett's left foot. Jedidah was happily peeing on it. My sentiments exactly. The reporter quickly made tracks for the nearest rest room.

Once back at the apartment, I hugged Jed for his bravery in taking on intrepid reporters. Then I took Jed out, fed Jed, played tug-of-war with Jed, flopped on the couch with Jed, then shared a plate of nachos with the mutt as we watched the Sci-Fi Channel's *Mummy* special. The current flick was *The Mummy Returns*. Original version. He really did look like Joe Hernandez. I fell asleep with the dog on my lap, hearing an Arab workman hissing something about curses. Neither dog nor girl stirred for the next ten hours.

Chapter 25

I'd been pacing in circles for a good five minutes on the sidewalk in front of MiaMaya Imports. Did I really want to buy Rafe and Lida Rose some kind of fake Mayan artifact for an opening night present? I'd found small, funny inexpensive trinkets for the rest of the cast. A can of silly string for the Humble brothers (representing the lasso.) A pack of trick cards with at least ten aces for Theo, who was playing Ace Royale. A mauve-colored blusher labeled "Primrose" for Amber, playing Polly Sue Primrose the ingenue. A video of the classic movie *David and Bathsheba* for Lindsay, since her character was Bathsheba Bombshell. An old fan magazine from the eighties with Michael Jackson on the cover and a headline saying "Jackson Gone Wild!" for Ben Collins, the actor playing Jackson Wild. I'd even found potted plants for the "live scenery" original cast members and daisy earrings for our accompanist. Maybe yellow flowers dangling from her ears would help lighten her up a bit.

My favorite present so far was an old vinyl recording of Vaughn Monroe singing about Daniel Boone. This was for Cyrus Boone, who'd let it slip at rehearsal the other day that Daniel was his middle name. As of yet, I hadn't purchased anything truly obnoxious for my best friend, or for Rafe Montez, whom I couldn't quite classify in my head as friend, foe, or—well, whatever.

Someone in the cast had mentioned that MiaMaya Imports had reopened a few weeks ago. I hoped to find a piece reminiscent of the Mayan works Rafe and I had seen at Fair Park. Perhaps one with a silly connection to our show. Even if all they had was an exotic clay vessel with hairless Chihuahuas singing to the moon that cost over $25 I'd get it. I owed him that much for paying my way into that exhibit and buying the ice cream. Also for saving my life when the railing broke.

A nice tinkly bell rang as soon as I opened the door to the shop. A smiling young woman behind a counter asked if I needed help and nodded affirmatively when I told her I just needed to browse. How does one ask a salesperson for aid in finding what one is clueless about?

I wandered the aisles for a good ten minutes, discarding evil-looking masks, plaster-of-paris dogs, statuettes of ugly naked gods, turquoise jewelry, and jade pendants. I stopped before a replica of that awful war serpent that had scared me at the museum but couldn't figure out any significance between his nasty face and anything in *Bad Business*. No snakes. Just guns, cards, and ropes. A solid brass goddess in less clothing than I wear at the beach who seemed to be engaged in a Bali fertility dance was a possibility. But we dancehall girls were clad in traditional frilly outfits complete with corset, petticoats, and garter belts. Our dances were closer to the French cancan than belly dancing of any kind. I kept it in mind as a last resort, and roamed through an aisle that didn't seem exactly organized. Jewelry had been tossed in among ceramic pots and giant iron columns. I saw velvet paintings similar to those at El Diablo's that were even trashier with images of all four Beatles and some former president; one of the Bushes. Or Reagan. It was a bad likeness. Masks were carelessly thrown on top of paintings and pots. I guessed MiaMaya hadn't yet gotten the knack for organization, or how best to display their goods for maximum consumer interest.

I did finally come across some outrageously huge feathered earrings in rainbow colors for Lida Rose (who would doubtless wear them with both her designer dresses and capri pants on alternate occasions).

I was about to go back and purchase the Bali dancer when I saw something glinting underneath a hideous squatty statue with the body of a baby and a face of someone at least fifty-five. I moved the sculpture over and discovered a mosaic about ten inches long and seven inches wide. It depicted a conquistador engaged in battle with a Mayan warrior scantily clad in a loincloth, feathered headdress, and jeweled neckpiece. The conqueror had tied up the man rather like a pig prepared for the luau. Next to the Mayan warrior was a girl wearing something akin to a string bikini in shreds. She was gazing at the conquering male with a look somewhere between lust and fear. Sacrificial virgin was the impression I got, but one who might well be happy to lose that status if the Spaniard was involved in the process. It was not the prettiest piece of art I'd seen, but Rafe would get all the double meanings behind it. I loved it.

"How much?"

The smiling salesgirl blinked twice when she saw the piece and tried to hide her laughter.

"Twelve dollars," she said apologetically. She should be apologetic. It looked like it could have been in someone's garage sale going for fifty cents.

I paid for the painting and for Lida Rose's feathered ear bobs and left MiaMaya, absurdly pleased with myself. I do love buying fun good-show gifts. For the first time since Jason's death I felt a real tinge of happiness.

I walked back across the huge vacant lot that separates the theater from MiaMaya Imports and strolled inside, grinning about my purchases and pleased to be out of the heat again. I glanced at my watch. I had a good thirty minutes 'til call time for "final dress."

The tech crew was everywhere, and everywhere they were was chaotic. Techies screaming, techies testing microphones onstage, techies testing headpieces to the conductor, to the stage manager and lighting booth, techies yelling at cast members to get off the stage. Orchestra members strolling in and warming up, each in a different key from his fellows. I smiled at everyone in turn and started to head for the green room where actors hang out before a show. (If one has never been involved in theater, I should mention that green rooms are seldom green. What they *are* are brown. Brown from coffee stains, brown from remnants of makeup that shouldn't rub off but does, brown from old age, and occasionally brown because a set crew finished up a set with too much color for background flats and decided the green room needed a fresh coat.)

I veered left before going to the green room to look for Jed, whom I'd last seen in the costume shop in

Thelma Lou's care. (The orchestra pit was now off limits to the dog since we were about to have real musicians.) My canine friend was snoring underneath one of the sewing tables. Thelma Lou was snoring on top of the other sewing table. They both looked serenely content. I gave Jed a quick pat and silently closed the door.

The green room was empty. The dressing rooms were empty. I checked my watch with the clock in the hallway.

"Oh, hell."

It had died. I was at least forty minutes late for call.

MiaMaya had presented me with cute gift bags that worked better than any wrapping paper and would serve as little carryalls for the presents, so I hurried back to my dressing room and stashed the gifts under my chair. At least I wouldn't have to lug Rafe's and Lida Rose's presents home tonight, then back tomorrow with the good show gifts I had for the rest of the cast.

I got into my first act costume and did my makeup in about five minutes, skipping the false eyelashes for now. I ran into the tiny room we were using for vocal warm-ups before shows and was greeted with a barrage of, "Where the hell have you been, Kiely?" by Lida Rose, Daisy, and, surprisingly, by Rafe.

He looked, I don't know, relieved to see me, as though he'd been watching that clock and worrying.

"Sorry. Sorry. I was out running errands and my watch stopped. Sorry. I will buy batteries tonight if some kind soul will drive me to an all-night store."

I squeezed next to Lindsay and Macy and joined in with the singing.

Rafe managed to squeeze in next to me after the

first set of scales. "Where were you? Don't give me this errand business. What kind of errands could you be engaged in just before final dress?"

I snuck a look at Daisy and Lida Rose. They were listening to Cyrus trying to hit a high note that was more in soprano range and arguing that Billie had never meant for that note to be taken up an octave.

"If you must know, Mr. Nosy, I was buying good-show gifts. Tomorrow's impossible for me. Lida Rose has managed to schedule my day from rising to theater call with media appearances at all local news stations. This was my last chance to spend my money."

That seemed to pacify him.

He grinned. "Whatdja get? Huh? Huh?"

I fluttered my unfalsified lashes at him.

"Well, never you mind, Mr. Montez. Suffice to say, you'll get yours, honey."

"That I will, Ms. Davlin."

The look in his eye changed from teasing to daring. The memory of that quick kiss in the prop room the day I'd found the garnet surfaced in my mind. I knew the same memory was floating in his mind as well. And possibly a few other anatomical areas.

Passionate glances during singing warm-up were not the best idea. I nudged him with my elbow.

"So, Rafe? You seemed a bit overly concerned when I was late? Worried about Delilah cutting out on final dress?"

His voice dropped to a whisper.

"Honestly? I was more worried that Delilah Delight wasn't going to make final dress. Lida Rose and I had been looking all over the theater for you and when we couldn't find you, she started moaning that you'd probably met with an accident and that it was all her fault for ever getting you down here in the first place."

"Good. She needs a guilt trip. Maybe if she has enough of them it'll teach her not to go telling outrageous stories all the time. So, you let her get to you?"

"I did. I am ashamed. But not sorry. You seem to have a knack for being in the wrong place at the wrong time and I couldn't help but wonder where that talent had taken you."

I stared at him, then snuck a quick glance at Daisy to make sure she wasn't starting a song that involved Rafe or me.

"Me? Me? You're the one I've seen with his butt sticking out of every damn set piece around here. You're the one who actually discovered Jason. You're the one who raced up the stairs and nearly got singed during the fire. You're the one who nearly landed on the Grand Piano twenty feet down in the pit. Either you're very accident prone or someone has it in for you."

For once he didn't scoff at me. He looked me straight in the eye. "I think someone has it in for both of us. I think someone is using the curse story for their own reasons to do away with Lance Lamar, Nick Nefarious, and Delilah Delight."

My mouth dropped open. Fortunately that was the right position to sing.

"Okay, everyone. One last time through 'Gamblers We' for the guys and the 'Bad Business' number for everyone, then it's back to dressing rooms before 'places.'"

Lida Rose waved her arms around. Rafe squeezed my hand lightly, then hurried back to his position with the guys. I stayed still and tried not to think about what he'd just said.

Ten minutes later we were done and back in our dressing rooms. I carefully applied my eyelashes and the remainder of my blush and lipstick and thrust out any thoughts of curses and accidents from my mind.

The five-minute warning could be heard over the intercom the techies had somehow managed to get working again. Then, "Places." Final dress was about to begin.

Chapter 26

Rehearsal had been finished for over an hour. It had been a terrific final dress. Nothing had gone wrong. Not a false note from the orchestra, not a missed cue by an actor, not a follow spot highlighting the wrong singer during another's solo. I admit to being very superstitious when it comes to theater traditions. I don't whistle in theaters (okay, fine, I've never been able to whistle anyway). If I'm in the vicinity of a theater, including high school cafeterias, I say "the Scottish play" rather than the real name of Shakespeare's tragedy (for anyone wondering which one, it starts with thunder, lightning, and three witches muttering). I believe in one other tradition. If final dress is a disaster, opening night will be terrific. It only follows that the reverse is true.

My fellow cast members were calling out good-byes and "meet you at El Diablo's." Normally I'm the life of the pre-show after–dress rehearsal party, but this particular night I didn't feel like going out. I didn't even want to go home. I gathered my belongings from the dressing room and my dog from the costume shop, and sank down onto the floor between the first row of seats and the orchestra pit, resting my legs over the new iron railing in a dancer's traditional "take five" pose.

I closed my eyes and made a conscious effort to shut out every noise. The box office staff and techies were the only people left in the theater that I knew of and they were in the lobby and scene shop, respectively, so no sound filtered through. The theater was totally quiet. But I was seeking more than silence. I wanted peace. I needed to block out the sight of Jason Sharkey lying in his own blood amidst thousands of shards of glass and a weapon straight out of an old Cecil B. DeMille epic. I hadn't told anyone, but I still saw that picture in front of me on a daily basis. I needed to banish it before I got onstage tomorrow night. I began to focus on my breathing. I tried to imagine cool blue lakes in mountain regions. I tried to imagine the ocean lapping onto a shore somewhere in New England. I tried every trick of yoga or theater meditation I'd ever learned.

But all I could think of were motives. Reasons why Jason had not been the best beloved actor at East Ellum. There were plenty. Theo, Lindsay, and Rafe had tolerated his bigotry in silence. Ham was in love with Amber and angry with Jason for getting there first. Hank would take up for his brother. Macy and Daisy might well have gotten tired of Jason's "from this girl to the next" routine. Macy's husband might have decided that he wasn't thrilled about their open marriage. Even the older cast had cause to dislike Jason Sharkey. He'd ignored Nathaniel because of his race. He'd hassled and tried to humiliate both Billie and Cyrus Boone. Fran and Shirley might have decided the actor was creating too much dissension at

East Ellum. Thelma Lou just hated the man on principle. And Lida Rose might think a murder was a great way to carry on the curse. A troublesome way, but great publicity.

Everyone had a motive to dislike. Were any of those motives enough to kill?

I started feeling twitchy. I got up and began stretching a bit. Jed followed me, begging me to play tug-of-war with one of his chew toys. One of us got a bit too enthusiastic, because the red-and-white-striped rag landed in the orchestra pit on a music stand. I figured I'd best dispose of the toy before some hapless musician was forced to touch the gnawed and doubtless damp toy to get it out of his way when he tried to turn pages.

The pit was in Down position, so I had to go backstage and use the other door leading from the kitchen to get in. I grabbed the toy, then shivered. The barest hint of a draft could be felt on my shoulders, now clad only in my leotard top and tank T-shirt for the walk home in the heat. I looked back at the door where I'd just entered. I'd closed it tightly behind me. I looked around the pit. In the far corner was a harp. It had obviously been discarded decades ago. I'd never noticed before. I hadn't even known it was there. But the sensation of air was coming from that direction. I moved the instrument. There was a door right behind it. I immediately inched away. If that door led to anything under the theater, forget it.

I turned away. Then I heard the voice.

"Please, Elias! Please, don't! Please let me have my life!"

It was a female voice; it was coming from the tunnel.

And it was followed by screams of intense pain. Screams I couldn't ignore.

I pushed the door open and found myself in a hallway. A dark hallway. I quickly backed up into the orchestra pit again. I stood beside the harp for a moment. Then the screams started again. I should have hauled it out of the pit and called 911. But when I saw the flashlight on the conductor's stand I felt guilty. I had to see what was wrong.

I tested the flashlight, and a beam the wattage of a police searchlight discharged. I could see clear to my apartment with the thing. I breathed out and my shoulders resumed a position under my neck, rather than by my ears. If someone needed help and needed it now, I couldn't use the excuse of the dark to turn away.

I pushed the door again and aimed the flashlight down the hall. Nothing. Nothing on the walls, nothing on the ceiling or the concrete floor. No one yelling or moaning. I took a few deep breaths to convince myself that I wouldn't be trapped forever under the theater, then I stepped farther inside. About a hundred yards down the hallway from the orchestra pit was a round room. To my right was a door, to my left were shelves that seemed attached to the wall. Below them on the floor was a mass of rubble that stretched all the way across the room in piles at least six feet high. It appeared that a cave-in had sealed this end of the hall. There was no way of knowing when.

I began to move toward the shelves, which were laden with boxes and what looked like old knick-knacks. Old props, perhaps. Maybe this was where the rest of the hundred-year-old *Bad Business* production pieces had ended up. I aimed the light in that direction and was about to explore the goodies when I tripped over one of the bricks in the middle of the floor.

The flashlight flew my out hands as I tried to save myself from taking a direct header into a shelf. As I crashed, I heard *it* crash, tinkle, then roll away from me. I scrabbled across the floor trying to grab it. The light went out.

I was in total darkness. I'm not talking a dim light. I'm talking *any* light. Total, absolute darkness. I lay on the floor listening to my ragged breathing and realized I saw nothing. At least when I'd been trapped in the pantry at Fran's there'd been a nice steady source of electricity.

I couldn't see and I couldn't hear, except for my heart beating and fighting to break out of my chest. Suddenly a scuffling reached my ears through the fog of fear. I thanked whatever guardian angel had my name on their job list for the week and yelled, "Hey! Whoever. It's Kiely! I'm in the room where the rubble is! Yoo-hoo! Hey! My flashlight broke and I'm in the dark! Need some help here. Hello!"

No answer. Not even an echo of my own *o*'s. I'd doubtless mistakenly addressed my pleas to a rodent as scared as I.

My skin prickled as my breathing grew louder. I reached out my arm to see if I could touch one of the shelves and get my bearings. It was like extending into a black hole of space. I felt completely disoriented. My arm didn't seem to belong to me. I crawled a few inches to where I thought the shelves should be. Nothing. I could have been as little as a foot away or as much as a yard.

Sweat was now racing down my forehead, front, and back. I started to rip every shred of clothing I had off my body. I did remove my *Grand Hotel* tank T-shirt but felt awkward and unbalanced as I did so. All the blood in my body had rushed to my head. No rational thoughts penetrated. I would have knocked my head against the wall to render myself unconscious but I couldn't find a wall close by. My heart, my breath, and soon my sobs were sounding louder and coming in faster. I felt I was screaming, but I couldn't hear myself.

Somewhere between panic and despair I forced myself to calm down. Then inspiration hit. A stupid inspiration, but better than trying to knock myself out. I would sing every song from *The Music Man* I could think of. The box office people might still be in the theater. Maybe someone would hear me. Or maybe Lida Rose would use her so-called extrasensory perceptive skills from White Rock Lake, know I was singing about her, and come get me the hell out of here.

I began inching toward any direction not blocked by stones and concrete, trying to find an exit. The hallway back to the pit had to be somewhere near. I'd seen one other door in this room that hadn't been blocked by rubble before the lights had been extinguished. I stayed on my hands and knees and blindly crawled.

"Ouch! Shit!"

My knees were crunching down on the sharp stones and cracked bricks from what I assumed was that caved-in ceiling. I was going to end up with some terrific cuts and bruises. Assuming I made it out. I carefully avoided what seemed to be a very large chunk of concrete but put my hand down on something sharp. I ran my fingers over it. It felt like a pin, perhaps a brooch. Whatever it was, it had punctured a small hole in my palm. I continued to hold it in my hand, needing something real to cling to. There was an object beside that pin. It felt solid yet somehow wrong. I moved my hand over the hard surface. And screamed until the sound of my own terror frightened me more than what was under my hand.

Bones. Bones and fabric. Not rodent bones, unless some demented phantom of the theater had once kept a rat for a pet and clothed it. I instinctively knew that what was beside me had once been a person. Female. I felt the sadness again. And heard the whisper of the voice, saying, "Please Elias. Please, don't. Let me have my life." Terror once more overtook me. I'm sure I passed out for at least a few minutes.

I awoke sobbing, praying, and yelling. That took up ten minutes. Then I got angry. It was time to get out. Now.

I inched forward again. Those inches turned to perhaps three feet. I extended my hand down to see if I could feel a door. Instead, I felt a space that had an airy quality to it.

"Thank God. Air. I'll give it a shot."

I managed to get to my feet and took a step forward. Then I took a step back. It was like a demented dance. The air, such as it was, came from what was more like a closet. No where to go from there and if that door closed on me once I was inside, I'd truly lose what was left of my sanity.

I sat back down and squeezed the pin I'd picked up earlier. Somehow having something tangible and sharp in my hand helped me to focus. I didn't want to die. I particularly didn't want to be buried alive.

I'd always figured I'd go in the middle of *grand jeté* at age ninety-six while demonstrating to some twenty-something dancer the proper form for split leaps.

That image made me smile and calmed me a bit. I carefully began to pat the space to find where that closet was, then avoid it. That took another five minutes by my inner clock.

Then I sat. I still had no idea where the entrance to the hall was. I was stuck. All the calm I'd built up left. I started sobbing again, then got mad because I had no Kleenex. Great. My bones would be found in another hundred years or so along with those of my new "buddy." Some snide archaeologist would comment on the fact that the dancer's nose had been running when she died, pointing out the ruined portions of the leotard as evidence of blotting. Which I now did. I inhaled to see if I was still breathing and got a whiff of something other than dust and decay. Popcorn.

"What in bloody blue blazes? Am I dead already? Did the angels carry me to some great carnival in the sky, complete with funhouse, popcorn, and cotton candy?"

I sniffed again. Popcorn. With butter.

"Oh my gosh! There must be someone in the theater above. Some kind, hungry, lunatic soul who has returned and is making mounds of popcorn in the kitchen."

It occurred to me that if I followed my nose, I might just be able to get the hell out of this dark chasm of dust and actually make my way into civilization again. Assuming I was correct about still being alive.

I stayed on my hands and knees and sniffed like Je-didiah following the scent of chili. (He loves chili.) I thanked every deity I could think of for being gifted with a good smeller, and silently apologized to my mother for complaining that my nose was so good I'd gained weight exploring every bakery in New York City.

I have no idea how long my journey took. I hadn't had the chance to get batteries for my watch, which wasn't luminous anyway. (Addendum to Christmas list for the next time I stupidly decided to go wandering through what could become blind territory.) I just kept inhaling and crawling and cursing when I scraped a knee and praying that this ordeal would be over soon.

I reached a door. I didn't care where it led. I opened it. I was back in the orchestra pit next to the harp. The light was so intense after the total blackness, I had to close my eyes and gradually become accustomed to my surroundings again.

"Hello? Anybody around?"

I looked around the pit. The music stands were still there. The piano was still there. (One leg looked as if it had a few teeth marks, canine size, from the previous week's rehearsals, but it was in place.) Jed was barking excitely from the floor of the theater over my head. No human had yet answered, so I assumed my popcorn-popping savior was still in the kitchen making a fresh batch. I started toward the entrance leading out of the pit to the kitchen. No one was there, either. The popcorn machine was empty, the cabinets with the food locked. This was bizarre. It had taken me at least twenty minutes to inch my way out of the tunnel, but that wouldn't have been long enough for whoever was cooking to get the popcorn ready and clean the huge machine.

I glanced toward the entrance of the orchestra pit. Don Mueller was calmly munching from the paper bag of popcorn he held in his hand. He smiled, waved a kernel at me, then disappeared.

Chapter 27

I should have called the police right then and there. But like any good heroine who needs life to get more complicated, I didn't. I just wasn't up to dialing Officer Krupke and company to explain that I'd spent half the night in a tunnel under the theater with a skeleton. To add to my idiocy, I decided I wanted to walk home. Past two in the morning and Kiely, the defiant and brave, was strolling through downtown Dallas as though it were Times Square at rush hour. I had to. I needed to be in open spaces or I'd start screaming again.

Jed was with me, so I wasn't overly afraid of being mugged. He's a sweetie but I knew he would defend me with every ounce of his now seventy pounds (no Kiely, no chili). I also figured any mugger within smelling distance would catch a whiff of my clothes and know this was not a person carrying a king's ransom in jewels or even a nice wallet filled with cash. I was also beyond angry at what had befallen me in the last few hours. I pitied anyone stupid enough to jump out at me. My feet were itching to kick someone, anyone, in any spot designed to provide maximum injury.

I needed to be out in the night air, with the Texas

stars above in the clear sky, away from dirt, bones, harps, and doors leading to blackness.

Three minutes into my walk I ran into a gay couple exiting the bar next to MiaMaya Imports. They were semisober, barely legal age-wise, and very concerned about this woman they spotted wandering down the street with a large playful puppy, wearing a filthy leotard top and jeans (me, not the dog). I calmly informed them that I'd just come from the East Ellum Theatre where I'd had a run-in with a tunnel, sans lights. They kindly offered to escort me home. I accepted.

The three of us (and Jed) had a great time walking the ten minutes to my apartment singing country and western songs I hadn't heard since I was a kid, and occasionally pausing to do a high kick or a spin in the street. Once we got to my Bennett Avenue home, I hugged my rescuers good-bye, got their names and numbers, and promised comp tickets for any performance of *Bad Business* they cared to attend. I'd been greatly cheered by this encounter after a near-death experience. It was nice to know that nice people who nicely took the time to help others were still left in the world. Not everyone stood ready to turn the lights out and leave claustrophobic dancers in the dark.

I was certain someone had been in that pit shortly after I'd entered the hallway. Someone had followed me, seen me fall, and watched as my flashlight died. Someone then deliberately doused the remaining lights. I knew this because after I'd grabbed Jed and my bag and thrown oodles of kisses toward the ghost of Don Mueller, I'd gone down into the orchestra pit for one last look around. The music stand that had been on the floor when I'd been looking for Jed's chew toy had been changed to upright. I didn't think the dog could have managed that little piece of housecleaning, especially from twenty feet above.

Once I was home, I tore off my clothes and jumped into the shower. I stood motionless under the heat and water for over thirty minutes. Eventually I took soap and washed off the remainder of the dirt and felt a bit more human.

I don't remember actually crawling into bed. The next time I was aware of anything other than throwing my Disney *101 Dalmatians* sleep shirt over my head, the sun was shining. I cautiously opened one eye. Ten A.M. Morning of opening night of *Bad Business* and some inconsiderate fool was pounding outside my apartment and yelling at me.

I staggered to the door. As I unlocked it, I recognized the voice of the irate screamer once it yelled, "Kiely! Are you ready? Open up!" at least three times. Lida Rose.

The woman entered, paused, then scrutinized my appearance with the eye of Richard Blackwell preparing to pronounce Worst Dressed for the year.

"Damn, Kiely! You look like crap."

"Thank you. Thank you for that comment. I can't tell you how much I needed to hear that after last night."

She brushed off my words and brushed by me as well, heading for the kitchen.

"Kiely? You're not dressed. Honey, you're not even awake. And you look like dog doo on a squished shoe. No offense. Did you not go home last night?"

She nudged me. "Hey! Did you get lucky last night?"

I promptly burst into tears and received a special Lida Rose bear hug. It felt great.

"I got locked in the tunnel last night."

She calmly moved me to a position an arm's length from her person and said, "Say again?"

"Don't you listen? I got locked in the tunnel under the theater last night. The one that leads from the harpist's door in the orchestra pit."

She wisely ignored this garbled interpretation of the location and seized on one word. Tunnel.

"There's a tunnel under the theater? How cool."

I pushed her away.

"It was not cool. It was like the first gate of Hell. Excuse me. I need coffee and I need it *now*. Would you care for a cup or are you going to stand there and bewail the fact that you were not locked up in dirt with a dead body for hours with me?"

That got her. "Dead body? You didn't mention a dead body before. Damn, Kiely, what on earth happened last night?"

I filled her in on my adventure with all the graphics and gory details. When I'd finished she shook her head and started to speak.

I immediately interrupted her. "If you dare to say, 'that's neat,' I shall personally pull out your bottle-dyed locks by their roots. In handfuls."

She looked offended. "Don't be ridiculous. This is not neat. This is serious. If you're right and someone deliberately left you there in the dark, you're quite possibly in a wagon full of danger. So, did you call the police?"

I stared at her as I swallowed a mouthful of coffee.

"Uh, no."

"Kiely. Why not?"

"Because all I wanted last night was to be out, to be free, to be clean, and to be home. Oh, I met the sweetest guys, too. Cute couple. They walked me home after they saw me when they were coming out of Madison's."

She threw her hands up to the heavens for assistance.

"Kiely Davlin! Not only do you fail to call the police, but you allow yourself to go home with two strangers who could have sliced your throat and left you for dead. And you think *I'm* brainless?"

"Oh, back off. The guys were great. I'm comping them for tonight's opening. I need to tell Neil Kincaid in box office."

She looked horrified. For a moment I thought she was about to chastise me for giving away perfectly good seats for free. Instead she began throwing objects out of her enormous purse, looking for her cell phone.

"Are you calling the cops for me?"

"Not yet. I'm calling the Channel Seven entertainment desk."

"You're what? Lida Rose! You can't bring more media into this mess. I swear, sometimes you act like a savant three-year-old with a demonic bent. Do *not* tell those vultures that your choreographer has been excavating tunnels. Please!"

She glared at me.

"You and I are supposed to be on television in ten minutes extolling the virtues of buying tickets to *Bad Business*. I don't think we're going to make it. That is why I am calling. Give me some credit for knowing where and when to garner publicity."

I gulped coffee and got dressed while she explained to some poor receptionist that the director and choreographer who were scheduled for their show weren't going to be on due to an emergency at the theater. Which was true. Lida Rose then dug even deeper into her purse and found the business card Officer Melinda Krupke had given each of us. She handed it to me along with the receiver.

"It was your misadventure. You tell her. And be sure they know a dead body is involved."

I took the card from her, looked at the number, then started to laugh.

"Are you getting hysterical with all this? What are you giggling about?"

"Look at this. Officer Melinda has a sense of humor. I knew I liked that girl."

She took back the card. There in black and white was a photo from *West Side Story* depicting the cops busting the gang members. Cute. Lida Rose and I spontaneously sang two verses of "Gee, Officer Krupke" to each other, then I picked up my desk phone and dialed the number. Melinda Krupke answered in person.

"Officer Krupke? This is Kiely Davlin. The choreographer from East Ellum."

I didn't know whether to casually mention that we'd recently met practically over the corpse of Jason Sharkey. I decided to skip that part. It seemed tasteless and unnecessary. She knew who I was.

"Yes, Kiely. I know who you are. And please, call me Melinda." She paused and I could almost hear the smile. "You'd probably find it a bit easier."

I bit my lip. "Undoubtedly."

"So, Kiely. What can I do for you? Any new information concerning Mr. Sharkey?"

"Yes and no. I don't know if this is related to his death or not. I just know something's up and it's not pleasant. I found bones. In a tunnel. Under the orchestra pit. It was dark and I don't know if they're human or not, but they sure felt big enough to be."

"We'll meet you at the theater."

I hung up and turned to Lida Rose.

"Wow! Fast action. She said she'd meet us there. Hey, how does she know that's not where I'm calling from?"

"You are such a technological dinosaur. Don't you have caller ID in Manhattan? Don't you know the cops have it in every station house?"

"Oh, yeah. My roommates and I don't actually have it since we're cheap and never there since we're on tour, but I know it exists."

I threw her purse at her as we started to leave the apartment. "I wish now I hadn't been so miserly. If I'd've seen your number weeks ago, I'd've never picked up. I'd be safely dancing the tango in Florida and been innocently unaware of dead bodies, broken railings, dirty tunnels, and ghosts in black tuxedos and tennis shoes."

Chapter 28

The cops made it to East Ellum exactly the same time that Lida Rose and I did. I know this because my dear friend narrowly missed hitting the nice white vehicle that plainly had the words "Dallas Police Department" on its side when she illegally made a left turn in front of them.

I refrained from pointing this out to Lida Rose since she was obviously eager to see the tunnel and its occupant, and was trying to beat the police to the scene.

Officer Krupke wasn't quite so reticent.

"Ms. Worthington? Did you know you nearly clipped my car ten seconds ago? Are you aware that one waits for the car either going straight or making the right-hand turn if one is turning left?"

Lida Rose smiled sweetly.

"I'm so sorry. I was trying to get here and have the doors opened for you and have coffee all ready, and look! I brought muffins and scones from this cute little bakery in Kiely's neighborhood."

I stared up at the sky and waited for the lightning bolt to crash through the skull of my best friend. Nothing. Clear. St. Peter et al. must be taking the day off.

Melinda Krupke smiled and took the cranberry-orange scone Lida Rose was offering.

"Since you're doubtless overwrought due to the circumstances of your choreographer finding another body on site, I'll let you off with a warning. I hate dealing with traffic violations anyway. I spent five years getting away from that particular detail."

She and Lida Rose smiled at each other. My best friend has a knack for dispensing charm in all situations.

Lida Rose crammed one of the scones into her own mouth and held it there while she pulled keys from her bag. This proved unnecessary. The door wasn't locked. I should have told her it had yet to be anything else since I'd first started popping in early to choreograph weeks ago.

Rafe Montez appeared in the doorway and studied me critically. "You look like you haven't slept in a week. No offense, but you look like crap."

"Thank you, Rafe. Thank you for that lovely observation after a night of hell. I truly appreciate it."

I promptly started to cry. Rafe took my right hand. Lida Rose took the other. Melinda Krupke slid past with Officer Carter in tow.

"Kiely, I'm sorry. What's wrong? I guess you really haven't slept? I guess since the cops are here something else is up?"

I sniffed. "Nice deductions. All of them. And just imagine how you'd look if you'd just spent the better portion of the last hour or two crawling through hell."

"What are you talking about? Last night's rehearsal went well. Nothing remotely hellish about it. Have you been hallucinating? Having run-ins that aren't so friendly with Casper the Ghost?"

I glared at him. "And just what are you doing back at the theater anyway? It's barely ten in the morning. I need more coffee. And throw in some of that Irish whiskey I know Thelma Lou keeps in the back cabinet."

He led both Lida Rose and me back to the kitchen. Our now-very-familiar-with-the-theater cops were already helping themselves to mugs of coffee. Rafe glanced at them, then at me.

"No booze. It's going to be a long day and you don't need to fall asleep tonight in the middle of Act Two."

He poured the necessary accoutrements into a new Styrofoam container and threw a very sharp look in my direction, but wisely refrained from any comment until the cup was in my hand. Once I'd taken a few swigs he began his explanation.

"I'm here because you did not show up at El Diablo's last night. You were not at your apartment. You were not honky-tonking at Sweet Ruby's. I thought you might have fallen asleep here, and since Jason's death I have been a little concerned about you roaming around the theater by yourself. Obviously I was right, since the police are visiting again. What's up?"

Melinda Krupke glared at him. "Excuse me, but I think I'm the one to ask questions. Although you did ask the pertinent one. Kiely? Care to explain why we're here?"

I started crying again. Rafe silently handed me the box of Kleenex that sits on top of the refrigerator in the theater kitchen. I blew and sniffed.

"Thank you."

I took a breath.

"Last night after everyone left, I found a tunnel under the orchestra pit. There's a door behind that huge old harp nobody's played for years. I decided to see where it went."

Rafe slammed his cup down on the counter so hard I was amazed it didn't splinter.

"You did what!"

"I heard someone screaming. Really. And hey. It had lights and a floor. There were no rats. I figured I was fine."

Rafe's right eyebrow shot high into his forehead.

"Are you insane? Jason Sharkey got murdered in the prop room a week ago and Kiely Davlin, the claustrophobic queen, is playing Girl Scout explorer and wandering around through underground tunnels by herself. How in humanity did you ever manage to make it out of childhood? Come to think of it, apparently you didn't."

I threw a pink packet of sweetener at him.

"Are you going to listen, or make nasty cracks?"

He threw a white packet of fake cream back at me.

"Both."

Melinda Krupke interrupted before we could start a full-scale fake food container war.

"Behave, children. Kiely? Please continue."

I nodded and addressed my remarks solely to the officer.

"It was not a fun place. Actually, I'd rather tour the Bowery at midnight in my underwear with the Hope diamond around my neck. It was nasty down there. I dropped my flashlight, and I was trapped for more than an hour. And I found a skeleton in the tunnel. Someone's buried there. Probably for a century or so. I felt fabric but, oh jeez, this is gross—no, uh, goo."

Absolute silence greeted this remark. Melinda was busy writing in her supercop notebook; she'd already heard this much when I'd called. Rafe and Officer Carter looked stunned. Lida Rose made herself useful by handing out muffins and scones.

The quiet continued for a good minute while everyone munched, sipped, and pondered the possibility that a dead someone had been residing under the East Ellum Theatre for decades.

"Okay, folks. Officer Carter and I will take it from here. Kiely? You said the door leads from the orchestra pit?"

I nodded and began to lead the two cops to where I'd started last night's journey. I stopped. I'd left around two A.M. and that pit had been in the Down position. It was currently in the Up position, barely below stage level. I turned to Rafe, who'd followed us from the kitchen.

"Did you bring this up this morning?"

He shook his head.

"I never even noticed it. I got here about fifteen minutes before you guys did. The front doors were open but no one was around. I headed straight to the kitchen to start the morning brew, then wandered backstage to check the props table before I heard y'all come in."

I shrugged. "I guess I forgot. I could have sworn. . . Well, doesn't matter."

The four of us stepped over the railing. Rafe hit the Down button and we rode to the bottom floor. I pointed out the harp and the door behind it. Melinda opened the door and put her hand up for me to stay behind with Rafe.

"We'll check it out. You said there's a cave-in and tons of rubble where the bones were, correct?"

I nodded.

She and Carter entered the tunnel with strong flashlights. Rafe and I sat in the chairs for first violin and drummer.

"Kiely, whatever possessed you to go tromping through tunnels last night by yourself? Damn, woman, you could have been killed? Don't you ever look before you leap?"

I smiled weakly. "Not in the dancer's manual, you know. One just trusts that one's partner will catch."

He frowned at me. "That's assuming one has a partner at the other end of the tunnel."

We both smiled at that.

"Rafe, I was about to run like a bunny. I don't do tunnels. But I swear I heard a scream. And someone saying, 'Please.' Once I opened the door, it just looked like a normal hallway. I didn't think I'd lose all light. And I sure didn't think I'd be keeping company with the skeleton of—whoever."

I looked carefully down at the floor where a piece of sheet music had fallen and opened to the second act song that the dancehall girls sing. It's called, "Aces and Death." I almost started crying again.

"Rafe? Please don't think I'm nuts. Well, more nuts than you already do. But—"

He interrupted with, "I don't think you're nuts. Nosy, perhaps. But not nuts."

I almost smiled. "You will. What I was about to say is that I'm wondering if those bones I found could belong to someone missing from this theater years ago. Someone who also played Delilah Delight in the very first production."

He sighed.

"I won't say you're nuts, but I will ask why you think that."

I shook my head. "I had the same sense of sadness when I felt that skeleton as I did when we were in the prop room and found that old earring. And I heard her voice. I did."

I stared at him and screeched semiquietly.

"Yikes! I just remembered."

I pulled my bag toward me and began searching for the object I'd hastily stuffed inside my bag into a wad of tissue last night. I'd been in such a hurry to leave, and so dazzled by the thought that I'd been rescued from near death by a ghost that I'd forgotten I'd even put it there.

I carefully unwrapped it. It had pierced my hand last night and drawn blood. Now I saw why.

"Rafe. Look at this. It's a garnet brooch. I grabbed it last night, then got so involved with trying to survive, I forgot I had it."

He took the piece from me, then peered intently at the stone from every side.

"This is a match, Kiely. I'd swear it on my degree in art. What did you do with that earring?"

"It's safely residing in a special box on my dresser at home. I was hoping to find the other ear, so to speak, and get them cleaned up. Maybe wear them to opening night party if I'd been able to locate the missing pair."

I took the brooch back from him.

"This is bizarre. A garnet earring in the prop room and a garnet pin by bones in the tunnel. Something bad happened to that poor girl."

Rafe shook his head. "You're letting your romantic imagination go haywire. This may not have anything to do with anyone from the *Bad Business* cast of a century ago. Let's wait and see what the forensic people have to say about your bones."

As if on cue, Melinda popped back out of the tunnel doorway.

"Forensics has nothing to say."

"What?"

I stared at her. She was almost as grimy as I'd been last night, and at least as miserable.

"Forensics will have nothing to say because forensics won't be involved. Kiely, your imagination must have been working overtime in the dark. There's rubble in there, yes. Cement and stone and dirt and one royal mess. But there's no skeleton. No bones. Nothing like that."

I stared at her.

"There has to be! She, I mean it, was sharing space with me last night. I know the difference between stones and the feel of human bones and I'm telling you, there was a skeleton there."

Melinda and Officer Carter looked at me with sympathy.

"I'm sorry, Kiely. Nothing there. Actually, the only fabric there was this T-shirt. With nothing wrapped around it."

She extended her hand. My *Grand Hotel* T-shirt I'd ripped off and blown my nose on and sobbed into and left hung sodden and limp from her fingertips.

"It's mine. Hey. Isn't that proof?"

She smiled but shook her head no.

"It's proof you were there and hot and upset. But unless there's a nice femur sticking out of this, it doesn't mean a damn thing. Sorry."

I began to protest. I was even prepared to go back

inside (as long as two cops, Rafe, and many flashlights went with me). Melinda stopped me.

"We searched everywhere. Even inside some sort of closet. Nothing. Empty boxes, lots of dirt, but that's it. I'm sure you thought you felt something, but I think it was only imagination and terror turning stones into something more gruesome."

I made one last plea.

"What about the fact that the orchestra pit has been moved since my little journey last night? Obviously someone came here and moved her. I mean, it."

Melinda gave me another sharp look. At least she was listening.

"What do you mean, 'her'? Is there something you've left out?"

I showed her the garnet brooch.

"I found this next to her. That's why I'm assuming those bones were female."

I didn't think I need mention the sadness I'd felt. That would clinch the "imaginative Kiely" theory for sure.

Melinda studied the pin, then gave it back.

"It's interesting, but without anything else, it doesn't mean much. That pin could have been lost any time in the last hundred years. By a very live owner."

She motioned to Carter to follow her out.

"Kiely, I'm sorry. I know you believe you stumbled on a very old body. But there's just no evidence. Call us if you find out something else."

They left. I sat with Rafe in the orchestra pit and tried not to start crying again.

He patted my shoulder.

"Would it help if I told you I believe you? That I

think someone did indeed come in after you left last night and managed to move those bones?"

My conquistador in shining armor.

"Yes. That would help very much."

"We'll search the theater and see if we can find anything more substantial to show the good officer."

I jumped up.

"Okay. I'm ready. Where do we start?"

He pushed me back into the chair.

"I was thinking we could explore tomorrow. Kiely, you may not realize it, but right now there are about fifty reporters outside waiting for all the interviews Lida Rose has promised them. Haven't you wondered where she is?"

Come to think of it, Lida Rose *hadn't* been part of the exploration. Instead, she'd been acting charming and unworried for the media blitz in the lobby. Lights, cameras, Brett Barrett, Channel Seven. The works.

I looked at Rafe.

"Hmm. What you're telling me is this is not the time to go traipsing through the theater yelling, 'Yo! Collar bone at three o'clock. to each other?"

He hugged me.

"You are a bright girl. Daffy, but bright."

He glanced at his watch. "It's nearly noon. Let's grab a bite, then get you home to rest. We open tonight, remember?"

I nodded. "I wish I could forget. But eating and resting sound like a plan."

We left the pit by way of the floor entrance and walked up through the kitchen. We could hear Lida Rose talking inside the lobby to what were doubtless a horde or reporters. The back entrance was the way to go.

As Rafe opened the door for me, he turned around.

"You never told me. How did you finally make it out? From the tunnel?"

I grimaced.

"I was really hoping you wouldn't ask me that."

"Why?"

"Because you're not going to believe me. And here we were getting on so well."

The left brow shot up.

"And why wouldn't I believe you?"

"Because my rescue was made possible by none other than Don Mueller. I smelled popcorn, followed my nose, and discovered the ghost of the villain with a bag of popcorn in his hand standing in the orchestra pit."

The other brow went up.

"My only comment concerning that bit of information is to say I'm glad you didn't repeat this theory to Melinda Krupke. You'd be in the Dallas Psychiatric Ward and we'd be without one Delilah Delight."

step, and I'd better find the food source [illegible] my forsaken soul
just fine. And [illegible] well be maudlin.

I checked the answering [illegible] the tenth time of the
evening.

"Trudeau, Lord. Most likely you know about a pretty
ex-Killing Cousins result. Going to play the Widow
Parmenter. Need [illegible] to [illegible] the scene putting
the nails on Theresa Two [illegible] worth almost with
Sefton Jackes in the opening part. See [illegible] for what was
so tongued exit open for today."

Chapter 29

I should have spent the rest of day at home playing
with Jed, watching movies on the Sci-Fi Channel, and
trying not to deal with the fact that we were opening
Bad Business on the Brazos tonight. Instead, I paced my
apartment wondering where the skeletal remains of
my companion from last night had been moved.

I knew in my own bones that I had stumbled across
the actress who'd originally done my role over a hundred years ago. Charity O'Sullivan. She hadn't survived
that tunnel. I had. I felt I owed her something.

I looked again at the brooch I held in my hand. An
antique brooch. A brooch that had pierced my hand
as I lay sobbing in the darkness last night. A brooch
that I knew belonged to the woman who'd unwittingly
saved me by giving a lifeline to sanity.

I hadn't told anyone but Rafe the identity of my
other savior. And Rafe's reaction had convinced me
to keep my theory quiet. Even Lida Rose might be
skeptical of a popcorn-munching ghost leading me to
safety. With the madness of trying to find one poor
lady's bones, no one had delved too deeply into how
I made it out of the black tunnel in one piece.

Pacing and thinking was doing no good except for
giving Jed a bit of exercise (he'd followed my every

step) and keeping me from raiding my kitchen for junk food. An idea hit me midstride.

I dialed the number for the costume shop of the theater.

"Thelma Lou? What do you know about Charity O'Sullivan? Is it true she went missing right after a performance of *Bad Business*? That the actors playing the roles of hero and villain were both found with bullet holes in their chests, but the body of Miss O'Sullivan was never found?"

Thelma Lou coughed.

"Almost. Makes a better curse story. But the hero wasn't shot. He's the one that told the police about the theater gettin' robbed. The rest of it is guessin'. Until you found what you found."

"Did you know the tunnel was there?"

"I knew there was extra storage under the theater and some sort of hallway. But I never went down there. I've got the worse case of claustrophobia known to humanity. Well, 'cept for you. I can't use a public restroom if the door's got a lock and no space underneath. I've gotta know I can crawl out if the door jams."

I had to laugh at the image, but not the feeling.

"I'm with you on that. I think it'll be a cold day in hell before I can even use a walk-in closet again."

"Kiely? I gotta go now. But you be careful. This ain't over yet. Although with Don watchin' over you, you'll be okay."

I hung up, laughing at the notion of Don Mueller in his villain's garb acting as my personal guardian angel. I liked it.

I finally lay down on the couch with Jed diagonally across my torso and fell asleep. *Bad Business* would open in four hours.

Lida Rose called at about five to ask if I needed a ride to the theater.

"Love one. It's too damn hot to walk. I'm leaving the air-conditioner on full blast for Jed to enjoy while I'm gone. I just hope he doesn't decide to chew it."

"See you in a bit."

She and George came by promptly at the appointed hour and honked. I squeezed into the back of the Volkswagen and listened to Lida Rose enthusiastically reeling off the names of all the wonderful, important people coming tonight who would bring checkbooks and keep East Ellum running for the next fifteen years. She carefully refrained from mentioning my adventure of the previous night. Whatever her reasons, I was grateful. George dropped us both off then went to grab some dinner before returning for the evening's performance at eight.

Lida Rose headed for the lobby instead of backstage.

"You coming with? I'm meeting some of the press people before 'Call.' I know Brett Barrett wants to talk to you. I don't think he knows about Charity O'Sullivan and the jewelry, but you might want to do an interview about the dancing to head him in another direction. Just in case."

"Oh, thanks so much. Fink. No way. I think I'll just hang in the dressing room for a while. You may tell Mr. Barrett I will be available for interviews for approximately five minutes tonight *after* the show. Then I intend to relax and enjoy myself at El Diablo's with many margaritas and several platefuls of nachos. I deserve it."

She smiled. "You do. If I don't get a chance to tell you, you did one marvelous job with the choreography. And you're wonderful as Delilah."

"Thanks. Same back at ya' as regards your brilliant directing."

We hugged each other.

I spent the next twenty minutes placing all the little good-show gifties on various dressing tables in both the women's and men's dressing rooms. Nametags were on each mirror, so I didn't have to try and guess who sat where. The only gift I held back was Rafe's. I wanted to give it to him in person.

Squeals of joy or laughter followed the discovery of the presents as each female cast member found her spot by the mirrors. I love giving good-show gifts. I could hear the men laughing in their dressing room as well. Time to give Rafe his present before he started feeling left out.

I had to show off my purchases for Lida Rose and Rafe to the ladies first.

"Whatcha think?"

Lindsay produced a fake pout. "I want those earrings. Lida Rose is going to go ape over them."

Amber just lifted her eyebrows.

"Tacky. Truly tacky. Lindsay's right, though. L. R. will love them. I think that orange shade in that feather matches those awful stretch pants she has."

Shirley Kincaid and Fran Watkins leaned over Amber's shoulder to see the goodies.

Shirley gasped. "My heavens. That little man in that thing looks just like Rafe does when he's hog-tied. I mean, not his face, but the way he's tied up to the spigot."

I glanced at her and ignored the use of "spigot" for "spit." "Notice the conquistador standing over him. Isn't that Rafe Montez to a tee? Cortez the Conqueror. Oh, yeah."

Fran shook her head and stifled a laugh.

"Is the lady on the ground representing you? I must admit, I want to see Mr. Montez's face when you present this."

Daisy had come into the dressing room to give some last-minute notes. She thanked me for the earrings, then stayed in a corner listening to the others. She and Macy had been studiously ignoring each other but couldn't resist taking a look at the mosaic. Both smiled for the first time since Jason's death. Macy even laughed.

"Cute, Kiely, cute."

I held up my hand. "Come on ladies, let's invade the men's territory."

Giggling like junior high school girls, we marched across the hall, knocked on the men's dressing room door, then boldly entered when a hearty "come in" was heard from Theo.

The guys hadn't quite made it to the makeup mirrors yet. They were engaged in a game of poker. Even Charlie Baines was gazing intently at the five cards in his hand.

I sidled up to Rafe who was standing in his black tux trousers and not much else. He was looking over Cyrus's shoulder at whatever cards Mr. Boone held. The sight of Rafe's bare chest distracted me momentarily, but I hung tough. I handed him the gift bag with "MiaMaya Imports" printed on it.

"For you, Rafe Montez, the conquering hero, even if you're currently a wicked villain."

He opened it, took out the painted mosaic, stared at it without speaking for a full minute, then literally fell on the floor laughing.

"Kiely! I love you. I will cherish this forever."

The "I love you" stopped me from saying anything. He was doubtless being flippant, but I realized I liked the sound of it anyway.

Theo grabbed the mosaic and howled. "It's you, Montez. Spittin' image. Damn. What happened? One of your ancestors pose for this during an off day from stealing lands from the peasantry?"

The other gentlemen joined in the teasing. Comments ranged from the rude and crude to the highly ribald. Our elderly castmates, Nathaniel and Cyrus, were by far the worst.

Lida Rose walked in to see what the uproar was about and had to fall into a chair to keep from joining Rafe on the floor.

"Kiely! You devil. This is wonderful."

I handed her the other gift bag. "For you, my beloved director. A little something to match your lovely turquoise duster."

She opened the bag and exclaimed joyfully over the earrings.

"I adore them. They are so, so, so . . ."

"Awful?"

She beamed. "Precisely."

She immediately undid the relatively sedate, dangling silver earrings she'd been wearing and looped the feathered earrings through.

"Kiely. Come with me a second, okay?"

We walked together toward the lobby of the theater. She stopped and looked to the ceiling as if asking for guidance.

"Kiely? First, thank you for the earrings. I adore them. You knew I would."

We hugged again. Then I stared at her. "What's wrong?"

She tried to smile. "I'm worried. We're about to go on in less than thirty minutes, and I have this horrible feeling in the pit of my stomach that a disaster the size of the last hurricane to hit Texas will blow through."

"I'd love to be able to reassure you, but after my little journey to the center of the earth after midnight, I wouldn't doubt that anything can happen."

She began twisting her new feathered earrings.

"Did I do the right thing? Letting this show continue? Letting Cyrus actually go on as the hero? Letting you go onstage after an ordeal with bones and dead bodies and tunnels? Please tell me this will all turn out all right."

I tried to smile. "Lida Rose. Honestly? I can't. But thanks for the opening night gift. If anything can keep away the gloomies and bad luck, this will."

She fluttered her lashes. "So, what did you think of your own present?"

When she and George had first come to pick me up, she'd presented me with a box containing a gorgeous blouse-and-skirt set that I could best describe as early Stevie Nicks: leather and lace. I had boots that went beautifully with it. Lida Rose had "suggested" I bring them from Manhattan the first night she'd called and told me to wear them for opening night. I'd put them in my dance bag. The skirt set was now in the box under my dressing table.

"I love it. It almost makes up for all the evil things you've gotten me involved in during the last twelve years!"

She waved her hand at me. "Think nothing of it. See you in the green room in thirty minutes. Time to meet and greet the elite."

We hugged again and parted company. I was on my

way to my dressing room to slap on my outrageously long false eyelashes when Rafe Montez appeared from the entrance to the kitchen.

"I need to talk to you. In private."

Chapter 30

There is a sentence made up of six small words that is guaranteed to strike fear into the heart of every woman who hears them.

That sentence is "I need to talk to you."

That sentence portends one of four options. None of those options are good.

The first (and worst) is "I'm married."

Number two is the oldie but goodie "I'm gay."

Three, "I love your sister," is right up there under "ouch." How does one respond to this without sounding like a jealous bitch?

Four is similar to three on the response level. It usually goes something like this: "I really like you, but I think we'd be better off as just friends."

When Rafe delivered that "need to talk to you" sentence, adding "in private" for effect, I considered going back into the tunnel and sitting out the conversation and the rest of my life. Less drastic was the option to set fire to *both* prop rooms, Kismet and the new one, thus creating a plausible excuse for running out of the theater, and never seeing Mr. Montez again.

I did neither. Instead, I mutely followed Rafe outside. That was the only area not entrenched with

reporters, actors, techies, florists, and Lida Rose, thus
providing the needed privacy.

Once we were behind the scene shop in the back of
the theater, Rafe led me to a trunk near the huge shop
doors and gestured for me to sit. When Rafe reached
out and took my hands I wasn't sure which scenario to
expect. Possibly all four. I could hear it now.

*Kiely, I'm married. To a man. But that's not the prob-
lem. I'm not in love with him. I'm in love with your brother.
I couldn't love your sister even if you had one. Oh, yeah. I'm
not really very fond of you and I don't even think we can be
just friends.*

I closed my eyes and tried to prepare for the worst.
I wasn't prepared at all for, "Kiely. I'm an agent with
U. S. Customs. The Art Recovery Team. I've been
working undercover since I started rehearsals with
Bad Business."

I stared at him. A dozen responses flashed through
my brain. All of them were mature and brilliant. I said
none of them. Instead I began to laugh. When the
laughter turned to hiccups, then died, I spoke.

"I guess that's one way to make use of a degree in
art. Lord knows, there's not much else."

He relaxed his grip on my hands slightly.

"You're the only person I know who could come up
with a line like that."

He kissed me, fiercely, then very softly. This was
going to make doing the show difficult. My brain had
turned to sheer mush. Oatmeal soaking in milk would
hold up better.

We spent an enjoyable five minutes or so exploring
lips, tongues, backs, arms and one or two areas hidden by costumes from the 1800s. Finally Rafe let me
go, then exhaled sharply.

"That was very, very nice. I could continue and even go a few steps further but we have about six minutes before call. And I need to fill you in on something."

I tried to lift one brow. Both went up but he got the idea.

He grinned. "So to speak."

I grinned back. "Bad man. Evil mind. Sorry. Okay. Go ahead."

He had brought a carryall bag with him for our little tryst outdoors. He reached in and pulled out my good–show gift of the mosaic of the conqueror.

"This came from MiaMaya Imports. Correct?"

I nodded. "Yeah. Why? You're not going to tell me it's actually some priceless artifact? To tell you the truth, it's probably made in China."

He turned the mosaic piece over and showed me where the cardboard backing was torn.

"It's what's *underneath* that's priceless. Almost literally. Kiely, there was a tiny conch shell carved like fish. A piece of real jade lies in the middle. Late Classic Mayan. I'd say around the year eight hundred A.D. It's currently in a safer place."

"I'm now totally confused."

He checked his watch.

"Great. Five minutes before call. I'll give you the high points. First, the Art Recovery Team. Yes, I do a lot of acting in shows, and I also teach art on occasion— it's a nice cover when I need for folks to be unaware of this particular occupation. I did grow up in Texas, but am based in Manhattan. Anyway, Customs got a tip that a smuggling operation was revving into high gear at the East Ellum Theatre. That was it. No pointers as to who, where, what, or why; you get my drift."

I nodded. The whole thing seemed nuts. Customs

agents and tips and smuggling weren't part of the everyday vocabulary of a dancer.

Rafe continued. "I'd met Lida Rose through George, who taught history at Jesuit the years I was in high school there. I knew she wasn't involved. I had a chat with her before auditions and told her I *had* to be in the show for professional reasons."

"She knows you're with Customs?"

He shook his head.

"No. She thought I had some big L. A. theatrical agent coming down to check me out for a part in a TV series. She doesn't normally precast, but in this case, she made an exception."

I interrupted. "What would you have done if she'd said no?"

"Told her the truth. Like I say, I didn't suspect her of anything. I just was afraid she couldn't keep a secret. I'll tell her tonight."

I laughed.

"Believe it or not, Lida Rose Worthington Rizokowsky is the one person in the world capable of holding a confidence 'til the earth implodes on itself."

"I couldn't take the chance. All I had to go on was that one very skinny tip. East Ellum Theatre. Smuggling. At least the location was specific instead of something like, 'Yo! Smuggling in Texas—have fun, guys.'"

"So?"

"So Lida Rose graciously casts me as the villainous Nick Nefarious and I started nosing around the theater without a clue as to what I was looking for. Then you, my sweet choreographer, kept popping in, which forced me to make up excuses as to why my face was in a piano or under a gaming table."

"Face, hell. I remember that day. Your whole torso was inside. I got a great view of your butt in the air. I might add, you came up with some interesting explanations for all your activities. I thought you were engaged in something illegal. I just couldn't imagine what."

I looked at Rafe's watch.

"You've got three minutes."

"So I have. Okay. Long story short, one of our agents in Dallas started looking at various import shops. Then another tip came in that simply said *My my. Mayan art.* So while the other agent was checking import shops that dealt in anything pre-Columbian, I started looking at everyone who had an interest in Mesoamerican art. Which, as you know, was practically the whole damn cast.

"When Jason died, I was thrown. He'd really been my chief suspect for dealing in stolen artifacts. Primarily because he lived quite well for an actor and I suspected him of having a little extra income. I thought for a while he'd had a partner. Macy or Daisy, even Amber, but nothing about those girls checked out. Since Jason was killed in the prop room, that seemed a good place to look for anything remotely connected to artworks. Zippo. The most interesting things found were those garnet earrings. And while I agree with you that they belonged to the original Delilah Delight, I can't see how that relates to smuggling artifacts. Which leads us to today when you, my wicked gift-giver, presented me with the key to it all. Something else hit me when I saw this. Joe had bought those crazy velvet paintings at MiaMaya's the day before he got run down. I asked Christa to take them off the walls and hide them 'til Jerry, my partner, can look at them and discover what's hidden behind them. I think that's why Joe and the dark-colored sedan had that meeting."

He sighed. "Joe's going to be upset when he gets to the restaurant tonight for the party and finds a different decor. Which is crazy of him to be doing anyway, but. Anyway, the agency now has a search warrant for MiaMaya. And information on exactly who owns it. They can handle it from that end. I'm staying here. For one thing, I don't want to blow a good cover."

He grinned, showing nearly every tooth. "I also told my superiors that no way in hell am I *not* acting in the opening night gala production of *Bad Business on the Brazos*."

"Uh-huh. Did you tell the U. S. Customs Bureau the truth? That you've been waiting for weeks for the chance to get on that stage and do high kicks?"

He kissed my hair. "I did not and they will not learn of this desire unless a certain lady spills the beans."

"Your secret is safe with me."

I looked up at him and grew serious. "All of them. Since someone else is involved in whatever smuggling is going on, I'd say there's a possibility you're in danger. I doubt anyone knows you're more than just a pretty face onstage, but Rafe, someone does know that you and I have been roaming around this theater poking into everything in sight. You've been searching for current felonies and ancient artwork while I've been looking to uncover mysteries from the not terribly distant past, but they don't know that."

I gasped.

Rafe grabbed my hand. "What's the matter? What did you just remember or think about?"

"Everyone in the dressing room tonight saw that

mosaic. Both dressing rooms. Including Miss Daisy the piano player, and Charlie. So it's very possible that we're both in a heap of trouble."

A muffled mechanical voice interrupted anything else he could say. The intercom system extended to outside the theater as well and our stage manager was yelling "Green room. Places in ten!"

Rafe kissed me again, then we began to stroll toward the outside kitchen entrance.

"We have much to discuss, Miss Davlin. Primarily, us. I did tell you I'm based in Manhattan, didn't I? This will work out quite well for later. Don't you think?"

"I don't think. Wait. Make that can't think. My poor brain is trying to deal with too much information while retaining whatever it is I'm about to do onstage in less than twenty minutes. Hey! Did I tell you I'm bringing Jed back to New York with me? The Wylers called the other night and we arranged a doggie adoption. Can you stand going on walks with the beast and me in the city?"

"Tell you the truth, Kiely Davlin, I like the idea of going anywhere and everywhere with you. Dog or not. Any objections?"

I stopped, looked into those dark eyes, and sighed. "Not a one."

Rafe hugged me.

"I almost forgot. I have a gift for you as well. This one's legal. And you'll be glad to know your mosaic present is still mine to treasure. I just can't keep the conch shell. It's already in the hands of Customs. The other agent I work with came and got it less than thirty minutes ago."

He reached back into his bag and pulled out a gift bag from Fair Park Museum. Inside was a small jade pendant replication of the jaguar god. The one I'd wanted when we visited the exhibit.

"Rafe. I love it. Thank you. For everything."

We were about to engage in another kissing session when the intercom sounded again. The stage manager voice seemed a bit miffed.

"Kiely Davlin and Rafe Montez! Places! You're late. Show starts in less than five minutes."

We ran, hand in hand, back inside the theater. If the last thirty minutes were any indication, opening night should be fireworks.

Chapter 31

"Gennel'men. Ah b'lieve the last hand is mine. Excuse me whilst I take m'winnins."

"Ah don't rightly think so, Mr. Travis. Seems to me that four aces beats three of a kind every day includin' Sunday. Now, ah'll jest take that pot."

"Not so fast, Mr. Lamar. I'd say my royal flush make those aces look pretty puny. Nothing personal, you understand. But *this* round goes to me."

"Jest hold those hands offn' the table, Nick Nefarious. If I 'member m'poker rules, a royal flush starts ace high, don't it? And since I've got four of 'em, you, sir, are cheating."

The sound of five chairs crashing to the ground and five guns cocking filled the air. I waited. The card players waited. No one even breathed. Tensions mounted to the point of explosion.

The opening chords sounded. "Gamblers We." Card players and dancehall girls slipped smoothly into the routine I'd taught a month ago. I grinned at Rafe (as my character Delilah Delight, of course) and he grinned back. Which wasn't quite in character for Nick Nefarious—an honest leer was more fitting—but the audience would never know the difference.

The show was going great. We'd made it to this

point in Act Three with nary a stumble. The orchestra
had kept the tempos lively, the actors were performing
with high energy, and even the elder members of the
company seemed charged up and were tossing out ad
libs worthy of stand-up comics in Vegas. The "Hog-tie
Hoedown" had gotten terrific applause and cheers,
Rafe's rope had held tight, no railings had split, no
fires were blazing, and no bones were falling out of
ceilings.

I hadn't had a free moment to think through all the
things Rafe had told me just before "places" had been
called an hour earlier. Smuggling at East Ellum and
MiaMaya Imports. Seemed implausible, but then again,
what a great setup. A theater stuffed full of props. Who
outside of an art expert would notice if strange pots or
paintings were real? And with an import shop nearby,
the "merchandise" could be disposed of quickly.

"Miss Delight? I have a proposition for you."

I wriggled my hips. "Yes, Mr. Nefarious? Jes' what is
it a gennelman lahk yourself would care to 'propose'
to li'l ol' me?"

The audience clapped. It was Act Three. By now
they knew pretty darned well what Nick Nefarious had
in mind for Delilah Delight. Rafe winked broadly at
the first row of patrons and ad libbed a one-liner.

"Sorry, boys, she's all mine, and so's the proposition."

More applause and cheers. Rafe returned to the
script, declaring Nick Nefarious's intent to take Delilah
on a world cruise on the *Brazos Belle,* "Soon's I finish up
winnin' the deed to the Primrose ranch once again
from Lance Lamar."

Hoots and whistles came from the crowd, along with
advice such as: "Don't do it, Delilah. He'll put you off
on the next boat to China."

"Go for it, Delilah. If he breaks your heart you can always kick him where it hurts."

Rafe whipped his head in the direction of the audience where the last comment had come from. He smiled, then tossed a handful of popcorn at the speaker, who couldn't have been more than fifteen.

In his Rafe, rather than "Nick" voice, he yelled, "Don't give this woman ideas, friend. Have you seen the boots she wears?"

More laughter and tosses of more popcorn.

We returned to the actual script and kept the pacing going onstage. The gunfight was fast approaching. For a second I shuddered, remembering that this was the scene where Don Mueller had been killed fifty years ago.

Cyrus looked tense. I didn't blame him. Things hadn't turned out so well the last time he'd performed these actions. I had to applaud the courage it had taken for him to get back on stage, to repeat lines that had led up to tragedy, and still manage to enchant an audience two generations removed from his first production of *Bad Business*. I caught Cyrus's eye and smiled at him from my perch at the bar behind the gaming table.

The moment had arrived. With a crash, tables were tossed over; and poker chips, paper deeds, and plastic bottles went flying. The dancehall girls all ran in front of the bar, then paused and intently followed the action.

Cyrus grabbed the gun from the table.

"You're a real villain, Nick Nefarious! You stole Polly Sue Primrose's land years ago. You cheat at cards and even made off with a horse from my good friend Ace Royale. You set fire to Billy Joe Bob and Bobby Joe Bob Travis's barn, tied up their Ma in her petticoat, and poured blue paint on their dog. I think it's time we put you behind bars once and for all."

Rafe, as Nefarious, sneered then laughed.

"You're a fool if you believe a mere jail cell can hold the likes of Nick Nefarious. And you're an even bigger fool if you think you're going to march me down to the sheriff's just because you wave a silly revolver in my face."

Rafe carefully positioned a tipped gaming table to stand upright, then placed his gun in the middle of it. He backed away two steps and faced Cyrus, boldly waving his weaponless hands.

"Care to make it a race, Mr. Lamar? A fair draw. Whoever makes it to that weapon first gets to shoot?"

Cyrus stood his ground.

"I'm not bargaining with you, Nefarious. There's a cell with your name on it sitting in town just awaitin' for you to fill it. Hands up, sir. "

Rafe laughed, then dove for the gun on the table. The script called for him to grab it, spin around, then shoot. Before Nick Nefarious can actually fire the gun, Lance Lamar shoots first. Cyrus steadied his own gun once again and prepared to discharge the blanks into Rafe's stomach.

Don Mueller stepped directly in front of Cyrus.

Don looked at me. I could hear his voice as clearly as I'd heard Rafe's and Cyrus's mere seconds before. The thought struck me that Don had had a great voice for an actor. Then the reality and import of what he was saying hit me.

"Kiely! Stop him! Live bullets!"

Not good. I was too far away to grab the gun from Cyrus. I whirled around and executed a spectacular kick in midair, neatly knocking the gun from Cyrus' grasp. The hisses and boos from the audience were accompanied by my teenage friend in row three who yelled, "Nice kick, Delilah."

From onstage I could now hear gasps and whispers.

"Kiely? What are you doing? I'm supposed to shoot!" Cyrus spat from under his breath. Rafe quickly ran toward me as I hissed back, "It's loaded! With the real thing!"

"Oh, my God. How do you know?"

"Him."

Cyrus and Rafe looked down toward the front of the stage. I began frantically performing kicks and turns so the audience would think this was part of the show. I vaguely saw Daisy Haltom in her perch at the piano throwing her hands up in shock over this marked departure from the script.

Cyrus whispered to me. "What are you talking about?"

"Him! Don Mueller. Damn! Don't you see him?"

Cyrus shook his head. Rafe looked sharply at me, then back at Cyrus. He took off his stovepipe hat, then held it in front of his face as he spoke.

"I'd rather assume Kiely's right. Cyrus. Let's change this scene. If Kiely can get the gun, um, she can aim it at you. Then Hank or Ham or Theo can lasso me again. We'll improvise a different ending."

He whispered to the twins. Both nodded.

I began doing cute little steps that would place me nearer the gun.

Someone beat me to it. "You little witch. How dare you interfere with my plan! It's time to settle your hash once and for all."

The audience had been eagerly waiting to see what the next twist would be.

Shirley Kincaid pointed the gun directly at me. She sniffed.

"Move, Delilah! Over next to Nefarious there. The lovers. How sweet."

I groaned.

Shirley with a live gun. The ditz of the theater. She probably thought Cyrus had frozen, scared, and wasn't going to shoot, so I'd changed the scene, but lost the gun in the process.

I smiled at her and tried to signal that all was not well with the piece of metal in her hand.

"Now, now, Miss Shirley. You don' rahtly know how to handle one of them firearms. So I'll jes take that, iffen ya don't mind."

Under my breath I muttered, "It's loaded, Shirley. Be careful! Live bullets!"

She smiled at me. And I knew. There was no reason to warn Shirley Kincaid about the ammunition. She was well aware that blanks had been taken out and live bullets placed in that chamber. She knew because she'd put them there. Shirley Kincaid. Murderer.

She shook her head and lowered her tone as well so the audience couldn't hear.

"I know quite well how to handle a gun. So stay where you are, you slut. I have a score to settle with you and the boyfriend. You, Charity, Noemi. All the same. Hot for villains. Ignoring the hero. Daddy was right. Trash, nothing but trash."

A shower of poker chips suddenly cascaded over Shirley's head from the direction of one of the Humble boys. She didn't even flinch. She smiled, then raised her voice to within audience listening range.

"Don't try that stunt again, Billy Joe Bob Travis. You and your brother are not in my plan. Yet. But there's six bullets in this gun and if my calculations are correct Mr. Nefarious and Miss Delight will only use up two. Leaving four. I'd be delighted to try my luck with you, Mr. Lamar, and Ace Royale if need be."

I found I was doing arithmetic in my head and reasoning she'd be a bullet short. I bit my lip. Not the time for math problems. I hadn't done so well on my SATs years ago and I didn't want to rely on my skills at subtraction to breezily assume any one of us would be safe.

Hank Humble, who'd thrown the chips, sank down in a chair near the upright game table and looked at Rafe for inspiration. Cyrus took a step forward toward Shirley. She raised the gun and aimed it in his direction.

"Stop right there, Mr. Hero. Lance Lamar. Delilah was correct. These bullets will indeed kill you."

I nodded frantically, trying to make Cyrus and Rafe aware that Shirley wasn't fooling.

Cyrus looked at my face, then halted his approach. Rafe stared at me as we tried to figure out how to stop the woman from shooting live bullets into what would soon be one dead dancer and art expert.

Shirley smiled at Rafe.

"Don't try any fancy footwork. Either of you. Nick and Delilah. Such an attractive, soon-to-be-demised little pair. With cousins yet. You've gotten far too involved with my life for far too long. I should have taken care of this before. But it's never too late to dispatch villains, is it? After all, it's part of the curse."

She actually turned to the audience as she made the last two statements. They loved it. I began screaming, "They're real bullets, you idiots! Don't you see? We're about to die!"

Nothing but more cheers. A nice willing suspension of theatrical disbelief had turned into stark reality. If we stripped naked and started break-dancing onstage it wouldn't make a difference. The audience would just assume we'd updated the show.

The incongruous thought flitted through my mind that Shirley's sentences and words had suddenly become very clear and concise. No cute mispronunciations, no mangled phrases or adjectives. Mrs. Malaprop's vocabulary was as clear as that of a classical actress accepting an Oscar for best performance in a Shakespearean tragedy. Which could happen soon (the tragedy, not the award) if Ms. Kincaid had her wish and killed Rafe and me before this eager audience.

A flash caught my peripheral vision. Thelma Lou. She was in the wings, wearing her rhinestone-studded pink silk shirt and jeans, and calmly loading what appeared to be a sawed-off shotgun. I shut my eyes and prayed for quick transport to anywhere else. When I opened them again, Lida Rose was standing next to Thelma Lou, obviously arguing that the last thing anyone needed at this point was another gun filled with real bullets.

"Is it live?" Lida Rose screamed at me. "Shirley's gun?"

I nodded. I kept thinking, "I can't die here. Lida Rose will be forever pissed that I never gave her the recipe for my brownies with Kahlua. Although, if I die, at least I'll finally get to meet Don Mueller in person. We can come back together and haunt Lida Rose for getting me in this mess."

This was not logical or clear-headed thinking. I shook the cobwebs from my brain and inched a bit closer to Rafe. I tried to gauge whether or not I was too far away from Shirley to kick. Either the gun or the woman's chin. I didn't really care which object my boots might connect with. I considered flying into a very high and very long leap across the length of the stage but knew I needed running room. I'm not a standing broad jumper.

Rafe was still trying to reason with the unreasonable lady now enjoying her moment in the light.

"If you dispatch this particular villain, Miss Shirley, you'll add murder to your crime of smuggling. Do you really want that? Don't you think this curse has gone on long enough?"

Shirley smiled. "I've *already* added murder. Twice, if my calculations are correct. What's two more?"

She sighed. "Enough of this chitchat, Nefarious. I'm tired and I'm ready to end this scene. There's a party to attend."

She lifted the gun.

Time turned into freeze-frame moments.

Rafe grabbed my hand and threw me to the floor. I landed easily, then rolled over onto my stomach, thinking I could crawl, then tackle her from the ground as Rafe tackled her from above. Rafe began moving toward Shirley in slow steps.

Shirley shot once, deliberately aiming toward the picture above the bar. After the screams onstage stopped there was total silence. Even from a now confused audience. Shirley stayed motionless, then addressed her next remarks to Rafe.

"I have perfect aim, dear. The next shot goes through Miss Delight on the floor there. Now step back, please."

Rafe stopped his forward motion. I looked up at him, then blinked. And blinked again.

Rafe Montez and Don Mueller both now stood in front of Shirley Kincaid. Both wore their black villain costumes. Both had a look of calm resolve on their faces. It was hard to tell where one began and the other ended.

Shirley's face turned absolutely white. She took a huge intake of breath that sounded more like a gasp. She'd seen Don. Back from the dead. Back to stop this killing.

Her hand unclenched and released the gun just before she fainted.

The lights went out all over the theater. Everywhere. Not even the exit sign glowed. It was as dark as the tunnel below the stage.

I was lucky. I had an advantage that no one else in the theater shared. I could still clearly see Don Mueller. But I knew that the only thing the audience and cast could make out was that column of light slowly filling the center of the stage. They couldn't understand how or why the gun lifted into the air. They saw it disappear into darkness, but didn't realize it had been placed in the secure pocket of a black tuxedo.

Don smiled at me, then faced the audience.

A rich baritone laugh filled the theater.

And a hailstorm of popcorn was sent hurling into the first three rows of the audience.

Chapter 32

"Daisy quit."

"She did?"

"Yep. Said we changed the script and she was upset she never got to play the song "Back to the Ranch, Polly Sue." After all that rehearsal. Said we were all horrible, rotten, and unprofessional."

Lida Rose poured champagne into a glass already three-quarters full, then studied it in silence. I did the same. We managed about ten seconds before we sank to the floor writhing in hysterical laughter, being careful not to spill the booze.

Lida Rose lifted her glass again and toasted the heavens.

"So, where's Rafe? Is he going to the police station with kindly Officer Krupke et al.?"

I shook my head. "They took our statements. When we could get a word in. Shirley kept wanting to talk. And talk."

I stayed by the orchestra pit. Lida Rose settled into one of the seats in the first row in the audience.

"So? What did killer Kincaid have to say? I was busy trying to get cast members calmed down, give the press some sort of statement, and make sure the opening night party was still on at El Diablo's. I still can't believe they let Joe out of the hospital. One more ridiculous event in a long chain of 'em."

"*I* sprung him. Joe claimed he would never forgive me if he missed the fun tonight." Rafe made this statement as he strolled down the aisle to join Lida Rose and me. He was still dressed in his villain costume.

"Incidentally, Shirley Kincaid is about one painting short of an exhibit. A taco short of El Diablo's *numero cuatro*. A scene short of a full act. You get my drift."

Lida Rose nodded vigorously. "I'm so glad she didn't kill either of you. I'd've been most upset."

I snorted. Bad move. Champagne zipped up my nose to sting sinuses already overworked from all the crying.

"Thank you, L. R. Rafe and I would have been upset as well. You do know the only reason that benighted elderly bitch didn't succeed in her nasty little plan was because Don Mueller grabbed the gun from her and put it in his pocket, which everyone else saw but thought they were seeing the gun just hovering in midair on the stage because they couldn't see Don's spirit."

Rafe groaned.

"Lida Rose, how much has she had to drink? She's rambling. And delirious. Don Mueller. Yeah, right. What *really* happened was Shirley dropped the gun, the lights went out, and that was that."

I frowned at him. "How do you explain the gun disappearing? How do you explain the popcorn sailing into the audience? And excuse me, Rafe Montez, but just *who* was that laughing? I'm telling you, it was Don Mueller. I know it and you know it."

Lida Rose put up her hands. "Stop. Halt. You two will never agree on this. So Rafe, any poop on the why of Shirley's nefarious deeds?"

I interrupted before he had a chance to say a word. "It's genetic."

Lida Rose whipped her head around to stare at me. "What? Kiely, what are you talking about?"

"Genetics. G, E, N—"

"I'm aware of the spelling. And the meaning. Just put it into some context."

"Sins of the father, L. R. Which were whoppers. Daddy Dearest was none other than Elias Henry. The first Lance Lamar."

I coughed as I was drinking, so Rafe took over.

"One century ago. According to Shirley, 'Daddy' was a great actor who had a thing for Charity O'Sullivan. He was married to Shirley's mom at the time, which didn't seem to deter him, but didn't thrill the original Delilah Delight."

I interjected, "Who happened to be in love with the unmarried Nick Nefarious. And was planning to elope with him after *Bad Business* closed."

Rafe nodded. "She never got the chance. Elias owned not only Henry's Five and Dime, but the antique store across from East Ellum. He used the underground passages in the theater to hide artworks and jewels, et cetera, then carry them to his store. There's a tunnel connecting the Kismet prop room to the orchestra pit to what is now MiaMaya."

I paused, and exhaled. "Which is where Elias stored the body of Charity O'Sullivan, the first Delilah Delight, after he shot her. The tunnel, that is, not MiaMaya or whatever the name of his store was back then."

Lida Rose waved her hand at me. "Wait. I thought she'd run off with the actor playing Nick Nefarious after robbing the box office."

I shivered.

"The reality is that Charity lay under the theater wrapped in a drop cloth until a cave-in sometime this year. Rafe and I found the cloth upstairs in Kismet. Nasty. We thought it was mildew. And I found Charity's bones. Then Shirley and her idiot grandson Neil moved her. Somewhere. Probably one of the trunks upstairs. I think Melinda Krupke will start looking there tomorrow.

"Shirley seemed disinclined to tell anyone where she and Neil had put Charity's remains this time. She pretty much ignored the question. Too busy apologizing to Rafe for trying to kill him. Which she didn't do to me, by the way. No "I'm sorry for locking you in tunnels, Kiely."

Rafe patted me on the head as he told Lida Rose, "According to Shirley, that 'little Irish tart didn't like Daddy.' I gather Elias wanted Charity to stay with him but she was going to go off with Nick Nefarious up North, to, as Shirley put it, 'play with the Yankees.' Second base? Anyway. She went on to muse over the fact that always has to be a problem with Lance, Delilah, and Nick Nefarious. Kiely is supposed to be dead, you see. Another 'Irish tart.' Cursed."

"Kiely?"

I zoned back in. Lida Rose was waving her glass at me. "Do you know if Shirley was responsible for Jason's death?"

I nodded. "Rafe? You heard more about that than I did. I couldn't stand to listen to a lot of her garbage."

He poured some champagne into a glass, then gulped it down.

"Shirley was afraid Jason would discover the tunnel in Kismet that ultimately led to MiaMaya. To quote Ms. Kincaid, 'That boy was a tramp. In and out of the prop room at all hours with women. No morals whatsoever. And smoking cigarettes. He could have started another fire.' She seems to have forgotten she killed him before that little blaze. Which she swears she didn't set—"

I interrupted him. "Don set that fire. To get our attention focused on the prop room and the program with Charity's picture. And her earrings. I heard her that night. Pleading with Elias Henry not to shoot her. To let her live."

Rafe ignored me.

"Never mind. It's my own theory. I'm communing with spirits. Sorry to have mentioned it. Forget I said anything. Go on. Tell her about Jason."

"Shirley snuck in and swung that scimitar at Jason. Who apparently was asleep after a night of—well, a long night. Then she pulled the cabinet down to make it look like an accident. She's not a stupid woman. Very, uh, resourceful."

Rafe had that right. In the last four weeks Shirley and Neil had attempted murder at least four times. They'd locked me in the closet at the party knowing I was claustrophobic. (Shirley's comment after telling me that Neil had been the one to close the door on me was, "You should really see someone about that, dear. Claustrophobia is no fun to live with.") She'd fired live bullets at us, semidecapitated Jason Sharkey, and played hide-and-seek with a century-old skeleton she'd hauled around the theater. And she'd done it all while continuing to run a successful smuggling operation and learn blocking for a show.

I wondered what kind of vitamin supplements she took.

Lida Rose interrupted my musings with another question. "What about Don?"

Rafe nodded. "She put the bullets in Cyrus's gun. Same story as her father. Shirley supposedly loved Don. Who really did love Noemi Trujillo by all accounts. Who happened to be pregnant with Don's child and made the mistake of confiding in our sweet Shirley. Who then persuaded her to leave town."

There was quiet for a moment until Lida Rose spat, "I'm so glad she wasn't able to fire that gun. And that you and Rafe are okay."

Rafe hugged her. "Thank you."

He turned back to me. "Neil was responsible for one other little accident. Which fortunately didn't end up in death. You didn't hear this since you were crying in the corner."

I raised both my brows at him. "Sorry. I don't deal well with getting shot at. So? What accident?"

"My cousin. Your favorite chef. Joe Hernandez."

I sat up.

"I knew it."

"Nasty Neil stole that dark-colored sedan you're so fond of, and ran Joe down that night. Ditched the car over in Plano in some junk yard."

"Reason being?"

"Joe had those fun velvet paintings on the wall at El Diablo's. Remember?"

I nodded.

"Salesgirl sold them, not knowing there were a few nice pre-Colombian gems embedded throughout."

He laughed. "Scattered throughout Elvis's white jacket. Looked like rhinestones."

I plopped my back up against the railing.

"Talk about nervy. And useless. The accident. No one ever would have noticed."

I lifted my glass toward Lida Rose. "More, please. Did I tell you what she said as she was being led off in handcuffs?"

Lida Rose perked up as she poured.

"Yes? Yes?"

"I quote, 'I'm tired. I want to go to the opening night party. I bought a new dress for it. It's pink.'"

"I love it. Mad as the proverbial hatter."

I sighed and looked up at Rafe. "I wonder what happened to Noemi Trujillo? Shirley didn't kill her, just sent her away?"

A new voice called out from onstage. We looked up. Cyrus and Billie Boone were crossing over to the steps leading into the audience. Cyrus was grinning as though he'd won the lottery and waving something in the air.

"I think I know. Pop the cork on a new bottle and start pouring."

"Cyrus?"

The couple made themselves comfortable in the seats across from us. Cyrus handed Rafe what turned out to be an old Playbill program.

"Take a look."

Rafe, Lida Rose, and I all peered intently at a black-and-white cover photo of a ballerina costumed in swan attire. Rafe handed it back to Cyrus.

"So? It's my mother. From before I was born. We've got an eight-by-ten framed in her studio at home. She did *Swan Lake* with New York City Ballet. She was like seventeen at the time."

Cyrus smiled. "I know. I went backstage to tell her

how great she was. Billie keeps every program from every show we've ever seen."

Rafe, Lida Rose, and I all waited. Nice to know Billie was a memorabilia addict, but there had to be a clincher.

Billie took over for her chuckling husband. "We've been trying to figure out where we'd seen Rafe before. I was going through my old programs, found this, and remembered he'd said Angelique Mauro is his mother. And that she'd been adopted."

Rafe frowned. "And?"

Cyrus stopped chuckling. "We heard Shirley Kincaid bragging about her murders and various shenanigans. She claimed Noemi had been pregnant with Don's child and she'd forced her to leave town."

Billie handed us a different program. It looked older.

"This one was never distributed. We made others after Noemi disappeared. But take a look."

I gasped like our sappy melodrama heroine. The *Bad Business* cast from fifty years ago stood in posed positions in front of the *Brazos Belle* anchor. A softer-looking Fran, a handsome Nathaniel, a bubbly, curly-haired Shirley. Two gentlemen of differing heights I'd never had the chance to meet. The ranchers, I supposed. Standing between Cyrus Boone and Don Mueller was a woman who could have been Angelique Mauro's twin.

Rafe grabbed the program. "This can't be my mother. She's barely fifty."

Cyrus sighed. "For a smart boy, you're really dense. That, Mr. Montez, is Noemi Trujillo. Look at her. Then look at Don. And if you still don't get it, look in a mirror. You're their grandson."

I could see it. The long lashes, the dark eyes, the black hair. A carriage and grace that screamed Spanish royalty.

But Rafe had something extra. A sparkle in the eyes, a funny quirk to the mouth. An expression I'd seen only in shadows, waving to me from the balcony as I danced.

I grinned. "Hot damn! I knew there was a reason Don and I got along so well. He's so much like you. The little tilt to the mouth. The way the villain's stovepipe hat sits on your head. Even the sense of humor."

As if he'd been waiting for a cue, Don Mueller appeared in the chair next to his grandson.

I couldn't help but stare. The resemblance was clear once one knew to look for it.

Don smiled at me, then grabbed a huge handful of popcorn from the ever-present bag. I smiled back.

"Hey, Don."

The necks that whipped around on hearing that innocent greeting would need chiropractic work for weeks.

Rafe groaned. "Kiely. Don't start that."

"I didn't. Don did. He's here. I swear. Can't you see him?"

His left eyebrow raised. Simultaneously, so did Don's. Damn. Ambidextrous movable brows from them both. Must be a genetic trait. Rafe frowned, then let loose with a baritone laugh that sounded exactly like his grandfather's.

"No. I don't see him and that's not fair. He's *my* grandfather and if anyone should be able to it's me. I mean I. I mean. Oh, forget it. I don't know what I'm saying. I've just been informed I have a ghost for a grandfather and my grandmother is MIA somewhere in New York. And you're over here flirting with the former."

Rafe cautiously checked the area around me. "Just where is he supposed to be?"

"He's currently snarfing down popcorn. And laughing. And whether you want to believe it or not, Rafe Montez, Don did save our lives tonight. First by warning me that the bullets were real, then by grabbing that gun from Shirley."

Rafe scowled again. "Nuts. You're just nuts. Shirley *dropped* the gun. And you just had a really good instinct that told you about the live ammunition. All the rest you imagined, my loony Irish love."

Lida Rose squealed as Cyrus and Billie shifted their eyes to her, then to Rafe, then to me.

"I knew it! I knew it! For once my matchmaking worked."

The eyes shifted back to Lida Rose. I felt like I was watching a manic Ping-Pong match.

"Don't go there, L. R. Madam."

Her tone turned serene and confident. "Honey, I'm *already* there."

I glanced at Rafe. He absently sniffed, then stuck his hand into the invisible (to him) bag of popcorn Don held. He pulled out a fistful and suddenly turned as pale as a conquistadorian hero could get.

He moaned. "I'm going insane. Where did this come from?"

"Him. Don. Loves popcorn."

Rafe made no response. He stared at the chair, then at the popcorn. He shrugged, raised his right brow, then took a bite and crunched.

Don slowly rose from the chair. When he stood, so did Rafe. Their movements were identical.

I let my eyes follow Don as he strolled down the aisle toward the back of the theater. When Don reached the double doors under the balcony, he turned and waved. I waved back. He tipped his hat to me.

I called out, "Thank you!"

Don winked. Then he vanished. My eyes continued to stare into the vacant space.

"I don't think he'll be haunting East Ellum anymore."

I turned back to Rafe and Lida Rose. "Of course, I may be wrong."

Lida Rose had stayed quiet for the last few minutes. I was about to ask her where her inventive little mind had gone, when she turned to me with a distinct gleam in her eye. I stiffened, then closed my eyes as she spoke four little words.

"Kiely! This is perfect! You know, I hate to admit this, but Shirley's antics really resulted in a much better ending than the original for *Bad Business*. Such exciting action. I wonder if we could stage it?"

I nearly threw my glass at her but decided simply to drink the contents instead. The woman was soused. Blotto. She'd forget soon enough.

Then again . . . Lida Rose. Trouble. The words go together like train and wreck. Like panic and stricken. Like. . .

I needed popcorn.